SEHMAH'S TRUTH

Beneath the Willow, Book I

A.J. Culey

ISBN-13: 978-1530695683

ISBN-10: 1530695686

A POOF! Press Publication

For my nephew, Calvin,
and my nieces, Ariana, Tobi and Josie.

Like Jennifer with her Samantha, I cannot imagine my life
without each of you in it.
You bring me endless joy and hope for the future.

THE END

THE FIRES BEGAN at the forests of Bipin. They spread in billowing waves of red, consuming the ancient trees in seconds. Those battling upon the fields of Shorel didn't notice when they became ringed in fire.

Sehmah stood in the middle of the battlefield, surrounded by death and chaos, a seething mass of writhing bodies on every side. In that moment, fighting for her life, surrounded by thousands of the living and the dying, she was alone. As the sounds of battle faded to a dull roar and her field of vision narrowed to that of the spinner she fought, Sehmah sank further into the isolation of war. Consumed by the battle, she was not aware of the flames that formed a halo beckoning at her back. Her red hair danced upon the wind, as if in harmony with the flames, but then its strands were burning, and from one second to the next, her form was engulfed in fire.

*

Hwanon was connected to the land. He felt the first tree's death, deep within the forests of Bipin. He felt it as the land died, as the trees burned to ash and their life force melted away. Turning from the garnonen he battled, he ran toward the forests. Weaving in and out of the warring and the dying, he raced to save their world.

Reaching for his power, he called forth the rains, though he knew it was too late. They both arrived at the forests, Hwanon and the rain, only to be consumed by the flames. The fires raced across the battlefields of Shorel, in increasingly bright waves. All who had fought there, all who had lived, all who had died, in one single moment, were burned to dust. The world became as nothing, ashes, words on paper, scattered to the farthest corners of the universe, then gone.

FINIS

*

More than any other place, it was the old tree with the darkened cavern beneath its blanket of branches that defined Samantha and Jonathan Whittier's childhood. It was beneath this tree where the twins lived out their dreams, where they spent hours creating an entire world filled with creatures of their own imaginations. It was here that Samantha became Queen Sehmah and Jonathan King Hwanon, where the two of them battled fierce creatures of darkness, where they lived out exciting adventures, destined to save an entire world.

Then everything ended.

Beneath their willow tree one final time, sixteen-year old Samantha wrote the end to their story. In slashing, sweeping lines of her pen, she killed their Willow Tree World, scrawling the word "Finis" at the bottom of the final page, bringing their childhood to its official end.

Jonathan was dead.

Journeys

WHEN SAMANTHA LEFT home the morning of her eighteenth birthday, four days before she was expected to walk across the stage in her high school graduation ceremony, she had no destination in mind. She simply knew she could not bear to face such an important event without her twin. Jonathan would never graduate from high school; his name would remain unspoken during the ceremony, and the graduation that should have been – the one where Jonathan walked across the stage moments before she did – would never happen.

Nearly two years had passed since Jonathan and their parents were killed in a car accident. During that time, Samantha had fantasized more than once about running, but she had always been strong enough to resist the temptation for her Aunt Jenny's sake.

She and Jenny had tiptoed around their apartment for more days than she could count, afraid that one single misspoken word would release the tidal wave of grief holding them both in its grip.

No more.

The bus to Willow Grove stood waiting, the acrid scent of its exhaust permeating the air around it. She'd never heard of the town it was headed for, but when contemplating the list of possible destinations, this was the only one that had caught her imagination.

Willow Grove.

Samantha boarded the bus, the ever-present grief intertwined with a sense of hope, that she might somehow find Jonathan and their lost Willow Tree World waiting for her at the end of the line.

*

"Willow Grove!" Samantha jerked upright. Had she slept? The sun was shining, so she must have.

"Everyone off," the bus driver demanded. "Willow Grove depot."

Samantha exited the bus and looked around.

Really, calling this a depot was too much. The bus stood in the parking lot of a local grocery store, and a small one at that, surrounded by dirt roads and rundown houses. There were no cars in the parking lot, no people standing around the store, no movement apparent through the store's grimy front windows. What had she been thinking, expecting to find some miracle answers here, simply because the name of the town had reminded her of home? There were no answers here because there were no answers anywhere.

Jonathan was gone and that's just the way it was.

She headed for the front of the store, planning to duck inside and find out how soon she could catch a bus back. She should probably also text her Aunt Jenny again, so she wouldn't worry. She was reaching for the glass door when she noticed the tree swaying in its reflection.

The willow stood across the street to the right, in the center of a small grassy area that housed a lone picnic table, swing set and slide.

Samantha walked back the way she had come, past the blue bus with the tiger lunging across its side, toward the first weeping willow she had seen since moving to the city nearly two years before.

It was beautiful. Perhaps even more beautiful than the old tree she and Jonathan once loved.

She moved beneath the willow's branches, heading for the

heart of the tree that called her so desperately. Resting her body against its surface, she inhaled the comforting scent of freshly mowed grass and tree bark. She rubbed her cheek gently across its rough texture, feeling as if she were embracing an old friend, embracing Jonathan.

Samantha sank to her knees, never breaking contact with the tree, not noticing when the rains began. She didn't hear the thunder as it roared, nor did she feel the water as it poured over the willow, drenching her form.

She did, however, see the brilliant flash of light and thought it was Jonathan calling her home. With his face in her mind's eye, she fell into the light, and just like that, was gone. Floating in the white.

There was no sound, no color, no texture to her world. She was

wrapped in cotton

floating in the sea

connected to everything

and to nothing

She was the world

the moment

the molecule

the essence of being

She was the beginning

the end

the everything

She was embraced

She was devoured

She was eclipsed

d e c o n s t r u c t e d

She was

reborn

REBIRTH

THE DYING LANDS

TAKEEM BALIL STOOD upon a mountain made of metal, surrounded by darkened skies and lands of gray. Far below, metallic beasts hurtled toward each other, colliding in a thunderous crash. The world disappeared then reformed into the blackened shell of the dying lands. He stood upon the battlefield of Shorel and the ashes of his father and his uncle, the ashes of the entire world, spun around him in swirling clouds of gray.

The Colors of Naya bloomed within the darkness, the ashes transforming, whirling faster and faster, and the world began to live again. Then, just as Takeem's heart quickened in remembered hope, the first flame burst forth. The waves of red raced across the fields of death, burning a path straight for him.

He and the world were burning, great piles of smoldering ash once more.

*

Takeem could taste and smell the ashes when he woke. His nostrils were filled with the scent of smoke, as if the fires of Shorel that had swept the battlefield twenty years before burned still.

Though Takeem washed and dressed in clean clothing, the smell of ashes and soot clung to his pores. He crossed the room, unlatched the window and pushed it open. Leaning out, he took in a deep breath of fresh air. The flowers and trees in the palace gardens were still shrouded in darkness. The reds and oranges of the rising sun pierced the night sky, chasing away the dark, the spreading light a different form of flame that transformed the world.

Why had he dreamt of the battlefield coming to life? It reminded him of the song he had heard as a child in the lands of the Sky-Blues:

"When ashes bloom amidst the endless fires of doom,
Royal, spinner and Sky will lay down the spears of war.
When life is born where innocents were laid to rest,
Royal, spinner and Sky will lay down the spears of war.
When the magicks wake and the darkness spins to light,
Royal, spinner and Sky will lay down the spears of war."

Was this the beginning of the End Song, told in every corner of the world – the beginning of the fall of the Royal-Blue reign?

It was possible. His dreams were not always phantom and mist. Sometimes they were more. If the end truly approached, he would have to decide. He would have to choose a side for real.

He needed to see.

Takeem strode across the room, pulled open the door to his chamber and checked the hallway outside. All was still silent in the palace corridors. It was early yet. Quietly shutting the door, he secured the latch, then hurried to the windows where he quickly drew the coverings closed.

He then climbed onto his bed and settled at the center. He closed his eyes and focused on the image of the battlefields of Shorel, as he had last seen them, ashen ruins of the dead. Takeem took a deep breath, held tight to this image and shoved his spirit outward, spinning it far away from the shell of his body. As his spirit spun away from the room, his body collapsed backward onto the bed.

A moment or a lifetime later, Takeem arrived at Shorel. Though he was only there in spirit and had no actual physical body, he still staggered upon arrival, dizziness sweeping through him as if his spirit was unaware that a physical body had not followed it to the dying lands.

Opening his eyes, he surveyed the world around him. Nothing had changed since his last visit. The battlefield in reality was as barren and dead as the one from his dreams. Twenty years after the fires of war, the entire battlefield still lay blackened in despair, nothing left alive for miles beyond its ridges. All those who had fought there, every last one of them, on both sides of the war, had been obliterated.

One battle.

One day.

Ten thousand lives.

This was the place where his father and his uncle, the king, had died; where his best friend, the Royal Nargnet, Hulak, had lost his mate; where the nargnet civilization had begun its inevitable slide into extinction.

Sinking to his knees, Takeem concentrated on his fingers. He sifted through the ashes of what once was, feeling the brush of their essence in every part of his physical and spiritual form. As part of his spirit mingled with the ashes, he lifted them high from the ground to spin into a gentle cloud that represented what he imagined his father, a man he had never met, and his uncle, the former king of Lutia, looked like. He manipulated the ashes so both men were smiling at him.

He imagined his father saying something his lying mother once claimed but didn't believe – that a Royal-spinner son was as good as a Royal-Blue one, that the mark of the beast was not to be feared. As he tried to manipulate the ash-men to make them speak, a wind rustled across the land and blew away the ashen remains of the men he would never know.

Takeem climbed to his feet. There was nothing to be had here – nothing real anyway. Here was the land of the dead. Here he found nothing but fantasies.

He might be Royal-Blue by blood, but he had no place in the world of Blues, for his spinner-wild eyes tainted his heritage, making him a nothing to the Blues of the palace. His father and uncle, two of the purest Royals to have ever lived, would have been no different than anyone else. They would have hated and feared him in equal measure, like all the rest, like his mother and his brother.

This was where Takeem belonged, walking the dying lands, a ghost in the real world, the only Royal-spinner alive in Blue territory. Clenching his fists, taking a deep breath, Takeem pushed outward and spun his spirit away again. A lifetime later, his spirit slammed home, jerking his body up then shoving it back to the bed. Darkness pressed upon Takeem and he slept.

ASHES TO LIFE

AT FIRST SAMANTHA thought it was snowing, but the flakes weren't cold.

Ashes. Ashes.

The nursery rhyme ran through her head as flecks of white and gray sprinkled down upon her.

And we all fall down.

Towering above her, the weeping willow tree was a huge pillar of ash. A canopy of thin, blackened limbs formed a roof above her head and ashes were slowly falling. The scent of tree bark had faded, leaving behind the smoky, pungent smell of scorched earth.

She was still enclosed within the willow's embrace, surrounded on all sides by its thin branches that trailed to the ground. How was she still alive? *Was* she alive?

Everything was so silent.

"Jonathan." She whispered his name softly, afraid that he would not answer, afraid that he would. As more ashes fell, light broke through the darkened canopy, allowing the shadows beneath the willow to brighten.

She was alone and the willow was weeping ashes, as if to mourn Jonathan's absence.

Samantha swept the trailing branches aside and stepped forward, away from the tree.

She stood in the middle of an enormous, unending field of

ash. Willow Grove had disappeared. There was no store, no bus, nothing.

She glanced behind her. The willow tree had crumbled to ash in the wake of her exit.

Her backpack was gone, along with her cell phone and money. Had they burned along with the tree?

Grayness stretched for an eternity in every direction. The sky, the land and the air smelled and tasted gray. There was an entire forest beyond where the willow had once stood, but that forest was a blackened, burned-out shell. The trees looked to be something from a horror movie, with ashes falling from their dead and blackened limbs.

In the opposite direction from the forest stretched an endless field of gray. Whatever had once lived upon that giant field was long gone; a blackened shell was all that remained. Her jeans and t-shirt were covered in the same ashy substance that blanketed everything around her. Worse still, her mother's golden locket was covered in ash. Samantha frantically rubbed the locket, trying to clean away the grime, but her hands were covered in soot. She brushed the locket against her shirt, but it was an ashen mess as well, and the soot clung to the locket's surface as if it belonged there. She couldn't even tell that the soapstone flower on its surface had once been ivory colored. She wanted to open the locket to make sure the pictures inside were safe, but was afraid of ruining them. Tears welled in her eyes, but she refused to let them fall.

A single leaf hanging from a tree caught her eye. Samantha reached out a sooty hand and touched her finger to the ashen leaf. At her touch, the leaf disintegrated, sprinkling more ash upon the ground. Turning away from the forest, Samantha stared out across the barren field.

"Hello!" She stepped away from the forest. "Is anyone there? Hello?" There was no answer.

*

Behind her, the ashes of the leaf she had touched fell to the ground and set off a cascading event. The forest rejuvenated, limbs unfurling, new life sprouting, the gray slowly overtaken by green. Behind her stretching into eternity, the world began to live again.

As she walked, she rubbed her thumb and forefinger together, dislodging some of the ashen residue left by the leaf. With each step, ashes exploded upward in a small cloud of dust before falling to bloom in the wake of her footsteps.

Leaves of ash stirred as she swept by, recovering their autumn colors. Green grasses sprouted in her wake; billowy clouds of white formed in the skies behind her; the skies themselves transformed from gray to blue and the dry riverbed filled with water. The river itself flowed in the path of Samantha's heels, tracing her footsteps in watery silence.

Samantha never looked behind her and thus did not see the colors forming at her back. Instead, she saw a gray world that stretched into eternity. She saw the end of everything – the ashes of what had once been and the ashes of what would never be.

She finally stopped, with the river swirling at her feet, touching then retreating from the heels of her shoes.

The entire world seemed to pause. The very wind held its breath, the leaves and clouds froze in anticipation, the land trembled then fell silent, all of them waiting. Waiting for her.

*

Where was she? And *why* wasn't Jonathan here with her? Grasping her locket with one hand, Samantha threw back her head, eyes tightly closed against the ruins of her life, and screamed as loudly as she could, "Jonathan, where are you? *Jonathan!*"

And the world whispered back to her, "hwanon, hwanon, hwanon."

His name, carried upon the wind, spoke deeply to her soul, and said that he lived; here in this time, in this place, he lived.

Samantha fell to her knees, her fingers digging deep into the ashes of this world, her tears raining down upon the land. Her locket sprang open and more ashes sprinkled upon the ground. She curled in upon herself, her forehead touching the newly recovered ground soaked in her tears and sprouting new life. "Jonathan," she whispered in a raw, broken voice, hugging the land with her fingers, hugging him.

*

And as she mourned, the ashes of the world spun themselves into life once more.

LOSING SAMANTHA

JENNIFER WHITTIER SAT at her desk in the police station, plowing through paperwork with more determination than care. At the back of her mind, thoughts raced in confusion. Samantha had sneaked out of the apartment that morning, allowing them both to avoid the situation. Today was Samantha's birthday, but it was also Jonathan's. Last year, Jennifer had chosen everything wrong. She had celebrated the day, but avoided speaking of Jonathan, and Samantha had erupted into tears and hysteria, raging at Jennifer and the world. Then she had barricaded herself in her room, refusing to come out for several days. How could they endure another day like that one? How could either of them survive endless days like this one?

Glancing at the clock on the wall, Jennifer realized it was fifteen minutes to shift end. She wasn't getting anything done here. She might as well call it a day. All of the cases she was working would be there tomorrow. They always were.

Tossing her typed report into her outgoing box, Jennifer stood and headed for the door, murmuring a half-hearted goodbye to her partner, Neil. She saw the look of resigned concern on his face, but didn't hesitate as she strode by. Everything was different between them, and had been for a while.

Her entire life had changed since Samantha.

She hadn't been prepared to become responsible for a teenager at age twenty-five. Her brother, Adam, had been twelve years older than her and raising twins by the time she was nine. As a result, her relationship with Samantha and Jonathan had always been more like that of an older sister than aunt or potential guardian. Yet now she was somehow expected to guide Samantha into adulthood. Some days, it seemed an *impossible* task. This was what she had been reduced to – whining in her head about the impossibility of raising her brother's beautiful, heartbroken daughter.

Most nights it was like this: working late, dealing with rush hour traffic, barely making it home in time for dinner. She entered the apartment, tossed the pizza box onto the coffee table and shrugged out of her coat.

"Samantha!" she called, "I brought dinner."

No reply.

Samantha's door was closed again. Lately, Samantha's door was always closed. Jennifer knocked quietly. "Samantha, are you coming out, honey? I brought pizza."

No answer.

This was not unusual for Samantha. Often Jennifer would come home to find her barricaded in her bedroom where no amount of coaxing would get her out. She hesitated to force Samantha to socialize if she didn't want to. She was particularly reluctant to force a confrontation today of all days.

Jennifer spoke quietly through the door, "I'll be out in the living room if you want to join me. I hope you had a good day, sweetheart." She hesitated, then whispered, "Happy birthday."

Hours later, Samantha had still not emerged from her room.

Jennifer now sat on the couch, her feet propped on the coffee table next to the open box of pizza. She had barely managed to choke down half a piece. The silence pressed in upon her, like a weight she could not escape.

She reached out and grabbed the bottle of wine she had opened. She had long since given up on her wineglass and simply took a giant swig from the bottle. She then held the bottle beneath her nose, inhaling its fragrance, the fruity scent somehow more comforting than its taste. Summers spent at her grandparents' winery, her brother chasing her around the barrels of wine, playing hide and seek with her, ruffling her hair, setting her on his shoulders to carry her out, all the while inhaling the essence of wood and grapes and some other scent she couldn't even define. The scent of home, of Adam, of family.

She took another drink. This wasn't her, sitting there in the dark, drinking, but she had no idea how to reach Samantha.

She studied the picture in her lap. Adam grinned up at her, joy in his face, his arms slung around the two twins, one on each side of him, the three of them so full of life together. If he could see how badly she was screwing everything up, he would be so disappointed. He and Katherine had trusted her to care for their children in the event of their deaths, and Jennifer was failing that trust. Adam would hate that she was sitting there in isolation, grieving all alone, letting Samantha grieve alone.

"Oh, Adam," she whispered. "I don't know what to do. Help me, please. I don't know how to do this without you, and now I'm losing her. Oh, Adam, we're losing her."

There in the silent shadows of her living room, Jennifer wept, unable to do more for her family than grieve.

The Gates of Lutia

"WHY DO YOU mourn so, fledgling?"

The voice was gentle, the snout that snuffled her hair not so much.

Samantha raised her head, blinking tears away to focus on the strange creature in front of her. The animal resembled a cross between a cat and a pig. Long fluffy tail, cat-like ears, sturdy, sleek body, gorgeous fur coat, pig-like snout. He was bigger than any cat or pig she'd ever seen though – three feet tall at least. He had a huge, black snout and his long, thick fur hung into his eyes, like that of a sheepdog. It was a brilliant shade of purple, with long strands of fire-red woven through it.

"What?" Samantha wanted to whisper the creature's name – she *knew* who he was. Those cat eyes and ears with the pig snout, it had to be him. But he was too small and he only had two curved, black stripes where there should be wings. It *couldn't* be him.

"I said, why do you mourn so?" The speaker stepped into her field of vision

The man was beautiful. There was no other word for it. A rich mass of dark blue curls swirled around his royal-blue face. Brilliant blue eyes stared down at her, framed by dark blue lashes and eyebrows. His lips were also blue, an even deeper and darker shade than that of his skin. When he spoke, his teeth shone whitely.

"Fledgling?" he rumbled.

Samantha stared, unable to speak past the awe she felt at confronting this hauntingly familiar man. Was it possible?

He reached down and offered his hand. Samantha took it, eyes widening as she noticed her hand was now clean. As the man helped her to her feet, she took stock of her appearance. Her jeans and t-shirt were also soot-free, and her mother's locket hung around her neck, the golden surface gleaming brightly in the sun, its soapstone flower ivory once more.

"My name is Arioan Balil." The man's voice interrupted her stunned observations. "I offer you friendship and peace."

Arioan was not one of the names she had expected, but it was close enough to Ari, to make her think this might be him. Ari, the older brother of Tak, the boy-hero of every story she'd ever written. "Thank you. M-my name is Samantha."

"This is my warrior-companion, Hulak." Arioan indicated the cat-pig at his feet.

Hulak, who might be Huk, the nargnet she and Jonathan had created together. Samantha placed a tentative hand on the creature's head between his two pointed, cat ears. She gently rubbed her hand along his forehead and murmured, "Pleased to meet you, Hulak. I'm Sam."

Arioan tilted his head in question. "Sam?" he asked. "Or Samantha?"

Samantha smiled. "Either one is fine. Sam is the short version of my name."

"Sam." Arioan tested it out. "Sam. I like it. It is tiny. Like you."

Samantha did not consider herself to be tiny by any means. She was barely an inch short of six feet; had, in fact, been this tall since Jonathan's death. Those final two years, she and Jonathan had been constantly growing, one of them falling behind only to shoot ahead a month later. They entered their fourteenth year two inches apart – he was five feet, five inches; she was five feet, seven. By the time he left her two years later, he had grown nearly a foot and was four inches beyond her. Sixteen years old and already six-foot-three. It seemed incredible that

someone so alive, so vibrant, could have died as a result of
something as mundane as a car crash. Since the moment she felt
that cord tying them together snap in half, she had stalled at five-
foot-eleven, as if the entire idea of growing without him was an
impossible one. She was five-eleven, and this man, who towered
over her by at least a foot, called her tiny.

"Hulak and I often come here." Arioan looked around, a
puzzled expression on his face. "Though it is much changed
since our last visit. We walk for hours at a time, to feel closer to
the ones we have lost. Quite often, we have found ourselves on
our knees." He glanced at Samantha. "To kneel and to mourn is
quite natural here."

Samantha nodded.

"You may join us on our walk, if you would like."

"Thank you. I'd like that very much."

It was at this moment that Samantha realized the world
around her was entirely new. Colors now stretched in every
direction, though she could still taste and smell the gray, its
smoky residue lingering in her nasal cavity.

Samantha reached up and enclosed her mother's locket in one
hand. The feel of the flower carved upon the surface comforted
her. The dead world had been left far behind, and the beauty of
the new world gave Samantha hope.

As they walked, Samantha felt a sense of peace descend upon
her. It was a feeling she had not had in twenty-three very long
months. Here in this place, with Arioan and Hulak beside her,
she felt an incredible sense of Jonathan's presence, as if he too
walked upon this land, one more companion at her side.

Hulak jerked to a stop, spun and stared in the direction they
had come from, his sharp teeth bared in a silent snarl.

"What is it, Hulak?" Arioan murmured to the beast, stepping
toward him, blue hand reaching out to stroke across his neck.
Before his hand could make contact, the great, furry creature
hunched down into a much smaller form, then with one
tremendous leap, twisted his body mid-air, lunged forward and
grew.

Hulak now stood taller than Arioan and he was not yet

finished. His thick coat shimmered for a moment, then where the two streaks of black parted the purples and reds along his sides, there sprang from nowhere two giant black wings. Hulak no longer resembled a pig *or* a cat, but something she had only seen in her dreams. He was everything she and Jonathan had imagined, down to each individual strand of fur.

He still had his pig-like snout, though it towered high above her now. His fur was longer and thicker than ever, and it was so brilliantly red, it might have been on fire. The purples had faded into the background, with only a streak here or there, somehow contributing to the overall effect of a giant beast of fire.

It was true—

A whistling sound filled the air and everything descended into chaos. Hulak plowed into Samantha and she went sprawling, his heavy paws pinning her to the ground. An instant later, he was gone.

The fresh scent of grass washed over her, comforting, a connection to home. Then she saw the arrow. It quivered in the ground, not two feet from where she lay, the grass around it losing its lush green color, turning brown in seconds. A strange chemical scent wafted toward her.

Arioan hauled her to her feet, snapping over his shoulder, "Hulak, now!"

The same whistling sound filled the air and Hulak lunged toward them.

Arioan vaulted onto Hulak's back and stretched out his arm toward Samantha. "Grab hold, quickly!"

Samantha grasped Arioan's hand and found herself aboard the beast.

Hulak made a great stretch and a leap forward, and they were in the air, flying.

Throwing her arms around Arioan's waist, Samantha leaned her cheek against his back and stared down at the ground where the arrow still quivered. The flowers around it had died, and the death was spreading. Purple flowers withered and turned black, the brown patch of grass slowly spreading outward, one arrow bringing death to the land itself.

Beneath her, Hulak lunged sideways, causing Samantha to yelp and clutch Arioan tighter. The whistling sound of an arrow burned her ears as it zipped by.

Hulak twisted mid-air, swinging his whole body around so that he faced back the way they had come.

A dozen men riding beasts pursued them far below. The men were dressed in black, their beasts a matching color – so dark they blended with the men who rode them and created the illusion of shadows creeping across the land.

The men raised their bows and fired as one unit.

Hulak turned and hurtled through the skies again. Their attackers fell farther and farther behind, their arrows falling uselessly to the ground, unable to span the growing distance between them. Each fallen arrow spread death upon impact until the blackened petals of a thousand dying flowers were all Samantha could see.

A massive metal gate rose in the distance. It stood alone, without the stone wall Samantha expected to see. Instead, there was a wall of men stretched outward on either side of the gate, facing their direction. The gate would be rooted deep within the land, Samantha knew, and the wall should have been rooted at its sides. The missing wall was not the only difference, however. Samantha was shocked to realize this gate stood completely open, though she supposed without the wall, there was no point in keeping it locked. She wondered if the men standing in the place of the wall would attempt to stop them from crossing over the gate, but none of them looked up. Instead they simply stared straight ahead, into the distance.

As they passed over the gate and its wall of men, Arioan said, "We're safe now. We're out of the warzone and headed home. Do you know why those men were after you?"

"Me? I thought they were after you."

Arioan was silent for a moment, then, "I suppose that's always possible. Well, they're far behind us now. With Hulak flying, we should pass through Sky-Blue territory fairly quickly and reach the palace by sunset. We can drop you off somewhere along the way or you may accompany us."

Samantha shivered at the thought of being dropped off in this unknown land, with no way to defend herself. "I'll go with you, if that's okay."

Arioan nodded and faced forward again.

This was unbelievable, but she couldn't deny the truth. Somehow, Samantha had been transported to the world she and Jonathan had created beneath their willow.

She wondered if she would ever see her Aunt Jenny again, if she would ever find her way home, if she even *wanted* to go home. On Earth, Jonathan was long gone, nothing of him left but memories. In this world, though, in *their* world, she could feel his presence, as if at any moment, he might appear and sling his arm around her shoulders once more.

Over the next several hours, as they flew over the territory Arioan had identified as belonging to the Sky-Blues, Samantha compared the world around them with the world she and Jonathan had created. The biggest difference was that all the walls of Lutia – the seven stone walls dividing their world – were gone.

In their story, the first wall of Lutia was originally built to keep the spinners out, though they had long since breached that wall. The War Zone stretched between the first and third walls. Between the third and seventh walls was Sky-Blue territory and beyond the seventh, far from the War Zone, seven walls deep from the spinners, lay Royal-Blue territory.

Here though, there were only gates and walls of men. Most of the gates were tightly latched, just as she had written them, and each gate had men stationed on either side where the walls should have been, though there were fewer men the deeper they traveled into Blue territory.

As they passed over the final gate, the sky darkened and Arioan called over his shoulder, "We've entered Royal-Blue territory and should reach the palace soon."

Samantha murmured an acknowledgement, her thoughts preoccupied. Although she had stood in the War Zone, somewhere between the second and third gates of Lutia, she had seen no evidence of battle. Had the war already been won? And if so, who were the victors?

Samantha's head throbbed in protest as her thoughts swirled with more and more questions, the reality of this land clashing with her deeply intimate knowledge of it. This was her story, hers and Jonathan's. It was their world. They had created it. Why then was it so different in all its familiarity?

The palace of Lutia appeared in the distance. It was exactly as she and Jonathan had imagined: a huge fortress of turrets and walkways, surrounded by acres of green.

DREAMS

FOR THE FIRST time in years, Sehmah and Hwanon visited Takeem's dreams.

The three of them played beneath the Shrouded One, running and shouting, fighting invisible enemies, forging an alliance that bridged worlds. As they played, the tree began to burn. First Hwanon disappeared, then Sehmah. Takeem was alone beneath the Shrouded One. Then it too disappeared and he stood once more upon the ashen fields of Shorel. In the distance, Sehmah walked, her red hair gleaming in the sun. At her back, the ashes of their world spun into life once more.

"Sehmah!" The world spun his words away and she never turned. She never saw him.

Then Arioan arrived, leaned down and whispered in her ear. Beyond Arioan, the Tekhlan, Royal assassins of the throne, rose in the distance, arrows pointed toward his brother, toward the girl he had only ever met in his dreams.

"Sehmah, Arioan, behind you!"

The arrows flew, but they did not connect with either Sehmah or Arioan. Hulak was suddenly there, and they were on his back, leaping skyward. The arrows that flew toward them thudded into the ground, spreading death as they fell. The thud they made as each one connected echoed through the lands.

Thump! Thump! Thump! Thump!

Takeem woke with a jerk. The pounding he heard was coming from the door. He staggered from the bed, clutching his throbbing head in his hands. Stumbling across the room, he swung open the door. "What?"

"Let us in." His brother, Arioan, shoved past Takeem, dragging behind him the girl from Takeem's dreams.

"Sehmah?" Takeem whispered.

"Shut the door." Arioan said.

Takeem closed the door and took a step forward, unable to look away from the girl who stood next to his brother. Her red hair hung to her shoulders, but hints of royal-blue peeked out at him. He wanted to see her eyes, but she was staring at his brother, just like every other girl he'd ever met.

"Sam, this is my brother, Takeem."

Sehmah's head jerked around. Her eyes were a soft sky-blue, but lighter than most.

"Takeem?" she asked.

Before Takeem could speak, Arioan said, "Takeem will keep you safe until I come back for you. Takeem, keep her inside this room. No one sees her. Do you hear me?" With these cryptic instructions, Arioan headed for the door.

"Wait a minute!" Takeem leapt forward, sliding between Arioan and the door. "What is going on? Where did she come from?"

"Hulak and I found her at the battlefields of Shorel. The fields have come to life again, Takeem, as has the great river of Lutia."

"How is that possible?" The river of Lutia had gone dry around the same time the fields of Shorel had burned. It rained so rarely now, but even when it did, the rain never touched the river basin, not at all. Now it flowed with life again.

"I don't know. Before I could discover any answers, the Tekhlan showed up. You must keep them from her. They will not hesitate to kill her."

"But why?" Sehmah exclaimed.

Takeem strode to Sehmah's side. "Yes, brother, explain to us why the Tekhlan are after her."

"I honestly have no idea," Arioan said, "but they won't be far behind us. They will have warriors riding all night to ensure their reports reach the palace as quickly as possible. I must consult with the queen before they arrive. Hulak is in the hallway. I will leave him to guard your door. Keep her safe, Takeem." With this order, he left the room, shutting the door firmly behind him.

SILENCE

JENNIFER WOKE WITH a horrendous headache and a crick in her neck. She was lying on the couch, her body twisted into an awkward position. Bright sunlight poured in from the living room window. She pulled herself to a sitting position and grabbed her cell phone from the coffee table. It was 7:15 and she already had a text message. It was from Samantha.

< luv u. going away for a while. don't worry. >

Going away? Jennifer quickly texted a reply, < where r u? >

She paced and waited and paced some more, but there was no answer.

She dialed Samantha's number and listened to the phone ringing. When it went to voice mail, she hung up and sent another text message.

< Sam, please text me so I know you're ok >

Every minute that passed felt like torture. Telling herself that a watched phone never beeped, Jennifer forced herself to get ready for the day. Carefully laying the phone on the back of the toilet so that it was within reach, Jennifer took a quick shower. Then, carrying the phone with her, she retreated to her bedroom, where she threw on some clothes.

Twenty-two minutes had passed since she sent the last text message.

Just because Samantha didn't answer didn't really mean anything. Maybe her phone had died and she didn't know

Jennifer was trying to reach her. Or maybe something terrible had happened.

It occurred to Jennifer that she didn't know how long Samantha had been gone. Had she even come home the night before?

Checking the time stamp, she saw it had come in after midnight. Samantha had been on her own since midnight, probably even longer than that since she hadn't heard her leave. Mind racing, Jennifer realized that Sam probably hadn't been in the apartment at all last night. While she had been sitting in the living room, drinking wine and feeling sorry for herself, Samantha had been off on her own, dealing with her grief.

Shaking, Jennifer made her way to the kitchen, where she phoned Neil and their captain to let them know she wouldn't be in that day. She then tried to trace Samantha's phone on their carrier's website, but the phone wasn't showing up at all.

There must be someone she could call, someone who might have an idea of where Samantha had gone, but the more she thought about it, the more she realized how isolated the two of them had become. In this city, there was no one Samantha talked about, no one the two of them ever visited, no one they called friend, family or loved one. The two of them were alone and cut off from the rest of the world, with no one but each other to turn to. That hadn't always been the case, of course. Once upon a time, Jennifer's world had been filled with friends. Back then, she'd actually had a social life.

The text she'd received had come through at 12:17 in the morning. Now Samantha wasn't replying, the silence oppressive. Anything could have happened since then.

She was probably overreacting, but Jennifer couldn't afford to pretend everything was okay. She would never forgive herself if something happened to Samantha because she ignored her instincts. Dragging in a deep breath for courage, Jennifer picked up the phone.

The Purge

SAMANTHA'S HEART POUNDED as she stared at Tak, the spinner hero of her world.

The boy she'd created long ago had grown into a man, as blue and almost as tall as his brother, Arioan.

His skin was a deep, rich color and his hair was striped in darker and lighter bands, like a tiger's pelt. A blue one.

His eyes were the same dark blue as his skin, with tiny stripes streaking across their whites. When those dark bands reached the edges of his eyes, they continued several inches across his skin in light sky-blue lines. The lines stretched down to the tops of his cheekbones and up to slice through his royal-blue eyebrows, stopping just above the ridge there.

Samantha stared at this vision from her childhood dreams. This man was an impossibility and yet here he was, exactly as she'd always imagined him – the hero of every story she'd ever written, the boy-man with eyes as wild as a tiger's, the Royal-spinner she'd created and adored as a child.

"Tak?" she whispered.

He smiled a brilliant smile, and stepping forward, swept her into a hug. He lifted her up so her feet left the ground and swung her around in a wide circle, much the way Jonathan used to. Being in Tak's arms was entirely different from being in Jonathan's though.

Setting her gently back upon her feet, Takeem placed his

hands on her shoulders and looked deep into her eyes. "Sweet Sehmah. It is wonderful to see you again."

Tingles radiated down Samantha's arms from where Takeem was touching her, and she shivered in reaction. Quickly pulling away from him, she forced his hands to drop. "My name is Samantha," she informed him. "Sehmah is someone long gone."

"Yes. It has been a very long time since we met in our dreams. Why did you go away? What has happened that your eyes have aged so darkly in sadness?"

Samantha shrugged. "Life happened and that is all."

"Life is often less than we would wish of it." Takeem reached out and caressed her cheek.

She jerked her head away, clenching her jaw against the urge to break down and tell him everything.

She stepped away from him and glanced around the room. It was terribly small, with only a bed, dresser and desk. There was just one window, small and too high for her to see out. There were no decorations anywhere and the floor was bare beneath her feet.

Spartan.

"What's happened here?" she asked.

"What do you mean, Samantha?"

"Nothing's the same. Nothing's right."

"I don't understand."

She hesitated. She'd written Takeem as the only spinner who stood with the Blues, a hero to lead them in the war against the rest of his kind.

"Samantha?"

"Shouldn't you be in the War Zone?" she blurted. "Or is the war over?"

"Not over, just ... different."

"Different how?"

"The Battle of Shorel happened."

Samantha stiffened. Shorel. The final battle she had written. "You mean when everything burned?" she asked.

"Yes. No one knows how the fires started, but everything was destroyed. Everyone on the battlefield, the nargnet nesting grounds, the seven walls of Lutia – all gone."

"The walls were stone," Samantha protested. "Weren't they?"

"Yes, and still they burned."

"But how? Most of the walls were nowhere near the War Zone."

"I know. The nargnet nesting grounds were at the farthest edge of Royal territory and yet they burned too. The only survivor from the battlefield that day was Hulak, and in twenty years, he's never shared his memories of the tragedy."

"It's been twenty years?" Samantha asked.

"Twenty years today."

Twenty years. And – "Hulak survived?"

"He did. No matter how terrible it was for the Blues and the spinners, it was worse for him. Because of that battle, Hulak is the last of his kind."

"The last – there were other nargnets?" She and Jonathan had only written the one. She'd never thought to create more.

"Of course. The Nargnet Nation was vast, once upon a time."

Had they done that, she and Jonathan? Destroyed the nargnets, doomed Hulak to be alone, simply because they had not thought to give him a family? "Why are the gates still standing?"

"No one knows. The land where the walls once stood is scorched black, yet the gates stand strong. Now the Skies guard the territories to prevent the spinners from invading. Most believe the spinners spun dark magicks that day, magicks to destroy everyone on the battlefield, to burn the nesting grounds and to crumble the walls of Lutia to dust."

Samantha sank down onto the edge of the bed. Her thoughts whirled. She'd written the fire to consume the world she and Jonathan had created together, to allow Sehmah and their beloved characters, Tak, Ari and Huk, to die with him. Instead, the fire had burned eighteen years before Jonathan's death, before she'd written their end story, and their world had survived beyond that fire. Did this mean the ending she'd written in the aftermath of Jonathan's death was still to come or did it mean this story's ending had yet to be written?

Their world still lived, as did Tak, Ari, Huk, and Sehmah. Could it be that Hwanon lived here too? Could Jonathan be here somewhere, lost within the story they created together? "Do you think it was a spinner?" she asked.

"We're in Year 130," Takeem said. "There are no magicks left for them to spin."

"What does that mean – Year 130?"

"130 AP – After the Purge."

"What Purge?"

"The Purge of Magicks."

"I don't understand. The magicks were purged? They're gone?"

"For a long time now."

"But if the magicks are gone, why are you still at war? I thought the fighting was because the spinners were using their magicks against the Blues."

"Maybe in the beginning, but not anymore. After spinning the spell to purge the magicks, King Torel banished the spinners to the outer lands. They now fight to reclaim their heritage and homelands while the Blues fight to keep them out."

"I saw the walls of men, but I didn't see any spinners. I didn't see any battles being fought."

"After the walls fell twenty years ago, everything was quiet for a time. My uncle, the King of Lutia died on the battlefield, along with my father. My mother inherited the throne, but she was pregnant with me at the time and the soldiers of that generation were dead. They all died on the battlefields, in the burning. As a result, we were at peace for the first time in a hundred years. Of course, that only lasted long enough for the spinners to train a new group of soldiers and invade again. It's why the men are stationed where the walls once were. The spinners now engage our men in surprise attacks, all along the outer perimeter. We're continually at war, pushing them back, but–"

A knock startled them both. Takeem opened the door to reveal Arioan with Hulak in his smaller form. "I spoke with the queen and she would like to meet Samantha," Arioan said.

Samantha crossed the room toward the two men. "I'm ready,"

she said.

"Follow me." Arioan left the room.

Samantha stepped into the hallway and Hulak brushed up against her. Takeem fell in step behind them.

They walked down the hallway and around a corner. Straight ahead was a narrow staircase. As they walked up the stairs, Samantha trailed her hand along the stone wall. Its rough texture helped ground her in reality. This was happening. She was in the palace of Lutia.

At the top of the stairs, they walked down another narrow corridor, ascended four more steps, turned the corner and entered a section of the palace that made Samantha's breath catch.

The passage in front of them was wide and lit every few feet by blazing torches. As Samantha passed by, their flames burned brighter, dying down as she stepped past them, only to flare bright again as she came abreast of the next one.

After several turns and a few more steps, these leading down, Arioan finally stopped.

By this time, Samantha was thoroughly lost. She'd never find her way back to Takeem's room or her way out of the palace if she suddenly needed to flee.

With a sweeping hand, Arioan indicated that Samantha should pass through a huge archway into a darkened room that stood to their left. "Please." Arioan bowed his head to Samantha.

Samantha hesitated. Hulak brushed by her to enter the room. The look in his eyes gave her courage. She followed him through the archway and down three stairs into a darkened room filled with flickering lights.

The walls were covered floor to ceiling with rows and rows of books. Samantha's fingers tingled with the desire to trace along the spines, to read the many titles, to explore through the pages of history and words.

In the center of the room was a sitting area with armchairs that looked big enough to accommodate a bear, the four of them arranged around a long table. The furniture stood in front of a circular fireplace made of some strange, translucent material.

Samantha could see through the flames of the fireplace to the other side of the room. The smoke from the fire rose up through a translucent chimney, to disappear into the ceiling.

To the side of the fireplace stood a tall woman whose entire being radiated power. The woman's skin and eyes were an even deeper, richer blue than Arioan's. Swirling around her shoulders and across her back was a living banner of flame – one moment fire-red, the next royal-blue, then a strange combination of the two. The colors moved freely, giving the impression of hair writhing in the wind. Beneath the writhing flame-hair, the woman's form was covered in a cloak of light. It hurt even to gaze upon her, for the sparkles that lit up the cloak blinded with every flash.

The woman stepped away from the fire and smiled at Samantha. "Welcome, my dear. Come sit down, won't you?"

Now that the woman stood farther away from the fire, her hair settled across her shoulders and no longer appeared alive. It was also completely royal-blue, no red in evidence at all. Her gown no longer sparkled, though it flowed as she moved, its stark white lines contrasting vividly against the brilliance of her deep, dark blue skin.

"Are you hungry?"

Just like that, a fearsome hunger rose within Samantha. She was so hungry, she could eat for days and not assuage the ache. Before she could answer, the woman said, "Come then, my child. Sit and eat with us. We have much to discuss."

Samantha sat in one of the armchairs. She took immediate comfort in the fact that Hulak settled at her feet, as if to guard her from danger, and that Takeem sat in the chair to her left.

The woman and Arioan sat in the chairs across from them.

"Samantha," Takeem said. "This is our mother. Queen Alatore."

"It is very nice to meet you, Samantha. Before we begin, won't you please help yourself to some nourishment." Queen Alatore swept her hand toward the empty table between them and from one moment to the next, a feast was laid out before them. The foods smelled divine.

Samantha's eyes widened. "I thought you said the magicks were gone."

Takeem reached for a plate then piled it high with food.

"There are some residual magicks left in this world." Queen Alatore said. "Some simply could not be contained and were molded into beings of magick while others still linger for anyone who can wield them."

"But ..." Samantha hesitated.

Takeem passed her the plate he had prepared.

"Thank you," she whispered. He had given her several triangles of bread with some unknown meat inside and a variety of fruits and vegetables.

"I may not be a spinner, my dear, but I am the queen. The Royal House of Lutia has always had the ability to spin some magicks, though nowhere near the amount the spinners could."

Taking a bite of purple fruit, Samantha was pleasantly surprised at its rich and tangy flavor. "So can you spin the magicks, Takeem?" she asked.

As soon as she asked the question, Queen Alatore's shoulders went back and she stiffened, as if in affront. Arioan's jaw tightened and Hulak raised his head and stared at Samantha.

"I have never been able to spin magicks," Takeem said. "I suppose the magicks that linger are not for the spinners to spin. Or perhaps I simply do not have the talent."

Samantha wanted to protest. She had created him. Of course, he could spin magicks.

"I suppose it is only natural that you would expect Takeem to have some abilities," Arioan said. "However, he has never shown any aptitude."

"Not even a little," Queen Alatore agreed cheerfully.

Takeem's jaw was now clenched tight, but he did not protest these statements.

There was more going on here than she understood. Everything was so different from what she and Jonathan had created. For one thing, the only queen in Samantha's story had been Sehmah. She never even gave Takeem and Arioan a mother, so Queen Alatore was someone entirely new to this story, which meant Samantha's role was completely unknown.

"Arioan tells me you were attacked near the Great River of Lutia, which I am also told flows freely once more." Queen Alatore stared intently at Samantha.

"I...yes. There were men riding beasts or something. They shot poisoned arrows at us."

"It was the Tekhlan," Takeem spoke flatly.

"Who are the Tekhlan?" Samantha asked.

Takeem was staring hard at his mother and did not look Samantha's way when he answered. "Royal assassins of the throne."

The throne.

Alatore was the queen. The assassins were hers?

"Arioan?" Alatore ignored Takeem's statement. "Was it the Tekhlan?"

At Samantha's side, Takeem stiffened even further.

"I believe so, Mother," Arioan said.

"Did you see them?" she asked. "Did they wear the red sash of the Guard?"

"I don't know. They were covered head to foot in black, so that even Hulak could not tell the color of their skin, or whether they wore the traditional sash. But their arrows destroyed everything they touched. They were Tekhlan poisoned arrows. Of that I have no doubt."

"You do not believe the spinners, with their dark magicks, could somehow spell an arrow to kill all that it touched?"

Arioan hesitated. "I suppose it's possible, assuming they have access to the magicks."

"If we Royals can manage to spin the few magicks that linger, Arioan, I guarantee you the spinners are able to spin a few dark magicks themselves."

"The magicks are gone from this world," Takeem said. "If the spinners could access any magicks at all, I would know of it, don't you think?"

Neither Arioan nor Queen Alatore answered him.

"If you think it was the Tekhlan, Arioan, then that is who it was," Takeem said. "So tell us, Mother. Why did you send the

Tekhlan after Samantha?"

"I doubt this was the work of the Tekhlan. I haven't sent the royal assassins after anyone, which means this was either a simple misunderstanding or, as I suspect, the spinners are responsible. Either way, Samantha, you are safe here in this palace."

"Thank you," Samantha said.

"Takeem, please take Samantha to the guest wing. Make certain she has everything she needs." Queen Alatore spoke briskly as she settled her glass of wine upon the table and stood.

"I won't leave her there alone, Mother," Takeem said.

"She'll hardly be alone, Takeem. The guest quarters are never completely empty. You know that."

"Exactly my point. She's almost been killed once today. We stay together, where I can protect her."

"Very well. You may choose a room in the guest wing as well."

Arioan surged to his feet. "Mother."

Alatore waved her hand at him. "It's only for one night, Arioan. Tomorrow we should know more about why she's been targeted and we will make a better plan then."

"Very well." Arioan didn't look happy.

Alatore smiled at Samantha. "You must be exhausted, my dear. We'll talk more in the morning. Arioan, with me." She swept from the room.

"It was very nice to meet you, Sam," Arioan said. "I will leave you with Takeem and I bid you both goodnight." With a formal bow, he left as well.

"Are you okay, Takeem?" Samantha asked.

"Do you see how she ignores me?" he demanded. "She only acknowledges my presence when she needs something from me, or when she wishes to belittle me. Otherwise, I might as well be a piece of furniture for all that she cares."

Samantha reached over and settled her hand upon one of his clenched fists. "I'm certain she cares, Takeem. She's the queen and must be very busy, but you're her son. Of course she loves you."

Takeem lunged from his chair. "I'm her spinner son and that's the truth. I may be Royal, but that doesn't make me Blue. I'm nothing to her. I'm surprised she didn't have me executed at birth."

Samantha gasped. "Surely not, Takeem. She's your mother."

Takeem stood in the center of the room, head bowed, fists clenched, dragging in deep breaths. "I'm sorry, Samantha. This is not well done of me. You deserve better."

"No, it's all right." Samantha stood and walked toward Takeem. "I know what it's like, Takeem, to wish for things to be different."

Takeem raised his head and looked at her. "Yes, I suppose you do." He asked her quietly, "Where is Hwanon, Samantha? Why is he not with you?"

Samantha's heart clenched to hear the question she woke with every morning. Where was her brother and why was he not with her? Closing her eyes, she could almost imagine he was there, standing beside her, whispering in her ear. She could almost hear his voice.

"Sehmah," he whispered.

"Hwanon," her mind sighed softly back.

"Samantha?" Takeem spoke quietly.

"What?" she whispered, eyes still closed.

"Where is he? Where's Hwanon?"

"Here," she whispered, seeing him in her mind's eye, standing tall, the warrior-king of their story. "He's here." Her eyes flew open. "I've been looking for him for a long time, Takeem, but now I know. He's here. In Lutia. Have you seen him?"

"I haven't, no. Are you certain he's here?"

"Yes, of course. I have to find him, Takeem."

"All right. I'll help you search."

Just like that. Samantha's eyes burned. *He would help her search.* Finally, after so much time, she would find Jonathan.

"Where do you think he is?" Takeem asked.

"I don't know. I just – I don't know."

"That's all right. If he's here, we'll find him. We can begin the search tomorrow. Will that work?"

"Yes, thank you." Something long forgotten rekindled and sparked to life.

Hope.

As Takeem led her toward the guest wing, Samantha tried to decide what she would say to Jonathan, if she found him and had the chance to speak with him again. What words would she share, what stories would she tell? If she could spend even one more hour in Jonathan's presence, what would she make of that hour?

*

The room Takeem gave her was luxurious and filled with gorgeous furniture, all of it somewhat foreign in design. The bed was completely round, covered in linen as red as any forest fire. A triangular chest of drawers stood against a wall and above it hung a mirror unlike any she had ever seen before. It was made of multiple diamond-shaped shards of glass. Each shard shone a different color, depending on the angle of sight. The shards overlapped each other, forming a shape she couldn't quite grasp, though the image lingered below the surface. Staring at that mirror, Samantha had a great feeling of both anticipation and foreboding. What would she see if she looked inside its depths? Would Samantha be there? Or would Sehmah-the-stranger be staring back?

Too terrified to look, Samantha settled on the bed. She closed her eyes and tried to rest, but all she could see were those flying arrows and the land that died upon their impact. Samantha launched herself from the bed, her eyes inadvertently falling upon the mirror once more. This time, though her heart pounded in terror, she stepped forward until she stood fully in the mirror's gaze, confronting the truth of her own self.

Samantha's hair had always been curly and red, her eyes a light sky-blue, and her skin fair with freckles scattered across her cheeks and nose. She had always worn her hair long, but when her family died, she had cut her hair in a fit of mourning. It now barely touched the top of her shoulders, though the curls were tighter than ever. The Samantha that stared back at her from the mirror's gaze was *not* the Samantha she'd grown up knowing. Her hair now had one solid strand of royal-blue that stretched from root to tip at her right temple. In addition, it looked as if she had dipped her hair into a gallon of paint, creating royal-blue tips about three inches long. Perhaps most shocking of all, however, was her skin. Now dotted a brilliant blue, all of her freckles stood out like a strange case of royal-blue chicken pox.

Spinning away from the mirror image showing her as she'd never seen herself before, Samantha strode across the room and flung open the door. Before stepping over the threshold, she glanced back one last time. From a distance, the mirror was so clearly in the shape of a willow tree she stumbled over her own feet, catching her hand on the doorframe.

Hulak lunged to his feet when Samantha opened the door. He'd been sprawled across the hallway, between her room and the one Takeem had chosen across the hall. He approached her now and nuzzled his nose against her hand. She gently stroked his head and leaning down, murmured softly in his ear. "I don't understand this world, Hulak. It's so different from what I imagined. I'm so different." Straightening up, she stared down the hallway, fatigue beating down upon her. She wasn't certain where she'd been going when she flung open the door, but everything was okay now. Knowing that Hulak stood sentinel outside her door, she was ready to sleep.

Leaning down, she hugged Hulak fiercely. Tonight, she would rest.

Tomorrow, she would begin the search for Jonathan.

THE BLUE TIGER

JENNIFER ENTERED THE apartment, exhausted and terrified. She had begun her search that morning by phoning every hospital in the area, but not a single teenager matching Samantha's description had been admitted. Jennifer had then, her heart pounding in dread, phoned the city morgues. She had wept with relief each time she hung up the phone.

Further attempts to call and text Samantha resulted in no replies and another check online revealed no information. Instead, the phone company's website said, "the device cannot be located because it is either not turned on or not in service", causing Jennifer to worry that Samantha's cell phone had somehow become a metaphor for Samantha herself.

Jennifer filed a missing persons report at the police station, but as Neil pointed out, Samantha was eighteen, legally an adult, today. She had also communicated via text that she would be away for a while. Neil didn't say it, but it was clear he believed Jennifer was overreacting.

She couldn't let it go though. She walked all over the streets of their city, searching for Samantha everywhere. She visited park after park, library after library, even the high school where everything was winding down, headed for summer vacation. No one she spoke with at the school had seen Samantha since the seniors' last day the previous Friday. For all of Jennifer's searching, she had no luck in uncovering even a single clue to

Samantha's whereabouts.

Jennifer's entire life revolved around helping others, but she couldn't help the one who counted on her the most.

She entered Samantha's sparsely decorated room and sank down onto the bed. No pictures hung on the walls; no trinkets littered the dresser top. It looked much the same as it had two years before, when this room served as a guest room for her niece and nephew when they came to visit.

Had Jonathan survived, they would have needed a larger apartment. Jennifer would have given up anything, would have *paid* anything, to have that option. This room was so wrong, without the trundle unit pulled out, without the two of them camped in here, or the three of them camped out in the living room, indulging in late night movies and giggle fests. They had lost so much, including the people she and Samantha had once been, and they just kept on losing.

Jennifer lay back on the bed and stared up at the ceiling. Directly above her head was one of Jonathan's drawings. It was of the willow tree that stood in the backyard of the twins' childhood home. The trailing vines were vividly real.

There seemed to be an image drawn into them. They were mostly green, but winking through here and there were various shades of blue. At first she thought it was the sky, but the blues took on their own shape until she realized that buried within the vines of their willow tree, Jonathan had drawn a blue-striped tiger.

Jennifer's tiger.

The Tekhlan

SAMANTHA WOKE EARLY the next morning, filled with a sense of purpose, perhaps for the first time since Jonathan's death. The feeling of unbearable grief that weighed upon her each morning was somehow lessened that day, replaced by a sense of Jonathan, one she had not woken to since the moment of his death. She felt his presence filling her room, as if he were waking when she was, as if he would walk at her side on this long journey of discovery, as they re-learned their world.

Samantha stood before the mirror and whispered to the willow tree, as if it were somehow the gateway to Jonathan. "Well, here we are, Hwanon. How is it possible our story burns so brightly?" Reaching out a hand, she touched one of the glass vines that trailed from the center of the mirror, from the trunk of her tree. "A willow tree brought me here, Jonathan. Did it bring you too?"

She stared into the mirror as if she might somehow see the shadow of her brother passing through its reflection, but saw nothing. She was convinced he was there anyway. She stared at her right shoulder, imagining he stood behind her, imagining he watched her from not so very far away, waiting for her to find him, waiting for her to pull him from this false world back to the real one, or perhaps waiting for her to turn from the false world of their birth toward this real world they had created together. Somehow, somewhere, he waited for her, and she would search for him to the ends of creation. She *would* find him.

She started for the door, only to be stopped by the sound of hooves, loud and drumming, that came from outside her open window. The sun had barely begun to rise. Her room was high off the ground, with windows that overlooked the main courtyards that stood directly inside the front gates of the palace. Those gates were now open and the courtyards were filled with a dozen black four-legged beasts. At their sides were men dressed in black. They looked like –

One of the men flung off his black cloak, revealing dark blue skin. He wore a black tunic and pants with a red sash around his waist. Were these the infamous Tekhlan, the assassins of the throne?

Shaking off her paralysis, Samantha ran out of the room and almost plowed into Hulak, who sat in the middle of the hallway. She grabbed onto his neck to steady herself and flung herself at Takeem's door. She pounded on it.

Seconds later, Takeem opened the door, fully dressed, ready for his day.

She grabbed his hand and dragged him into the hallway. "Come quick, Takeem. I think the Tekhlan are here."

"What? How do you know?"

"I could see them from my window."

"Stay here." Takeem hurried into her room, only to reappear a few seconds later. "It's definitely the Tekhlan." He crossed back into his room, emerging a few moments later with two long, curved blades that he slid into a holster that was strapped to his back. "Let's go find Arioan." Grabbing Samantha's hand, he pulled her down the hall behind him.

They raced down several passageways before finally arriving at Arioan's rooms.

Takeem flung open the door and pulled her inside, but Arioan was not there.

"Should we go to the queen?" Samantha asked.

"I'm not certain. I don't know if we can trust her. The Tekhlan do her bidding."

"Do you think she sent them after me? Or after Arioan?"

"No," Takeem said. "She would never order the Tekhlan to

assassinate Arioan. He's the heir to the throne. If she sent them, they were there for you. Let's go." He led the way to the end of the hallway where a tall, semicircular table stood against the wall. Above the table was a charcoal drawing of a willow tree. It looked like Jonathan's work.

Samantha took a step closer. Something blue was hidden in the branches.

A loud, mechanical click sounded and the wall, drawing and table shifted outward together, exposing a hidden doorway.

"What did you do, Takeem?"

"Pulled the lever inside here." He closed the table's drawer and reached for the edge of the wall. He pulled the opening wider, revealing darkness beyond.

Hulak brushed by Samantha and entered the darkened space. Samantha followed. She inched her way forward until she felt Hulak's fur brush her hand. There was a stale, musty scent that permeated the area.

Takeem entered behind her and pushed a second lever. The door closed, sealing them in darkness.

Samantha whispered, "Takeem?"

"Just a moment, Samantha. It will take me a moment to…" A loud click echoed through the room and four torches blazed to life.

They stood at the top of a long stone staircase that twined downward. Samantha shivered at how easy it would have been to stumble down them in the dark.

"This way." Takeem grabbed one of the torches and led the way down the staircase.

Each stair was wide and curved, requiring several steps forward for each step down.

Several moments later, Takeem stopped and pulled another lever in the wall. A portion of the wall beside Samantha rose into the ceiling, revealing another dark passageway. Once more, Hulak led the way.

There were alcoves within this passageway. Each alcove had a stone bench on two sides and a slanted wall between them.

"Where are we, Takeem?" Samantha whispered.

"These are the spy tunnels of the Tekhlan."

Samantha froze. "The Tekhlan?"

"Don't worry. The Tekhlan have not used these tunnels since my father's time. Perhaps they no longer know of their existence."

"But—"

"But what?"

"How do you know of their existence? I mean – you're not –"

"No. I'm not one of the Tekhlan. Even if I wanted to be, they would never accept a spinner into their ranks, even a Royal one. I know of these tunnels because my father was once the leader of the Tekhlan. He died before I was born, but I found his war logs when I was ten. I've read them all and have found all the passageways hidden in the palace. In all the years I've been walking these halls, I've never met anyone inside them – not my mother, not my brother, not one of the Tekhlan. We are safe here. I promise you."

Samantha forced herself to start moving again. To take her mind off the Tekhlan, she asked, "Why is Arioan heir to the throne?" It didn't make sense. Hwanon was the only king in their story. Though Jonathan had occasionally tried to convince Samantha she should make Takeem a king, neither of them had ever considered Arioan a candidate.

"Because he's Royal and I am not."

"Of course, you're royal, Takeem."

"Not royal enough. In Lutia, our skin and eyes denote our rank. Arioan is destined to lead while I'm an abomination."

"Don't say that, Takeem."

"It's true. The spinners are impure, the magicks we inherit a taint that infects our eyes, spreading marks of the beast across our skin.

"But you said you have no magicks."

Takeem shrugged. "It's why the Blues hate me. They don't really believe I'm without power. They expect at any moment I will spin them into darkness."

"That's ridiculous. You're the Royal-spinner."

"Yes, but that doesn't make me Royal-Blue. I'm not one of

them and they'll never let me forget it. My mother and brother
are no different." He stopped in the middle of the hallway.
"Enough of this. You and I have no power to change what is."
He stepped into one of the alcoves. "That doesn't mean we'll
allow the Tekhlan to determine our fates though." He settled on
one of the benches. "Come." He pointed to the bench across
from him. "Sit and let us see what we can discover."

Takeem reached over and lifted away a long, black rectangle
that hung from hooks on the wall to reveal a small sliver of a
window. Samantha inched closer. The window looked down
upon the library where they had met the queen the night before.

"What are we watching for?" she whispered to Takeem.

"Just wait," he whispered back.

Alatore's voice reached their ears a moment before she
stepped into view. "Why was I not told of this immediately?"

"You had no need of this knowledge." The speaker was male,
his voice firm.

"Clearly I did. Had I known, I could have acted from the
moment she arrived at the palace." Alatore stormed across the
room, grabbed a wineglass from the table they had sat around
the night before and took a drink. Swinging around, she shouted,
"Now everything is at risk. How dare you not keep me
informed?" She flung the glass she held across the room where it
shattered against the wall.

"We can still control this situation, my queen." The speaker
strode across the room toward Queen Alatore. It was the man
Samantha had seen in the courtyard. The red sash around his
waist had an image painted on it. From this angle, Samantha
couldn't tell what the design was.

"That's Yezyr, the leader of the Tekhlan," Takeem whispered
in Samantha's ear. His breath caressed Samantha's ear and neck,
causing her to shiver in reaction.

"Does the Council know?" Alatore's voice was quiet, defeated.

"Not yet. If you give us the girl, there is no need to involve
them."

Samantha clasped a hand against her mouth to keep the
whimper of fear from escaping.

"And if I do not?"

"Then your accord with them will surely be forfeit."

Silence filled the room for a moment. Then Queen Alatore spoke again. "Very well. See that it is done quietly. The girl is on the third floor in the east—"

Samantha did not hear what else was said because Takeem slid the cover over the window, grabbed her hand and dragged her out of the alcove. They ran down the hall back to the staircase and raced up them.

"Where are we going, Takeem?" Samantha gasped as he led them past where they'd originally entered the tunnels and continued running up the stairs.

"To the roof."

Several flights later, Takeem stopped and pulled open a door. Sunlight poured in.

Samantha walked out onto a long, flat segment of roof and froze.

A man stood waiting for them. He was completely Royal in color, from his hair to his eyes to his skin. He was dressed in black, with the Tekhlan's red sash around his waist.

Samantha whirled to warn Takeem, but he was already there, sweeping in front of her to face the Tekhlan on his own.

"Devix? What are you doing here?"

Takeem knew this man?

"Why are you with her, Takeem? A death order's been placed on her head. If you refuse to hand her over, they will execute you as well."

Samantha took a step back, brushing up against Hulak. His presence gave her comfort.

"I thought they transferred you," Takeem said. "You're supposed to be in Sky territory."

"I was. My unit was called back. For her." Devix nodded to Samantha. "They say she's a traitor. You need to disassociate yourself from her, Takeem. The Royals need little provocation to order your death."

"I won't abandon her."

"Why not?"

"She's Sehmah."

Samantha jerked to hear that name again. Why was he calling her that? She'd told him –

"Your dream-companion."

He'd spoken of her to Devix?

"One of them, yes."

But it was supposed to be two. Sehmah and Hwanon.

"Then you need to go. Quickly. I'll hold them off, if I can." Devix stepped to the side.

Takeem hesitated. "Will you be all right?"

"I'll be fine."

Takeem grabbed Samantha's hand and pulled her toward the center of the roof. Hulak followed, transforming into his larger form, wings exploding from his sides.

"Wait."

They stopped and turned, Samantha terrified Devix had changed his mind. Her eyes widened when he clasped Takeem's shoulder, jerked him forward and hugged him tight. "Be safe." He pushed Takeem away again. "Now go."

Takeem turned to Hulak, vaulted onto his back and leaned down toward Samantha. "Quickly, Samantha."

With a strong sense of déjà vu, she reached up.

Takeem grabbed her arm and swung her in front of him onto Hulak's back. "Thank you, Devix."

"You have your mother's list?"

"What? Yes, but she's the one who sent the Tekhlan–"

"Don't believe everything you hear, Takeem. Trust your mother. Trust the list. Now go!"

Hulak lunged forward.

Three men burst onto a roof across the way, bows and arrows pointed at them. Devix shouted, arrows flew and Hulak dove off the building.

They plummeted fast, the wind a roar in Samantha's ears, a pressing weight upon her chest.

Hulak spread his huge wings wide, caching the air currents and hurtling them back up.

The three men on the roof were down.

Devix was running from one side of the roof to the other.

Hulak hurtled them around a corner of a building, over a walkway and around a tower.

Samantha caught a glimpse of an arrow and then someone fell from that tower, red sash marking him as one of the Tekhlan.

Hulak hurtled over another walkway, where Royal-Blue faces stared up at them.

Across the way, Devix raced from one rooftop to the next, making leaps of huge distances, dispatching arrows at incredible speeds. More would-be assassins fell from rooftops and towers.

Far below, additional Tekhlan poured from buildings. They raced toward pitch black beasts tethered to platforms similar to those used when boarding planes, only these had stairs leading to incredibly tall beasts.

The Tekhlan raced up the stairs, and within moments, were riding for the gates.

"He's not going to make it," Takeem said, drawing Samantha's attention back to Devix and his race across palace roofs.

Three assassins waited on the final roof, their arrows no longer pointed toward them, but instead toward the adjoining roof.

Devix raced toward the gap between the two buildings and leapt.

"No!" Takeem shouted.

The Tekhlan released their arrows.

THE RIVER

THE WOODS WERE silent. The sun winked through the leaves, casting pockets of light amidst the dark. Nothing moved but the shadows.

She waited.

Maybe he wouldn't find her. Not this time. If she stayed still. If she didn't move.

The roar of a tiger echoed through the woods. Birds took flight.

The tiger's paws made an almost silent thudding sound as they hit the ground. Thwap. Too close.

The soft snap of a twig, the rustling of leaves.

He was hunting her.

Another roar echoed through the woods. Nothing moved.

The tiger surged onto the path. He opened his mouth and roared.

She turned and ran. Feet pounding the terrain. The chuff of the tiger at her back.

Off the path.

Not that way.

Down the incline.

Not that way.

Toward the river.

Not that way!

She plunged into the river. Stopped. Caught her breath. Safe.

Not true.

The river was never safe.

He was watching her.

She pivoted slowly, knowing what she would see. The blue-striped tiger stood on a boulder a few feet away. The moment she looked into his royal-blue eyes, he lunged.

ALATORE'S LIST

TAKEEM HADN'T SPOKEN a word since they'd left the Royal palace far behind.

Samantha didn't know what to do. She sat in his embrace, comforted by his presence, his arms strong around her waist, when she should be the one comforting him.

The last they'd seen of Devix, he'd been falling between the two buildings, arrows having ended his mad race to save them. Hulak had flown by so quickly, Samantha wasn't even sure whether Devix had managed to kill his assassins before falling.

"I'm so sorry about Devix, Takeem."

No answer.

After a few moments, Samantha tried again. "It was truly the most beautiful thing I've ever seen though."

Silence, then, "What are you talking about?"

"Nothing."

"No. What do you mean? That wasn't beautiful. That was death."

"I didn't mean his death. I meant his life. He loved you so much and he gave his life to keep you safe. There's nothing more beautiful than that."

"I didn't trust him."

"What do you mean?"

"He was like a father to me, practically raised me, but I stopped trusting him long ago."

"Why?"

"Because he was Royal and a member of the Tekhlan. Because both the Tekhlan and the Royals hate what I represent."

"Magicks?"

"Exactly. I'm a spinner, capable of spinning the magicks that don't even exist anymore, and everyone hates me for something I'll never be able to do. I was certain Devix hated me as much as everyone else and so I did not trust him. I was cold and hard and still he gave his life for mine."

"Because he loved you."

Silence.

"Yes," Takeem finally said. "And it breaks my heart."

Samantha closed her eyes against the grief she heard in his voice. Against the grief she held in her heart. She knew this song. It was endless and dark.

Time for something new.

"Where are we going?" she asked.

"The list Devix mentioned. It's one my mother gave me when I was very young, maybe four or five. It's a list of Sky-Blue families who are loyal, who will protect me against everyone and everything, including the Tekhlan."

"But–" Samantha leaned to the side, so that she could look up at him. His jaw was rigid with tension, his gaze fixed above her head. "But your mother was going to give me to the Tekhlan – are you certain the people on the list can be trusted?"

"I don't know, but Devix said I needed to trust her, to trust the list. He died protecting us. I have to believe him. Otherwise, nothing makes sense."

"If Devix knew about the list – I mean he's a member of the Tekhlan. Won't the other members know about it too?"

"My mother gave me the list when I was very young. She told me the people on it would protect me from the Tekhlan. I don't think she'd share it with them."

"But she's the one who sent them after us in the first place."

"And the list she gave me was intended to save me from them."

Samantha didn't want to hurt Takeem's feelings, but she didn't trust Alatore at all. She settled her arms on top of his, squeezing gently. "What did Yezyr mean, when he said her accord with the Council would be broken?"

"I'm not certain. I've never heard of any accord between them."

"Well, who's on the Council?"

"A group of Royals who serve as advisors to the throne." Takeem rested his chin on top of her head and caught her right hand with his, threading their fingers together.

Samantha closed her eyes. He made her feel safe, protected, *loved*. "I wonder what kind of accord it is and why she was willing to sacrifice me to keep it intact."

"I don't know. My mother does not confide in me."

"But you believe we should trust the names on her list?"

"I think we should try anyway, if only because Devix has earned our trust."

"All right. Who's the first name?"

"Pyral. She lives in the village of Belia, close to the fifth ring of Lutia."

"How long will it take us to get there?" she asked.

"Maybe another hour or so."

"How long will it take the Tekhlan to catch up with us?"

"Hulak is the last of his kind. Even the fastest krutesk will take three hours to travel the distance he can in one, even with us on his back. We should be fine, at least from the remaining Tekhlan at the palace. It's the Tekhlan stationed in Sky territories we'll have to worry about now."

"There are more of them?"

"Of course. However, most serve in Royal territory, which we just left, or in Sky territories closest to the War Zone. Since our first stops aren't close to either, we should be safe enough."

Taking comfort from these words, Samantha relaxed into the rhythm of the nargnet's flight, the comfort of Takeem's arms lulling her into a sense of peace. Her eyes closed and her thoughts drifted.

ADAM'S GIFT

JENNIFER WOKE WITH a start. Her heart was pounding, her ears ringing from the roar of her tiger. For one brief moment, she couldn't understand why she was in Samantha's room, sleeping on her twin bed, then it all came rushing back.

Samantha was missing.

As Jennifer lay there beneath Jonathan's willow, staring into the bright blue eyes of his hidden tiger, she felt alone and lost. She sat up and stared at the floor for a moment, then pushed herself to her feet. Stepping away from the bed, she tripped on the bedspread and fell to her knees. She grabbed the offending blanket and flung it away, in the process revealing the space beneath Samantha's bed. The gleam of honey-colored wood caught her eye. Recognizing the edge of a treasure, she reached under the bed and pulled out Samantha's willow tree box.

The box had been sanded to perfection, then stained a gorgeous honey color. Its hinges gleamed gold at the corners of the lid, where a willow tree had been lovingly carved upon its surface. Her brother Adam had made this box for Samantha and another one to match for Jonathan. Adam, who had no talent whatsoever for carving or for carpentry or really for any type of woodwork at all, had somehow managed to create two perfect treasure boxes, one for each of his children. The boxes were so similar it was almost impossible to tell them apart, unless you knew where to look. Deeply buried within the roots of the trees on the surface of each box, Adam had carved the twins' pet names for each other: Sehmah on Samantha's box, Hwanon on Jonathan's.

At the time of his death, Jonathan's box had held treasure beyond worth – an exquisite collection of artwork that he had completed over the years. His creativity and imagination were stunning.

Now Jennifer held Samantha's box in her hands. What clues to Samantha's whereabouts might it hold?

THE FIRES OF SHOREL

BY SAMANTHA WHITTIER

This was it. Of all the battles he had witnessed, this was the one Huk had foreseen, the one battle that would determine their future. It was Tak's first skirmish as a future king, Ari's one opportunity to gain vengeance for their father's fall, Hwanon's final chance to heal this world. Above all, it was their last opportunity to win this war.

Huk, the Royal nargnet, flew across the sky, a red beacon of warning to all those who would fight against them. Tak was seated upon his back, his father's sword clutched in hand, ready to engage the enemy. The sky was filled with the sound of beating wings as nargnets and brekzors battled in ferocious lunges.

Huk's red claws raked through a brekzor's neck, blood spraying the sky red. Flinging the brekzor away, allowing it to fall, he turned and was speared from below. Grunting from the force of the blow, he struggled to stay in the air, but a second spear caught him and he was falling. With a great, thundering crash, he was down.

Tak was flung from Huk's body when they landed. Disoriented, he staggered toward the nargnet, desperate to save him. When the sword plunged through his heart from behind, Tak felt nothing but an icy coldness that spread swiftly through his frame. As he fell, the last thing he saw was Huk's burning red eyes, his dying eyes.

Ari witnessed the moment everything went wrong. He saw the spear that ended a world, the spear that took down the royal nargnet, the spear that landed his brother, the next king of Lutia. He raced across the land, desperate to beat the nargnet to his dying place, but there was not enough time. The nargnet was down, then Tak as well. In a terrible moment of grief, Ari came to a skidding stop in the middle of the battlefield and screamed. In that moment of inattention, Ari's world went dark, his head removed in one decisive swing of an enemy's sword.

The fires began at the forests of Bipin.

ARIOAN'S NEED

SAMANTHA CAME AWAKE with a start, images from the final story she had written racing through her head. Huk gutted from below, Tak impaled from behind, Ari beheaded. And the horrid scenes that followed, the fires that consumed.

"You okay?" Takeem's voice rumbled above her.

"Yeah." She straightened her spine, pulling forward a bit, away from the comfort of Takeem's embrace.

"Bad dream?"

Samantha shrugged, scrubbing her face with her hands. "I'm okay," she muttered.

"We're almost there." Takeem pointed toward some houses in the distance. "You can see the village of Belia ahead."

"Do you think they'll know? I mean that the Tekhlan are after us? Are you sure we can trust them? You're the Royal-spinner, but I'm not anything. I mean I'm not a Blue."

"It'll be fine, Samantha." Takeem pulled her into his arms so that her back was once more resting against his chest. He wrapped his arms around her and squeezed gently. "Trust me. We won't stay long, but we need some help."

Before she could reply, Hulak plummeted downward. Samantha cried out and grabbed hold of Takeem's arms in fright.

Takeem shouted wildly with laughter as Hulak barreled toward the ground, the wind whipping past them, making

Samantha feel as if she could be plucked from Hulak's back at any moment. She closed her eyes and whimpered, the wind snatching the sound away. Or maybe she hadn't made any sound at all. Maybe she was still dreaming, still on Earth, far away, in the apartment sleeping, waiting for Aunt Jenny to wake her, to force her to face life again.

"Nice flight, Hulak. Wasn't that incredible, Samantha?"

Samantha opened her eyes and looked around. They were on the ground. Stopped. She had missed the entire landing. Come to think of it, she had missed the last one too. One of these days, she was going to keep her eyes open and figure out how Hulak managed to go from a giant nargnet in flight, to a standing still position on the ground.

Takeem slid from Hulak's back and helped Samantha down.

There were a number of people standing around, watching them silently. They all had light blue skin and pale blue eyes and hair.

One woman stepped forward. "Why are you here?" Her eyes were fierce and angry.

Samantha edged toward Takeem so they stood side by side.

"We're here to see Pyral," Takeem said.

The woman crossed her arms. "Pyral has no interest in speaking with a son of the Tekhlan."

"What about the son of a queen?" Samantha asked.

"The son of a queen?" the woman repeated. "A mendacious queen perhaps, a pretender queen, a lying -"

"Enough, Kerina." A voice rose from the back of the crowd.

The woman confronting them whirled to face another. "You should not be here. Danger enshrouds them."

"As it does us all." The new arrival had short, mostly white hair, with a few light blue streaks in it. Other than some laugh lines around her eyes and mouth, her sky-blue skin was smooth and creamy. "I am Pyral."

"Thank you for seeing us." Takeem bowed and introduced himself and Samantha.

Pyral studied the two of them for a long moment. "Well, come on then. I don't have all day." She turned and walked away.

Hulak shimmered to his smaller size and the three of them followed.

Kerina let out a soft huff of frustration and rushed past Takeem to walk at Pyral's side.

She led them by two cottages up onto the porch of a third one. She pushed the door open and went inside.

Kerina stopped at the door and glowered as Takeem and Samantha went by. As they entered the cottage, Kerina followed, shutting the door with a distinct snap. She leaned her back against it and crossed her arms.

They stood in a large room with a wooden table and chairs. "Have a seat." Pyral waved at the table and disappeared through an archway into another room of the house.

Takeem led Samantha around the table to the far side, pulled out a chair for her, waited for her to sit down, then settled onto the chair next to her. Hulak padded over and stretched out on the floor behind them.

Pyral bustled into the room with drinks and plates of food. "Come, Kerina," she said to the woman at the door. "Join us at the table."

Kerina sat across from Takeem.

Pyral settled beside her across from Samantha. "Eat," she ordered.

When neither Takeem nor Samantha reached for the food, Kerina growled and grabbed a sandwich. Shoving it into her mouth, she glared at Takeem as she chewed.

Takeem passed a sandwich to Samantha, who murmured a quiet thank you, then took one for himself.

"So, why are you here, then?" Pyral asked. "I assume it's because you need help."

"Yes." Takeem set down his sandwich without taking a bite. "We had to leave the palace suddenly without provisions. We need food, water, clothes, and a place to stay tonight, somewhere safe, if possible."

Pyral shook her head, making Samantha's heart sink. "I always thought it would be Arioan coming to me for help, not his younger brother."

"Why would Arioan come to you for help?" Takeem asked.

"To claim the throne, of course."

"You think Arioan would conspire against our mother to claim the throne before his time?" he asked.

Pyral laughed. "Of course not, but there are those who know the truth, and they will do everything in their power to ensure your brother never inherits the throne."

"The truth? What are you talking about?"

Pyral stared at Takeem in silence for a few moments then said, "So Alatore's lies still hold. Do they hold for Arioan as well, I wonder."

"What lies?" Takeem demanded.

"It is not for me to share those tales. Just know that Arioan's need is at least as great as your own, Takeem."

"I seriously doubt that. Arioan has never been in danger of being executed for the color of his skin."

"You might be surprised, Takeem."

"Will you help us or not?" Samantha burst out.

Pyral glanced at her. "Perhaps. However, I require honesty in return for my help. Why do you come here now, Takeem, burning through the first name on your mother's list? And who is this young woman who accompanies you, this woman who is not purely Blue, yet not spinner either? What dangers have you brought to our door?"

"This is Samantha. We have no idea why, but the Tekhlan are after her."

"And what is your plan, Takeem? To run until you cannot run anymore? That did not work so well for your mother."

"I don't know. Truthfully, we have no plan, other than to survive the Tekhlan."

Pyral stood up. "I wish you well, Takeem, though I do not hold out much hope for your survival. You both may stay here tonight, but I expect you to be gone by morning. Several packs with provisions will be left on the porch for you. Safe journey." With a quick bow, she left the house.

Kerina stood, then with one final glare in their direction, exited as well.

There was only one bed in the cottage. Though Takeem offered to sleep on the floor, Samantha would not hear of it. They could share the bed, she declared, her heart fluttering a little at the thought. And so they settled down, with Hulak stretched out on the floor beside them. The two of them lay on their backs, arms at their sides, and stared at the ceiling.

It was awkward and weird.

Samantha rolled toward Takeem and settled her head upon his chest, an arm around his waist. He immediately wrapped his arms around her, one hand at her waist holding her close, the other hand at the base of her neck, fingers playing with her hair. Feeling safe and warm for the first time since her family's deaths, Samantha's eyes grew heavy and she slept.

She dreamt a willow tree grew around them in the night. It exploded from the ground beneath the cottage and stretched upward, breaking through the roof and stretching all around, enshrouding the entire home beneath its branches.

She dreamt the willow tree shared the story of Arioan's need with her and Takeem.

BRENIN / VUKEL, 31 YEARS AGO

FLIGHT

Brenin paced while he waited for his brother to arrive. The large room was empty, as were the surrounding barracks, a reminder that he should be on the wall. His shift was supposed to have begun ten minutes before, but Liden had switched the schedule last minute, demanding Brenin meet him in the main hall of the guards' quarters. The change worried him. He couldn't afford to bring attention to himself.

"The king's back." Liden announced from the entryway.

"Is Vukel with him?"

"Of course."

"Where are they?" He had to get to Alatore before they did.

"It doesn't matter, Brenin. You need to stay away from her."

"I won't do that. You know how they are." Brenin pushed past Liden, but his brother caught his arm.

"Wait."

"What is it?"

"They've announced the wedding. She's to wed Vukel in the morning."

Brenin jerked away from his brother's hold and started to pace again. "She would never agree to that."

"She's the king's sister, Brenin. She's not meant for the likes of us. We're soldiers at best, and Sky-Blue ones at that."

"Vukel's a soldier."

"He's not a soldier, Brenin, he's the leader of the Tekhlan. He'll kill you if he suspects you've touched her."

"It doesn't matter. I have to get her away from here. We need to leave tonight." He headed toward the sleeping quarters. He was mostly packed, had been since Alatore told him –

"Brenin, please, listen to me." Liden followed him into his quarters.

Brenin grabbed two bags from under his bed and checked the area quickly. Had he forgotten anything?

"Brenin."

"I'm not abandoning her, Liden. We thought we'd have more time, but we always planned to leave. She's too good for them. You don't have to come with us. Just don't interfere."

"Not come with you? Brenin, I have no choice. You're my brother. You take her, they'll execute me after torturing me for everything I know. You make this choice, you make it for all of us, not just for you and me and her, but for our parents and all of our brothers in all of the territories, for their children, for their children's children, for all of our line. You make this choice, we burn or triumph together."

Was Liden right? Would this choice haunt his entire family for the rest of their lives? Liden had worked hard for his position as lead guard on the wall. He was Sky-Blue, but still had risen far in the ranks. If they left, he'd lose everything.

If they didn't leave, Alatore and his child would pay the price.

"Alatore needs me. This is her chance, to get away from their influence, to make a difference for all of us."

"A difference? She's Royal-Blue, Brenin. Worse, she's the sister of the king and descended from a long line of Royals who dedicated their lives to destroying anyone not Royal enough."

"I know, but Alatore's not like that. She loves me, a Sky-Blue, and she wants our child to inherit the throne."

"A Sky-Royal?"

"Or a Royal-Sky. I suppose it depends on the color of the

child's skin."

"It'll never happen, Brenin. They'll execute the child first."

"She's pregnant."

"What?"

"She just found out two days ago. We were going to leave next week."

"Brenin, I warned you. How could you be so—" Liden shook his head.

"I'm sorry, brother."

"It's too late for sorry. If they discover the truth, they'll execute you and her and the babe."

"It's why we have to get Alatore out. The chance of my child being born fully Royal is unlikely at best. Both their lives end the day the child is born."

Liden sighed. "Tell me you have a plan."

"Alatore knows the way to the nesting grounds. We're going to travel there, beg the nargnets for help."

"And if they refuse you? You'll never get over the walls without their aid."

"I know. It's our only option though."

"Fine. Get to Alatore. Tell her we leave when the moon is high. I'll secure us some mounts."

"Thank you, brother."

"Just go."

*

Six weeks later
Sky-Blue Territory: the Village of Soryn

Vukel and the Tekhlan had been in pursuit of the Sky kidnappers for more than a month now. Though the Tekhlan spread the word that to keep the Royal heir from her betrothed was to face charges of treason, punishable by death, the Skies remained silent as to her whereabouts.

In the end, it did not matter though, for as Vukel pursued them through the territories, it became clear the Sky was headed home, undoubtedly believing he would find protection in the village of Soryn. Instead, he simply brought death home with him.

Soryn was closer to the fourth wall than the third, but still in the mandatory service zone. The Skies between the third and fourth walls of Lutia were fodder for the war. Everyone knew this. They fought and died young in defense of their lands, in defense of all Blues.

Alatore should never have met this Brenin of Soryn.

However, Brenin had nine older brothers, all of whom had served so well they'd been promoted again and again. When one of them had been offered an opportunity to work in Royal territory, he'd negotiated to bring his youngest brother, Brenin, with him. Brenin had just turned thirteen, the age of mandatory service at the wall. That someone had allowed this, had allowed a young man of able body to escape his duty was unbelievable.

This boy had become a man, not on the battlefields where he belonged, but in Royal territory, safe from the War Zone. His brother had helped him secure a job protecting the palace gates and while his king had headed for war, Brenin had stayed behind, safe from harm. While Vukel was striking down the spinner army, this Sky-Blue deserter had been courting his beloved. The more Vukel thought about it, the angrier he became, until all he lived for, all he dreamt about was killing this Sky-Blue refuse who dared to strive for more than he deserved.

When they reached Soryn, Vukel's rage had turned to cold resolve. Alatore was his. She had always been his. He would kill the Sky-Blue and any who harbored him, to ensure the Skies learned that lesson well.

Four towers stood at each of the four corners of the village, two men in each. Eight men to protect an entire village from the assassin force of the throne.

Vukel climbed the eastern tower, a shadow unseen, unheard.

The two men on watch spoke quietly above him, their soft murmurs the only sound this night. One of them laughed.

Unbelievable. They were not even worried, not even a little afraid. Having heard the Tekhlan were searching villages for the Royal heir, they should be terrified.

Leaping upward, Vukel silently swung over the railing and landed with a soft thud inside the tower. He threw three knives in swift succession.

The laughing man fell dead from a knife to the throat, a second in his chest.

The final knife lodged in the other man's heart and he was down as well.

Vukel waited a moment to see if an alarm was raised. Nothing. A perfect execution. He quickly retrieved his knives and sheathed them. He then waited for his men to attack.

As morning light began to streak across the sky, the Tekhlan rode from the hills to the west. As they approached the village of Soryn, the western bells rang in alarm.

The Tekhlan and Skies met at the western border to the village, the Skies demanding to know why the Tekhlan came armed for war, the Tekhlan demanding the Skies hand over the Royal heir. As the Skies protested their innocence and blocked the Tekhlan from entering the village from the west, a group of villagers mounted krutesks and headed east.

Vukel had his arrow ready, but he wasn't certain which rider to target, which one was Brenin. It shouldn't matter because any Sky between him and Alatore was a dead Sky, but he couldn't be certain which rider was Alatore. They were getting closer. Brenin would be one of the riders closest to her. Which one. She would be near the center.

One of the rider's hoods blew back displaying her Royal hair.

Vukel loosed an arrow.

One of the riders fell.

Vukel loosed a second and a third arrow.

Two more men fell. The other riders did not stop, but instead raced around the fallen riders and continued out of town.

Vukel launched himself across the tower and shot another arrow after them. As a fourth man fell, he notched a fifth arrow and drew it back to let the arrow fly. In that instant, as his fingers loosed the arrow, Alatore launched herself from the horse she rode. She slammed into one of the other riders, the fifth man, the man Vukel had just targeted. The arrow slammed into Alatore's body from behind.

"No!" Vukel's roar was echoed far ahead.

The other riders circled back and collected both Alatore and the man she had saved. A few moments later, they rode away, Alatore's body cradled in one of the Skies' arms.

Vukel's bow clattered to the ground. His legs buckled and he landed on his knees. He could not feel anything. He should be pursuing them, but couldn't manage to stand.

He'd shot his betrothed, the king's sister.

When he finally climbed down from the tower, he discovered the men of Soryn had engaged the Tekhlan and had died for their efforts. The town was in disarray, women and children weeping everywhere.

Vukel wanted to burn everything to the ground, to wipe this town from the planet.

He would not though. This was not the town's fault.

It was that bastard, Brenin's. He'd taken Alatore from her home, from the safety of Royal lands, and had brought her here, to the land of the Skies, kilometers from the war zone, and made her a target of the Tekhlan, the walking death of the throne.

If Alatore died, by Vanadevi's name, she would be avenged.

THE BIRTH OF A ROYAL-SKY

SEVEN MONTHS LATER
The War Zone, Year 100 AP

"I have news from the Sky villages, sir." Vukel's second in command, Petrar, said as they walked toward the king's tent.

"Tell me."

"They're saying a Royal-Sky has been born. They're saying this child is destined for the throne."

Vukel frowned. "A Royal-Sky? That is absurd. No Royal would—" He came to a dead stop. "What exactly have you heard, Petrar?"

"Just what I told you. Nothing more. Just that a Royal-Sky has been born."

"Born to whom?"

"I do not know, Vukel. No one is saying."

"How do they know the child is a Royal?"

"I assume because of the color of its skin or that of one of its parents."

"Has anyone mentioned her at all?"

"Not at all. Not once by name. I've heard the occasional rumor of a Royal-Blue woman in the Sky-Blue villages, but each time I investigate, it's never her."

"He said she was dead."

"He may have lied."

"I know, Petrar. I've known since the moment he said it. If she's still alive, though, where is she?" Vukel began walking again. "No matter. Whether this supposed Royal-Sky is Alatore's or some other woman's half-breed child, the result is the same. The Skies are now talking about one of their own attaining the throne." Vukel stopped at the entrance to the king's tent and turned to Petrar. "Very well, then. Thank you for letting me know, Petrar. I will inform the king."

Petrar nodded and walked away.

*

"A Royal-Sky?" King Sorelion shook his head. "There is no such thing. By definition, a Sky cannot be Royal. A half-breed's lines will always be contaminated."

Vukel nodded. "You're right, sir. However, there is the possibility…"

"What is it, Vukel? Just say it."

"We never found Alatore's body. Brenin claimed she was dead, but if she was pregnant and he knew it…"

"He would say anything to protect their child."

"Yes."

"That child would be my nephew."

Vukel nodded. "Yes."

"What are the chances of the child inheriting the throne? Tell me honestly, Vukel. He's impure. That should disqualify him. Right?"

Vukel sighed. "I know you want me to say that, sire, but…"

"No. I want you to tell me the truth. Be honest. What are the chances if the child is Alatore's, if he is my nephew?"

"The Royal Nargnet chooses based on honor and blood, sire. While the human king must be descended from the ancient lineage, that does not mean those lines must be pure. I believe if the nargnets found a spinner from the ancient line, whom they deemed more honorable than any Blues of that line, they would mark even a spinner for the throne. There would be no hesitation over a Sky-Blue."

"We are at war. How any of us might be found honorable under those circumstances is a mystery. Indeed, I was surprised Hulak chose me, but then there really were no other choices, not at the time. Alatore was too young. And the others..."

"Their hatred of the spinners was much more fierce than your own."

"Only because I had not been to war yet. Now my hatred would rival any of theirs." Sorelion shook his head. "My youth worked in my favor." He froze. "And now there is a child out there, possibly my nephew, innocent, no doubt full of honor. If I die on the battlefield tomorrow..."

"It is highly likely the nargnet would choose the child."

"What do you suggest I do, Vukel?"

"Track the mother. Discover the truth of the child. If this is all an elaborate hoax, we end the threat as quietly as possible. Similarly, if the child is your nephew but is more Sky than Royal, we make him disappear."

"And if he is more Royal than Sky?"

"That is your decision, sire."

"No, Vukel. I believe it is yours. If this child is my nephew, we both know that means the mother is Alatore. If you are willing to raise her child, to pretend he is yours, I will not stop you. The child must never know of his Sky origins though, and of course, he will never inherit the throne. Alatore must agree."

"And if she won't?"

"Then she will have made her choice and will have to bear the full weight of its consequences."

"Very well."

"Take half the men for the hunt."

"Sir, they are your Royal guard, here to protect you. It is better if I go alone."

"No. You will take half the guard. The men need some time away from this war. And you, Vukel, you need to know that when the time comes, you have the full weight of the Tekhlan at your back."

"Yes, my king."

PRESENT DAY

THE SHROUDED ONE

SAMANTHA WOKE, HEART pounding. The world was pitch black. She couldn't see anything, though she was still lying curled into Takeem's side. "Takeem, are you awake?" she whispered.

"I am."

"It's so dark." She used her hands to push herself to a sitting position and looked around. "It's too dark, Takeem."

"It's just the night, Samantha."

"No, it's the willow tree."

"The what?"

"The willow. It grew in the night. It -"

"You mean the Shrouded One? You dreamt of it too?"

"I need to find the door. We need to get some light in here." Samantha climbed from the bed and with her hands out, began walking toward where she remembered the door stood.

"Samantha, answer me. Did you dream of the Shrouded One too?"

"What's a Shrouded One?"

"The tree of creation. They're mostly gone now, ever since the purge of magicks. If a Shrouded One truly grew in the night, it would be a blessing for all the inhabitants of this village, past and future."

"I found the door." Samantha yanked it open.

It was lighter on the porch than in the cabin. Beyond the porch, a veil of willow vines had fallen, blocking out the rest of the world.

Fur brushed Samantha's fingers. Hulak, in his smaller form, stood at her side. She turned and stared into the cabin.

Light had filtered in, just enough to break the deep dark.

"Takeem," she whispered, staring at the trunk that stood to the right of the bed. It was huge, taking up much of the cabin's floor space.

Takeem jerked, scrambling away from the tree. In his haste, he fell from the bed, landing hard.

"Are you okay?" Samantha gasped, stepping forward.

"Fine." Takeem leapt to his feet and rushed toward her, an almost panicked look on his face.

"What's wrong?" Samantha asked as he joined her and Hulak on the porch.

Takeem leaned over, hands on his knees, gasping for breath. He flung an arm back toward the tree whose trunk had broken through the roof of the cottage. Samantha imagined it towering high into the sky, its branches and vines stretching out from the center of the roof, enclosing the entire cottage in his sphere. "It's a Shrouded One," Takeem said, "and we're still beneath it."

"I know." Samantha smiled. "Isn't it beautiful?"

"No. Yes." Takeem stood upright, but kept his back to the door and the trunk of the tree. "It's holy, Samantha. We shouldn't be here. Beneath its branches."

"But if it didn't want us beneath its branches, it wouldn't have grown here. And how did it manage that anyway? How long have we been asleep?"

"I don't know."

They stood on the porch, Samantha staring at the tree, Takeem staring at the porch stairs, where vines of the Shrouded One drifted against the lowest step.

After several long minutes of silence, Takeem spoke again. "I dreamt of my parents and of Arioan when he was a babe."

"I dreamt of them too," Samantha said.

"Is that why Pyral calls my mother the Mendacious Queen? Because Arioan is not a true Royal, but instead is the son of a Sky? I've never even heard a rumor questioning his parentage.

Everyone believes my mother was pregnant with Vukel's child when she was taken."

"Brenin said the babe was his."

"Yes, but Arioan has no Sky in him. Maybe Brenin was delusional. Maybe he kidnapped my mother when she was pregnant with my father's child and somehow convinced himself the babe was his."

"Then why did she throw herself from the horse?" Samantha asked.

"What?"

"When Vukel shot that arrow, she saved the Sky he was aiming for. Why would she do that?"

"I don't know."

"Are you sure she was kidnapped?"

"What do you mean?"

"Brenin said they were planning to leave together. Are you certain Alatore didn't leave of her own accord?"

"I'm not certain of anything anymore."

They stood in silence for another moment, then Takeem said, "We should go. We've lingered too long here."

They gathered their things, including two packs of provisions they found on the front porch as promised, then descended the porch steps. As they reached the bottom of the stairs, the vines that separated them from the world lifted and parted.

They emerged from beneath the willow to discover the entire town had gathered, including Pyral and Kerina. Many of those gathered were kneeling as if in prayer. All of them stared at Samantha and Takeem with something that looked like awe on their faces.

"What have you done?" Kerina asked.

"I'm so sorry about the damage," Samantha said. "We're not sure how it happened."

"The Shrouded Ones all died in the aftermath of the purge," Pyral said. "There are only two left in all of Lutia, yet one grew overnight through the cottage while you slept. What manner of spinners are you?"

"We're not spinners," Samantha said. "I mean, at least, I'm

not a spinner."

"And the magicks are long gone from this world." Takeem worked on tying their packs together with a piece of rope. "There are no magicks left for me to spin."

Hulak transformed into his larger form and Takeem slung the packs across his broad shoulders so that they hung down at his sides.

"There may be no magicks for spinning, but there are magicks left in this world," Pyral said. "There are the Shrouded Ones and there is Hulak and there are the Mozkola. Do not forget that some magicks simply could not be purged. Now it appears some are making their way back to this world." She stared at the Shrouded One. "We thank you for the Shrouded One you have gifted us with, young Takeem, and wish you safe journey."

"My thanks, Pyral." Takeem helped Samantha board Hulak, then clambered aboard himself. "Blessings of Vanadevi upon all of you."

Hulak lunged forward and took them to the skies.

Treasure Beyond Worth

The moment Jennifer opened Samantha's box and discovered the pages inside she recognized their story. It was the same story she had found in Jonathan's box, told through his artwork. Samantha had not wanted his box or any of its contents, insisting Jennifer keep them all. And so Jennifer had kept the box in her room, unaware of the true meaning of his drawings, unaware that Samantha's box held the written words to accompany the story Jonathan's pictures told.

From Samantha's stories, Jennifer now had a name for the creature with the pig snout, black wings and fiery red coat that Jonathan had drawn: Huk, the Royal nargnet, guardian of the sky.

She also had a name for the people drawn in shades of blue – the Royals, the Skies and the spinners. And the amazing portrait of Samantha, plunging a sword into the neck of a chelinga, now had greater meaning, for she had read the final story of their war.

It was while reading these stories that Samantha's whereabouts came to Jennifer, like an epiphany. Samantha would have wanted to feel close to Jonathan on their birthday. For this, she might have gone home to Harrisonville – to the cemetery where Jonathan was buried or to the weeping willow they had played beneath throughout their childhood.

Harrisonville was where Jennifer would continue the search.

THE MENDACIOUS QUEEN

THE SUN WAS setting when Hulak, Samantha and Takeem finally arrived in the village of Tilkna. They had stopped along the way for a few calls of nature and to eat lunch, but otherwise they had been in flight the entire day. Samantha could barely stand when they dismounted and asked to speak with Marin.

The village of Tilkna was full of suspicious Sky-Blues who were even less accommodating than those in Belia. Marin was unavailable, they were told. Takeem said they would wait and then he set up camp, right there, in the middle of the town square.

"This is a terrible idea," Samantha protested. "The Tekhlan are after us. We're too exposed. What if–"

"The villagers don't want us here, in the middle of their square. It's too dangerous," Takeem explained. "Be patient. They'll send Marin because they want us gone, and I'm guessing that's her right there."

A tall Sky woman with a banner of sky-blue hair and fierce blue eyes stormed toward them. "What is this?" she demanded. "Why are you here? You do not belong here and we do not need the trouble. Go home."

"I'm afraid we can't," Takeem said. "We need help."

"And you came to us? Why would we help the son of the woman who brought nothing but grief to all Skies everywhere?"

"Because my mother once told me the Skies are honorable

and that you, in particular, will always do the honorable thing."

"A pox on honor. Do you know who I am? I am the granddaughter of Stavo, the niece of Telan, the daughter of Joien, the victims of your mother's perfidy and lies. That she thinks I would help her, that she thinks I would shield you, from anyone, for any reason-"

"The Tekhlan pursue us," Samantha spoke quietly. She recognized something in Marin, something that seethed inside Samantha herself. Anger. Bitterness. An ocean of grief.

"The Tekhlan," Marin hissed. "Isn't that like Alatore? To unleash the Tekhlan once more upon the unsuspecting Skies. I suppose she still upholds that fiction she chooses to tell from one corner of the world to the other."

"What fiction?" Takeem asked.

"Still denying the truth, I see. What is it that you're here for, Takeem? Another village to burn for those of the Royal line? Is Tilkna next then? The next Volya? The next Lieria?"

"You're right. The Tekhlan were harsh in their condemnation of the Sky villages and the innocent died along with the guilty. I-"

"There were no guilty." Marin snapped. "Unless you count your mother, that hateful, mendacious queen, and your father, the man she betrayed us all for."

"I-I don't know much of what happened here in the villages thirty years ago. I know that the Skies paid a steep price and for that I am truly sorry."

Marin stalked away, then stormed back. "I hate those vile Tekhlan and you can tell them I said that." She flung back her head and roared to the stars in the night sky, "I hate you, you sorry bastards." She paced in front of them, waving her hands to punctuate her words. "What is it with this Royal family? Sending the Tekhlan after each other, fleeing into Sky territories, unleashing the Tekhlan among us, as if the life of a thousand Skies is less worthy than that of one Royal-Blue." She stopped, hands on hips, staring into the distance.

"Fine," she snapped. "I will help you, but not because I care one tiny bit about your pathetic lives. I will help you because I burn to make those Tekhlan bastards pay. I hope they suffer in their pursuit of you."

Silence. Takeem finally cleared his throat and said, "Thank you, Marin."

"Don't thank me. Tell me what you need and then leave, before we end up paying for your miserable lives in Sky blood again. If you think Yezyr is any less evil than your father was, you are sadly mistaken. He will tear us all apart in a heartbeat. Now what do you need?"

"We need a place to stay for the night and some answers. We have no idea why the Tekhlan are after Samantha. You seem to know a lot about them. And apparently about my mother as well. What–"

"I know nothing that can help you in this quest. I will not speak of your mother or the past. As for the Tekhlan, your companion is different from them, of a color unseen in this world. That is all they need to condemn her. They probably revile her, as they undoubtedly revile you, the Royal-spinner heir."

"There's more to it than that," Samantha said. "They were after me before they'd even seen me, from practically the first moment I arrived in Lutia."

"I cannot help you."

"Do you know someone who might have the answers for us? Somewhere we might go?" Takeem rushed out his questions.

"Perhaps the Book of Ages."

"The Book of Ages?" Samantha repeated.

"I-I don't think–" Takeem said.

Marin whirled around. "No, you don't. You Royals never think. You never think of consequences or what you might be unleashing upon an unsuspecting world. The Book of Ages is housed deep within the War Zone, in the Lixorlan mountain range where the Mozkola roam free. It might have your answers, but you will have to walk the Trail of Truth to receive them, and I doubt seriously that the son of the Mendacious Queen has any truths in his heart to share. You may stay here tonight, but I want you gone at first light." Marin stormed away.

Takeem headed back to where he had set up their camp a few feet away. He knelt upon the blankets Pyral had provided and sat there in silence, staring at the ground.

After a few moments, Samantha tentatively asked, "Did you understand any of that?"

"No." Takeem grabbed a stick and poked at the ground. "Well, some of it, yes, but most of it, no. I don't understand what's going on here, why everyone is so angry with my mother. I mean, yeah, I'm not happy with her, but that's because she's a terrible mother. It's her attitude toward anyone not Royal enough. She hates the Skies *and* the spinners, but honestly, I think she hates me even more. I'm her son, you see." Takeem tossed down the stick and stared into the distance. "I should be a perfect Royal. Instead, I'm the enemy everyone loves to hate."

"Oh, Takeem." Samantha flung her arms around his neck. She pressed her cheek to his and squeezed him tight, as if in holding him, she could somehow mute his grief and with it, her own.

Takeem gently hugged her back, his hands cradling the back of her head, his fingers sifting through her hair.

After a moment of silence, he pulled away. "Marin is right. The Book of Ages may know why the Tekhlan are after you. It might even be able to answer all the questions I have about what happened in the Sky-Blue villages thirty years ago. The problem is the journey will be difficult. We'll be flying deep into the War Zone and the Mozkola are a danger as well."

"What's the Mozkola?" Pyral had mentioned it as well. The name wasn't familiar to her. This world was so different from what she and Jonathan had created.

"They're beings of darkness created when Torel purged the magicks from Lutia. The magicks that were so dark and vile they could not be contained were spun into the Mozkola. They live in the mountains far from here and as long as we stay away, the world is safe from them."

"And if we go there?"

"The Mozkola do not visit the Holy Shrine of Vanadevi for fear of its light. If we can make it to Vanadevi Mountain without them realizing we have trespassed upon their range, we should be safe. The Mozkola are not the only danger, however."

"What else is there?"

"The Trail of Truth. The Book of Ages will incinerate anyone who touches it if it deems they do not have the right. We'll have to walk the Trail of Truth to prove our worthiness. The trail is an arduous climb up the mountain and then I hear there's an even more difficult journey once inside the Shrine."

"You hear? You've not been there before?"

"The Shrine is for the Royal line of Lutia. The Book of Ages is for the king or queen to read and no other. I've never been allowed to step foot in the shrine, for fear that I would contaminate its holiness with my spinner skin. As I am not the king, I do not have a right to touch the Book. Truthfully, nor do you. It's entirely possible the book will incinerate us for having the audacity to try."

"Is there anything else we can do? Anywhere else we can go?"

"Honestly, Samantha, I'm out of ideas. We have three more names on my list. We can try them, but what are they going to do for us other than try to hide us from the Tekhlan? And given the reactions of Pyral and Marin, I do not hold out much hope the others will be willing to take such a risk."

Samantha was silent for a moment then said, "I think we should go ahead and try the Book of Ages. The Tekhlan would never expect us to go to the Shrine, right? I mean you're not the king, so why would you go there?"

Takeem's eyes widened. "I hadn't thought of that. You're right – the Shrine may actually be the safest place for us right now." He fell silent for a moment, then said, "All right. We'll set out tomorrow morning, first thing. We should try to get some sleep now. First light comes early."

While Takeem took care of their campfire, Samantha headed to the pile of blankets he had spread on the ground. Hulak was in his smaller form, already stretched out along one edge of the blankets. Samantha lay down on her side facing him. She reached out and gently stroked his fur. He smelled like the wind and nature, of earth and home. A few moments later, Takeem settled down behind her. He slid his arm around her waist and pulled her toward him so that they were spooned together. He buried his face in her hair and she listened to the sound of his breathing until she drifted off to sleep in his arms.

VUKEL, 30 YEARS AGO

VILLAGES TO BURN

The village of Volya was silent. No one stood guard, though they had to have known what was coming. Word had spread to all the villages between the third and fourth walls of Lutia – the Tekhlan were on the move. They were sweeping through village after village, interrogating and killing, in search of the Royal-Sky.

Vukel had tracked the mother and half-breed child to Volya. Most of the Skies claimed to have never seen the woman, let alone her child. Most were not even certain the child truly existed. Those who believed he did, admitted they had never set eyes upon the child. They had no idea of the child's name, nor did they know with whom he traveled. When pressed, they admitted they were not even certain the child was a boy.

As light dawned in the morning sky, the Tekhlan poured across the village of Volya, dragging Skies from home after home. Children and babies wailing. Men shouting. Women struggling. Finally, the entire village was gathered in the fields that lay fallow to the north of the village and forced to kneel there. There were only Skies among them. No Royal-Blue faces, no Alatore, no Royal babes.

As Vukel looked out at so many Skies, he didn't know which scenario was worse – that Alatore was truly dead or that she had been living all this time in squalor with the Skies.

Where were they and why were these Skies protecting them, committing treason to do so?

"Where is the king's sister?" he demanded.

Silence.

"Who is the leader of this village?"

"I am."

"Who said that?"

An older man struggled to his feet at the center of the Skies. "I did."

Petrar grabbed the man's arm and shoved him forward. "Walk."

The Sky-Blue walked toward Vukel. As he moved through the crowds of Skies, he touched the heads of several in passing, murmuring soft words of comfort.

His actions displayed his weakness. Of course, the man cared. Any good leader would. But to show this to the enemy was a mistake. Now Vukel knew how to break him and his people.

When the Sky stood before him, Vukel nodded to Petrar.

With a well-placed kick to one knee, Petrar sent the Sky to the ground.

The man straightened his back and lifted his head high. Everything about the Sky screamed defiance, from his hate-filled eyes to his clenched fists to the insolent look upon his face. This man did not believe the Royals were his betters.

He would learn different.

Vukel circled the Sky. The man's skin was light blue, of course, as were his eyes and his hair. His hair was a shade darker than his skin, but still well within the Sky tones. There did not appear to be any evidence of Royal genes. He was a Sky through and through.

Placing a hand on the man's head, Vukel looked out over the Skies kneeling before him. "Tell me where the king's sister is and no one will be harmed."

The Sky, showing no fear of Vukel, the walking death of the throne, jerked his head back and spat at him.

"So be it." Vukel took hold of the man's head and with a quick jerk, snapped his neck.

Many in the crowd gasped and cried out. Others began to cry.

Allowing the man's body to fall, Vukel demanded again, "Where is she?"

"Please," a young Sky woman said. She knelt on the ground with her head bowed. She darted a quick look at him, tears pouring down her face, before jerking her eyes downward again.

This was a woman who knew her betters.

"We do not know, sir. We heard she died. Then, lately, we heard the Tekhlan were searching for her again, for her and her son, but we have not seen them, sir."

"If you have not seen them, why are you so certain the child is a male?"

The woman cringed and darted another quick look at Vukel's face. "Please, sir, I am not certain." She hunched forward a little, speaking frantically, "I assumed. I should not have. I am sorry."

Vukel stared at her for a long moment, then nodded and turned to Petrar. "Burn the village."

"No!" Though many in the village cried out in protest, none fought back.

A few moments later, the first building began to burn.

"Where is the child? Where is its mother? Tell me." Vukel strode back and forth in front of the Skies, waiting. No one answered.

More buildings went up in flames. Soon, the entire village was engulfed. The Skies watched from the fields as their homes burned. Still they said nothing.

What was it about these Skies, these villagers that made them feel as if they could defy the throne? Was it the mother – Alatore or some other woman? Was it the child? What would convince any Blue to risk sanction by the Tekhlan?

Every village they had visited over the past month had been the same. One village had seen her, another had not. One village caved, the next did not. A few killings at each site had gained him nothing. It was time to make the consequences of plotting against the throne very clear. It was time to place the fear of the Tekhlan into the hearts of every Sky in existence.

Dragging in a deep breath, Vukel stared toward the mountains in the distance and proclaimed, "This village is found guilty of treason. You have collaborated with those holding the Royal heir hostage, denied the representatives of the throne, and defied your king. The punishment for treason is death. May Vanadevi have mercy upon your souls."

"No!" The sounds of panic, anger and defiance spread through the crowd.

Turning to Petrar, Vukel gave him one final command, then walked away.

Faced with death, the Skies surged to their feet as one unit and began to fight. They fought for the children in their midst, for the elderly, for their loved ones, for the continuation of their lines. Still, they were slaughtered.

The Tekhlan were the well-trained assassins of the king, and the Skies, though trained on the battlefields of war, were still no match for them. In the end, the villagers perished but for one small child who was left alive, crying in the midst of devastation, a single witness to the consequences of betraying the throne.

*

Forelia watched as Vukel approached. She wished her mate, Hulak, was with her. Perhaps he could have stopped Vukel. Perhaps he could have made him stop and think. But this was so much greater than her, so much greater than Hulak.

Her heart was breaking. This day, this horrible day, along with so many others, would be etched upon her soul forever. Was this what it had been like for Hulak, in the days of Torel? She knew it had to have been hard serving as the Royal Nargnet, warrior-companion to a monster-king, but until she and Vukel began this journey, she had never understood how truly horrific it must have been. As she had endured the passing of days, watching as her own warrior-companion slaughtered countless innocents, she had come to the realization that Vukel and the human king, Sorelion, were as monstrous as Torel had ever been. Now she and Hulak served two monster-humans, one of them a king and the other the king's Royal assassin.

Humans had brought this world to ruin. The nargnets had
wanted to leave in the aftermath of the purge more than a
hundred years before, but Hulak had argued in favor of staying.
He believed the nargnets could provide a stabilizing force,
possibly saving the entire world from ruin. He just hadn't realized
the world's ruin was already upon them.

With a huge sigh, Forelia knelt lower to the ground so Vukel
could mount her back. He was so small compared to her. For an
instant, she was tempted to break their sacred companion bond.
For one moment, the blood-red lust of a nargnet's fury swept
across her vision and she imagined raising her paw and using her
blood-red claw to sweep across his neck, to end all of their
misery.

"Let's go, Forelia."

Vukel's voice brought her back from the edge as he settled
upon her back. What had happened to this man, Forelia
wondered as she slowly stood to full height and spread her wings.
She had once thought him a great and honorable man. The
years at war had changed him though. He had once, a long time
ago, advocated negotiating peace with the spinners. Now,
though, after twelve years of fighting them, he embraced his
hatred for them, as Sorelion did, as Torel had done. The humans
had left a legacy of hatred across generations of men, and that
hatred was consuming Vukel. It was consuming them all.

Lunging forward, Forelia raced across the fields, away from the
smoldering ruins and the Tekhlan's killing grounds. As she ran,
she enjoyed the feel of the breeze ruffling her fur. She launched
her body skyward and for a brief moment, could imagine that all
was right in the world. It was a beautiful day, bright and sunny,
no clouds in sight. The breeze felt gentle and kind and –

"Take us to the next village, Forelia, the one two kilometers
south of here."

The village of Tilkna. Vukel didn't even care enough to find
out the names of the villages they terrorized or the names of the
victims he killed. He simply swept in and swept out, and the
villages between the third and fourth walls of Lutia paid the
price.

*

Another village – Tilkna. Another search. Still no evidence of a Royal-Sky. Still no proof that Alatore lived.

Vukel had spent the hours traveling, trying to decide whether one village would be enough. He'd concluded it was doubtful. He would allow these villagers to decide their own fates though. Should they give him what he needed, he would spare their lives. If not, they would pay the price, as the last village had. After much consideration, he devised a strategy he hoped would minimize the bloodshed here.

This time, Vukel had his men gather the villagers of Tilkna in the town square. He stood on a raised platform, watching as his men lined them up. Once the villagers were in place, his men formed four lines, building a human wall around the Skies. His men faced him, drew their blades in one swift move, crossed the blades with a clash of sound, then in perfect unison, turned to face the Skies, blades crossed in front of them, held at the ready. It was pure intimidation, but it worked.

Raising his head, he nodded to Petrar who stood at his side.

Within a few moments, a Sky-Blue was shoved to his knees before him. The man's skin was the lightest of blues. So light, he seemed an abomination to Vukel. His hair was only slightly darker than his skin. He had several warrior braids at his temple. This far from the palace, this close to the battlegrounds, those warrior braids marked the man as one who defended the wall. Vukel pondered a moment what the loss of this village and the last one might mean for the war. These villagers were the front line.

There were other villages though. And others meant for the wall.

"What is your name?" Vukel asked.

"I am Stavo, the leader of this village." The Sky's eyes were royal-blue. An unwelcome surprise. He truly was an abomination, the result of a mating between a Sky and a Royal, designation Sky first for the color of his skin.

This was the type of leader the Skies chose – a Sky-Royal half-breed whose impurities were so visible they could never be hidden away. This man's lines would never be pure again; the contamination would spread forward to every product of his bloodline.

This was how spinners had once been made.

The child they sought, the Royal-Sky the villagers spoke of, would have Royal skin. His eyes would hold the truth of his heritage though.

"Stavo," Vukel said. "Where are they?"

"I do not know, sire."

Vukel stepped back.

Petrar slit the man's throat and shoved him to the floor of the platform.

A pool of blood spread from where the man lay.

Petrar turned and nodded to another of the Tekhlan.

The Tekhlan grabbed a second man from the crowd and shoved him toward the platform.

A Tekhlan standing at the base of the stairs caught the man's arm and dragged him up them to where Petrar and Vukel waited.

Petrar shoved the man to his knees in front of Vukel.

The man knelt next to the body, in pools of blood.

"What is your name?" Vukel asked.

"Telan."

"Where is she?"

The man, Telan, stared down at the body on the platform and did not answer.

"Where is she?" Vukel demanded again.

Telan lifted his head. Madness glittered in his strange eyes, a ring of sky surrounded by a ring of royal.

Vukel shuddered. Abominations filled this village.

"If I knew where she was, I would defy you still," Telan spat.

"You dare —"

"Unclean," Telan growled. "You are the dark shadow of our world, the creeping filth that devours us whole."

The man's head flew from his body and rolled across the platform. His body collapsed.

Vukel lowered his blades, no memory of actually drawing them, no memory of using them to decapitate this insolent Sky-Royal.

These Skies actually believed themselves better than their Royal leaders, believed themselves strong in the face of the Tekhlan.

He would show them different.

"Bring me a child."

A few moments later, a young girl was shoved to her knees before him.

Chaos erupted among the villagers, as they cried out in protest.

The child was crying, wailing for her mother. She was tiny, no older than five. Her wispy, Sky-Blue hair was baby soft when he settled his hand upon it.

Vukel drew in a deep breath and strengthened his resolve.

The Skies were weak. If they ruled, Lutia would fall and the spinners would win the war. He would not condemn the Blues to a world where spinners ruled. If he had to sacrifice this innocent, if he had to sacrifice ten thousand villages of innocents, to keep the Skies from ruling Lutia and to save the Blues from the spinner race, he would.

"Where is she?" he asked the crowd of Skies.

As if these words were the spark needed to ignite the world, several Skies leapt forward to attack the Tekhlan. They were struck down.

A few more attacked, enraged, and they too were cut down.

The Skies were surrounded by the Tekhlan on all sides and still they attacked. They were farmers who had been sent to war, who had learned to fight on the battlefields. They had not been trained like the Tekhlan they faced, and yet they could not contain their need to fight. They had no chance, yet they fought because the Skies were all emotion. If they ruled Lutia, they would rule as they fought – from an emotional state – and in doing so, they would make Lutia weak. Lutia would die, as the Skies were dying now.

Vukel waited until the chaos subsided. Though a number of

bodies now littered the ground, many Skies still knelt, eyes lowered, cowed by the events taking place.

Two of the Tekhlan stepped forward, dragging the child's parents between them. While the Skies had fought, these two men had held their captives back, not allowing them to join the chaos. The parents had to survive, in order to bargain for their child's life.

"Please," the Sky female cried out. Her knees buckled and the man holding her allowed her to fall. "Please," she begged, scrambling up the platform's steps to reach Vukel. "Please leave my baby alone, oh, Vanadevi, please!" She tripped on the top step, sprawled flat, struggled to her knees and crawled to him. Clutching at his leg, she begged, "Please, please, please, sire, anything you want, anything, please, please, please."

"Where is the king's sister?"

The woman wept and sobbed, shaking her head. "I don't know," she sobbed. "I don't. Oh, please, please…" Turning to face the Skies below her, she begged, "Tell him, I beg of you, if you know, please, please, tell him!"

Silence.

The woman wailed in agony.

Vukel tightened his hands to keep the girl's head from moving, wrapped a few silky strands around his fingers and yanked.

"Mama! Papa!" the child cried out.

"Where is she?" Vukel asked, tightening his grip.

"Lieria!" The father shouted.

Was he simply giving an answer to spare his daughter or did he truly know?

"Lieria," the man gasped out again. "I attended the meetings when they arrived. It was agreed."

"Joien, no!" someone whispered from the crowds.

"It was agreed," he continued, a broken man, harsh sobs catching in his throat, "if the Tekhlan arrived, the heirs would ride for Lieria. Please, I beg of you. Spare my child."

Vukel lifted his hands from the child's head and headed for the stairs.

Behind him, the mother and child clutched each other,

wailing.

As Vukel passed the men holding the girl's father, he nodded to them.

They dropped their arms from the Sky and he immediately lunged forward, racing up the stairs onto the platform. Hitting his knees beside his wife and daughter, he caught them both in his arms. Huddled together, the three of them wept.

"Give them a few moments, then bring the father and child," Vukel murmured to Petrar. "We ride out in ten."

PRESENT DAY

The Mystery of Alatore

SAMANTHA WOKE TO discover a willow tree had once more grown around where she and Takeem slept.

"Marin," she whispered.

"The granddaughter of Stavo, niece of Telan," Takeem said.

"Daughter of Joien. Do you think Vukel killed her father too?"

"Based on her rage, I would say yes. No wonder she hates me. Everyone knows the history of Vukel's search for his betrothed. I'd heard that Volya was burned to the ground, its residents found guilty of treason, but I never imagined, never really understood what that meant."

"It's not your fault, Takeem. These events happened long before you were born."

"Still, I am of his blood, and he was nothing but a monster." Takeem stood and began to pace. "Did you know – the Royals tell the story like it's the greatest of romances. The leader of the Tekhlan pursuing his betrothed to the end of the world, destroying village after village until he finally rescues her from the clutches of her kidnappers. It wasn't romantic though. It was a nightmare."

"Do you think she loved him?" Samantha asked.

"My father?"

"Yes. I mean, could anyone love a man who would do that, who would destroy so many innocent lives?"

"I don't know. I hope she loved him because if she didn't, what a terrible waste of lives for a woman who doesn't love you."

"Yes, but even if she did love him, don't you think that love would die when she discovered what he did?"

Takeem shook his head. "I just don't know. My mother's never been anything but a mystery to me."

*

When they emerged from the Shrouded One, they discovered the villagers waiting for them, as had those of Belia.

Marin stepped forward. "How is that a Shrouded One grows around you as you sleep during the night?"

"We don't know," Takeem said, "but ever since Samantha arrived, the Shrouded Ones have been coming back to the world."

"My uncle and grandfather were killed not far from this spot. Right around where the trunk of the Shrouded One grew. I've lived with my rage over their deaths my entire life. Now a Shrouded One has grown to honor their passing and I find my rage is gone. Your family owed this village a blood debt, young Takeem. That Shrouded One there has more than repaid that debt. May the blessings of Vanadevi be upon you." She bowed her head and walked away, the rest of the villagers following in her wake, many bowing to Sehmah and Takeem as they went.

"Wow," Samantha whispered. "They really love willow trees around here."

"I told you. They are holy trees. We should go. It's a long journey to the Shrine of Vanadevi."

They packed quickly, then climbed onto Hulak who launched them into the skies.

Samantha stroked Hulak's neck, remembering Forelia's love for him and her sorrow for all that he had endured. It was amazing to know Hulak had a mate, to realize more nargnets existed than the one she and Jonathan had created.

Except they didn't.

Samantha's hands clenched in Hulak's fur as Takeem's words came back to her:

Hulak is the last of his kind.

Taken by the Shrouded One

THEY'D PASSED BOTH the fifth and the fourth rings of Lutia and now approached the third ring. Samantha could feel the tension rising in Takeem's body as they flew closer to the War Zone. He was focused on getting to the Shrine as quickly as possible so they could find out why the Tekhlan pursued them. Samantha, however, was more interesting in asking the Book of Ages about Jonathan. The opportunity to find her brother was worth any risk.

It wasn't right that she was living out the story they had built together without Jonathan by her side. Instead it was Samantha and Takeem, flying across the world. It was strange to realize that all those other moments, when it had just been the two of *them*, Samantha and Jonathan, it had always been Takeem who was the shadow at their side, a spirit they felt more than saw, a shadow-warrior to fight at their backs. Was *Jonathan* the shadow-warrior now? It felt as if he rode the wind as they rode the nargnet, surrounding them with his presence, unseen yet keenly felt. Samantha closed her eyes and breathed him in with the beauty of the day. She could feel him, right there, right then, in that moment… her twin, her best friend, her lost brother, coming home to live again.

"Look," Takeem spoke into her ear, interrupting her reverie, shattering the moment.

She opened her eyes.

"That's Volya."

Samantha stared down at the village as they passed over it. The buildings were blackened shells, no movement anywhere, just an eerie, black ghost town, building after building a scorched ruin. "Why did they leave it like that?"

"It's a warning."

"Of what?"

"Of the penance for standing against the Tekhlan. And there is Lieria." Takeem pointed to a village far ahead. From a distance, it looked like every other village they had passed. As they got closer, though, it was like a ghost town. No people, no crops, no animals grazing.

"It's deserted," Samantha murmured.

"Yes. The buildings still stand, but no one will live there. My father finally caught up with the kidnappers and rescued my mother there. Not one villager survived his wrath. The Skies claim the ghosts of those who died still wander the buildings of Lieria."

Samantha shivered. "It's horrible. They left it standing as another warning?"

"Exactly. The penance for standing against the throne."

"I hate it, Takeem. I know he's your father, but–"

"I know. I never knew him. I always hoped he would be the type of father who wouldn't mind if his son was marked a spinner." He waved his hand at his striped eyes. "I'm guessing that was a foolish dream."

"Do you still think Arioan was Vukel's son?"

"I don't know."

"Because if he was Brenin's, maybe you're right. Maybe he wouldn't mind your spinner eyes. After all, he raised Arioan as his own, right?"

"I guess so. He died less than a month before I was born, so I never really knew him. I have no idea if he accepted Arioan or just tolerated him. I'll probably never know. There's so little in my life that makes sense, I'm getting used to not understanding any of it. It's just the way it is, I guess."

Just the way it is.

Samantha thought about those words as they flew through the afternoon skies. As they flew over the third ring and entered the War Zone.

Just the way it is.

Was that the answer to the question she lived with every single moment of every single day? It was what she had been thinking right before she was transported here, right before she saw that willow tree back in Willow Grove. It was time to accept what was, she had thought.

That Jonathan was gone and that's just the way it was.

That he was nowhere because that's the way it was.

Or was it that he was everywhere? Everywhere that was here. Everywhere in Lutia. Because that's the way it was.

"Blessed Vanadevi." Takeem's voice interrupted her thoughts.

"What is it?" she asked, glancing up.

Takeem stared toward the land below with a stunned look on his face.

All she saw were fields stretching for miles in every direction and a giant river cutting those fields in half.

"Take us down, Hulak!"

Hulak descended, sweeping toward the land in a death-defying rush. The wind roared in Samantha's ears as they hurtled downward. She flung herself forward, hiding her face in Hulak's neck. She was missing it again. Forcing herself to open one eye and then the other, she clutched Hulak's fur and stared at the ground as it approached at a terrifying speed.

When the nargnet's paws connected with the land, she barely felt it, though she flinched, expecting a horrendous jolt and crash. Instead, the descent leveled out until they raced at breakneck speed, Hulak barely touching the ground at first, as they flew more than ran, then with ever-increasing contact between land and beast, began to run more than fly. His paws pounded the terrain as they hurtled across it.

The moment Hulak shuddered to a stop, Takeem flung himself off the nargnet's back and hurried across the field.

It took Samantha several moments before she finally stopped shaking enough to push herself up from the nargnet's neck and look around. Would she ever get used to those landings?

"Unbelievable, Huk," she exclaimed. "What is it about you and Takeem?"

Hulak blew air from his snout, and it sounded like he was laughing at her.

Samantha gracelessly clambered down from Hulak's back, muttering all the while. "You didn't fly this way when it was Arioan and me, so I'm starting to think that you're showing off for Takeem."

Hulak huffed in response.

"And where did he go anyway?" she demanded. "I don't see any shrines so I know we're not there yet."

"What did you do?"

At the enraged roar, Samantha looked up, her eyes widening as she watched Takeem storm toward her, a furious look etched across his face.

"*What did you do?*" he shouted again.

"Wh-wha-what are you talking about?" Samantha gasped.

"Look at this place. *Look at it.*"

"It-it's a field, right?"

"Of course it's not just a field." He made a sound of disgust.

"Well, what is it then? What's wrong with you?"

"What's wrong with me? *Look* at this place!"

"You keep saying that, but I don't even know where we are. It's a field with flowers and a river. There's nothing here."

"Exactly. There's nothing here. Nothing. Look at it. Do you think that you had the right, to take it all away, as if it never happened, as if no one died here in this spot?"

"What are you talking about?" Samantha looked at Hulak. "What is he talking about?"

Hulak simply stared at Takeem with a great and dark sadness in his eyes.

"What do you mean, I took something away? I didn't take anything."

"Of course you did. It's just like when you made those Shrouded Ones grow."

"I didn't make the Shrouded Ones grow. That was you. You're

the spinner. It had to be you."

"Me? I've never made a Shrouded One grow in my life. Besides, Arioan said you were responsible. He said you made this place come back to life. This place, with all its darkness, this place that was dead three days ago." Takeem's voice broke. "This place where my father and uncle died." He sank to his knees and buried his fingers in the soil.

Just as Samantha had done when she first arrived in Lutia, searching for Jonathan.

"I walk here every week, at least once, to sift through the ashes of what we lost, to feel closer to the father I never knew."

Arioan had told her something similar about this place – that he went there to feel closer to the ones he had lost. *"To kneel and to mourn is quite natural here,"* he'd said.

"Now there's nothing left of him," Takeem said. "Nothing left for me to mourn."

Samantha hesitated, then knelt beside him, gently placing her hand on his shoulder. "I'm so sorry, Takeem. I didn't know. But I didn't do anything, I promise."

"Of course you did. Arioan picked you up right over there by the Great River of Lutia. He said when he found you, the fields had come back to life and the river was flowing again. I know it was you. I know you did this. I saw you in my dreams, bringing life back to the dying lands. This land was completely scorched, a blackened shell when I was here just a few days ago. How can you not understand what you've done?"

He leapt to his feet and swept his arms wide, as if to encompass the entire world. *"This* is the battlefield of Shorel, by the great forests of Bipin, and it lives today as if no tragedy has touched this land. What gave you that right?"

Samantha didn't know what to say. "I'm sorry, Takeem, I'm so sorry if somehow by being here I've made this land heal itself, but I didn't mean to, I promise you. I would not take it from you, this place, if I could have stopped it, I... I just..." She scrambled to her feet. "I don't know what's happening, Takeem. You say I did this, but I'm not magic. I don't have any special abilities. I can't heal the land or – or do anything special!"

Though she had created this world and it now somehow lived, she didn't feel any different than before. Maybe if she found Jonathan, things would start making sense again.

"We should be traveling, Takeem. The Tekhlan are hunting us and we're not safe here." She looked around. "It's too exposed."

"I need a moment. I need a lifetime. Just leave me be." He turned away.

Samantha wanted to say something, wanted to take away his pain, but nothing she could say would make things better. There was no cure for grief and loss. She knew this better than most and because she understood, she would give him space while honoring those who had died on this battlefield. Those she had killed in sweeping, slashing strokes of a pen. Even though she had not understood she was killing Takeem's family. Even though she had not planned for this to be the result. She still felt as if she were responsible.

She and Jonathan had planned the war and she had penned the battle.

Tears burning in her eyes, Samantha walked for quite some time, hand clutching her mother's locket, taking comfort in the feel of the carved flower pressing into the palm of her hand. She walked until she was certain she would not break down. Then she settled on the ground to wait for Takeem. However long it took. She would wait. With this thought swirling in her head, Samantha closed her eyes and focused on her breathing. With each inhalation, she pulled in the scents of spring. With each exhalation, she relaxed into the embrace of an imaginary willow at her back.

She inhaled. Waiting for Takeem.

She exhaled. Waiting for Jonathan.

Takeem sat in stillness for so long, his mind a dark cloud of angry thoughts, he might have completely forgotten Samantha and the Tekhlan who pursued them, were it not for Hulak. Hulak had eventually shimmered into his smaller form and settled next to Takeem, keeping him company in his grief and fury. Time passed and Takeem might have sat there forever had Hulak not finally lifted his head from his paws, lumbered to his feet and nudged Takeem hard enough to break his reverie.

Takeem tried to recapture his sullen anger, but Hulak nudged him again, demanding his attention. "What is it then?" he asked.

Hulak looked out across the field.

Takeem scrambled to his feet. "Is that what I think it is?" Far across the field there stood a Shrouded One. "How did that get there?" He glanced around frantically. "Where's Samantha?"

Hulak pushed his head up under Takeem's hand so that it rested upon the crown of his head.

"Very well, my friend. Show me."

Hulak reared up on his hind legs, settling his front paws onto Takeem's shoulders, and stared into his eyes.

Scenes rolled across Hulak's eyes. Takeem standing, his back to Samantha in the left orb, Samantha turning and walking away, walking across to the right orb, walking and walking far into the distance. She walked so far Takeem wondered if she was leaving them. Finally, she settled on the ground, naturally sinking into the meditative pose of his people's holy ones. Her hands fell, palm sides up, to the tops of her knees. Her back was straight, her eyes closed. She seemed the picture of tranquility, sitting at the very center of a wide and open field, so calm and serene as she waited for something.

A tiny sprout of green appeared over her shoulder, followed by a dark and tangled vine. It grew to become a great and magnificent trunk stretching toward the sky. It rose at her back, blocking the sun, enshrouding her, yet she never stirred, never once glanced back or up to see what blocked her light. She simply sat in her pose of serenity, and the trunk grew until it appeared to become a part of her. It rose so high, with still only a few tiny green sprouts at its very top, no leaves, no greenery, simply a dark and magnificently aged trunk, hovering, waiting at her back.

A wind swept across the plain, causing her hair to lift off her shoulders and twine its way around the trunk. Had her hair grown longer while she sat there? Everywhere her hair touched, a tiny green leaf sprouted and twined itself up and around. Her hair moved and the vines moved until it seemed as if her hair had become the vines. In the shadow of the trunk, her strands no longer appeared red and blue, but green, the green of the vines now reaching toward the sky, now stretching out and away from the trunk of the tree.

As Takeem watched, in amazement and horror, the trunk sprouted new branches arching out away from its center and from these branches there came ever-increasing vines of green, creating a blanket of greenery above Samantha, completely blocking the sun, enshrouding the entire area. The vines stretched out away from the branches and down, moving in a sort of graceful, yet horrifying dance. Slowly these vines blocked Samantha from his view, twining their way toward the grassy floor until they brushed the land, the vines twisting around the flowers there, so they locked everyone out, so they locked Samantha within.

Takeem sank to his knees. "I should have stayed with her." The past two nights, when she'd been taken, he'd been with her, a link to their world, sharing the visions with her. This time, though, she'd been all alone when the Shrouded One enveloped her.

According to legend, time had no meaning beneath the holy trees. Some companions chose to remain with their trees for decades, even centuries, before emerging to an entirely new world. Others stayed for only a short time, returning to change the world they had been born to.

When would Samantha choose to emerge?

Resting Place

JENNIFER HAD ARRIVED in Harrisonville an hour before. Though she was exhausted and wanted nothing more than to check into a hotel and get some much-needed sleep, instead she had come here, to the resting place of her family.

It was quiet in the cemetery this morning, and though neither she nor Samantha had visited in the two years since their family's deaths, their graves looked well cared for. She wondered if Samantha had already visited the day before, whether she was the one to care for these plots or if the residents of Harrisonville were tending them. It comforted her to think that perhaps the people of Harrisonville still watched over her brother and his family, that those left behind in this town would continue to care for their graves when their family could not.

Perhaps that had been her mistake: not forcing Samantha, not forcing herself, to come back, to face the past, to grieve as they needed to grieve. Instead, she had simply buried herself in work and unsolved cases and allowed Samantha to bury herself in depression, and neither had come to terms with anything.

"I don't know what to do, Jonathan," she murmured. She had thought, when imagining coming here, that she might want to speak with Adam, as she often spoke to his picture back home. She thought she would turn to his memory, in her frantic attempts to find his daughter. Instead, however, it was to Jonathan's memory she reached out. Jonathan was the key to finding Samantha.

"What should I do, Jonathan? Wait here? Go back home to wait for her there? Search the town?" During the final hour of the trip into Harrisonville, Jennifer had made phone call after phone call, at times waking the people she called. She had called everyone she could think of: all of Jonathan's friends, all of Samantha's, all of her brother's, all of Kate's. No one had seen Samantha yet, but everyone knew to be watching for her. Still, Jennifer had expected to find Samantha here, at the cemetery, by Jonathan's grave, by their parents' graves. If Samantha had come here, however, it could have been more than twenty-four hours before Jennifer had. If that was the case, Samantha could have already come and gone.

Now that she was here, and Samantha wasn't, Jennifer was terrified to continue the search. She had only one other place she thought Samantha might be. If she wasn't there, if she wasn't beneath their willow, Jennifer didn't know what she would do.

The wooden box she had carried with her into the cemetery caught her eye. The willow tree carved on its surface shimmered in the sunlight.

It seemed a sign.

Jennifer grabbed the box and stood. Stepping forward, she settled her hand on Jonathan's tombstone. "I'll find her, Jonathan. I will."

Jennifer left the cemetery, convinced that she would find Samantha in the backyard of her childhood home. She had to be there because, unlike the cold grave Jennifer left behind, beneath the willow was where Jonathan's spirit surely thrived.

READING LUTIA

SAMANTHA WAS UNAWARE of the world around her. She was lost in her own thoughts, wondering how this story had become so unfamiliar to the one who had created it. Takeem had called this place the battlefield of Shorel, had said his father and uncle had died there. But Samantha had not written those deaths into that battle. The Battle of Shorel was the end story to their Willow Tree World, the one she had written in the aftermath of Jonathan's death, the one where the five of them had died. How was it the battlefield she'd burned in her story had burned for an entirely different generation?

She sank deeper into her own mind, until it seemed as if the entire world had opened itself to her thoughts, as if the story she had written, the story that was spinning itself into new directions and new storylines, now opened itself to her, allowing its author to transform herself into its reader.

VUKEL & FORELIA, 20 YEARS AGO

WAR

"Alatore's going to be a problem," King Sorelion predicted as he watched his commanders exit the tent.

"When has my wife been anything else?" Vukel asked. He tightened the red sash around his waist. "She has no respect for the sanctity of the throne."

"True." King Sorelion paced. "My sister has always been an unusual Royal."

"And now she carries a potential heir."

"The second potential heir."

Vukel scowled. "We've made arrangements for that. The boy will never attain the throne."

"Agreed, but as I said, Alatore will be a problem."

"She has no choice in the matter. We made our intentions clear and she will simply have to abide by them."

"I guess we'll see how well she does at abiding."

Vukel laughed. "Not so well, I predict. Still, As soon as the winter snows are upon us, I will take the boy under my command, as promised."

"Excellent. This is for the best."

Before Vukel could respond, the horns of war blared. The two men grabbed their swords and burst from the Royal tent. Two nargnets, fierce and battle-ready, came racing toward them. Vukel and the king launched themselves onto the backs of the nargnets as they hurtled by.

Grasping hold of Forelia's neck fur, Vukel hunkered down and watched as the third wall of Lutia approached. With swift and powerful beats of their wings, the nargnets passed over the wall and entered chaos. There, between the second and third walls, the many beasts and peoples of Lutia battled ferociously. The land teemed with chelingas, garnonens, and krutesks; the skies with nargnets and brekzors. And everywhere, on land and mid-air, those of Lutia were dying.

The sounds of war permeated the world, and though he had seen this scene played out day after day for what seemed his entire life, Vukel felt as if it were for the first time. He would never acclimate to this world of death and war, he thought, even as he urged Forelia toward a brekzor, even as he raised his sword and prepared to kill the spinner standing upon its back.

The clang of their swords, their slide against each other, the pulsing hate he saw shining fiercely from the eyes of the spinner he engaged, the shouts and battle cries that filled the air around him, the surging strength of Forelia below him... all of these combined into one throbbing moment, filled with life and death as his vision narrowed to the ferocious battle he waged mid-air. Despite the fierce movements of Vukel's nargnet and the spinner's brekzor – snapping jaws and writhing bodies, whipping tails and fiercely beating wings – Vukel and the spinner both managed to dance their deadly dance upon the backs of their war-companions.

Swords slashing and clanging, blood flying, nargnet mind-roaring and brekzor snarling, their forms swirled and danced mid air, until finally, with a roar of his own, Vukel vaulted from the back of his bucking nargnet to land upon the shoulders of the snarling brekzor. As the brekzor whipped its head around, trying desperately to tear the intruder from its back, Forelia snapped her great jaws around that reaching neck, ripping with all her might so that blood sprayed the skies red. The brekzor shrieked and plummeted a spiraling death roll, taking the spinner and Vukel with it.

They barely noticed as the brekzor fell, for they were locked in their own deadly battle. Dancing upon the back, then the belly, then the back of the rolling brekzor, they stabbed and slashed and raked at each other, each of them reaching desperately for that fatal wound.

The brekzor crashed into the trees of Bipin, catapulting the spinner and Vukel into the air. Vukel landed amidst the branches of a tree. For one instant the tree held him in place and then with a great thundering crash, the branches broke and he was plummeting downward. Grasping for anything to hold onto, he lost his sword, but managed to stop his fall. Hanging from the branches, gasping for breath, he realized this might be a battle from which he would not return. Pulling himself onto a branch of some weight, Vukel drew the two korelian blades strapped to his back, took a defensive position and listened.

From a distance, he heard the sounds of battle. What he did not hear, however, were the sounds of his enemy approaching. Nor did he hear the sounds of his nargnet. He had fallen a good distance from the top layer of the forest. He would have to climb quite a bit to reach the sky and somehow signal Forelia.

Sliding his blades back into their sheaths, he climbed as quickly and quietly as possible. Every few branches, he stopped to listen to the forest around him. It was eerily silent. No birds, no animals, not a single sound to indicate life in the teeming forests of Bipin. It was as if all of life waited to see the outcome of this deadly battle.

When Vukel finally reached the top layer of the forest, he wondered if perhaps he should have climbed downward instead of up. Though he now stood perched on the topmost branch of the tree, when he gazed at the skies around him, all he saw was a tangled mass of brekzors and nargnets, all engaged in battle, none of whom were his Forelia.

He felt the tug of his companion-bond and saw the bright red and gold that were Forelia's colors alone. She raced toward him. His eyes widened when he saw the color of hers. They had gone from their normal golden color to flaming red.

Vukel flung himself facedown upon the branch, and shuddered as a wave of fire whipped across the top of his body, close enough to singe his hair and clothes. Hearing a shriek of horror, he looked up and saw the spinner he had battled on a dying brekzor, burst into flames and fall from his perch atop the tree opposite Vukel's, the spear he held poised to launch falling with him.

Forelia whipped around in mid-air and flew back toward him. With a cry of joy and maddened relief, Vukel leapt up and away from the tree to land on her back. He flung himself forward onto her neck, whispering his thanks in her ear. Swinging her head around to affectionately puff air his way, Forelia arched upward toward the sun, then quickly plunged downward, taking them both back into the thick of battle.

Vukel didn't see the spear that ripped through Forelia's underside until he felt it pierce his leg, stabbing them from below. Forelia fell.

Spiraling downward, the nargnet flapped her wings as fiercely as she could. Vukel scanned below for a safe place for her to land. There was nowhere but in the midst of horror.

Lying across Forelia's neck, Vukel embraced her and murmured in her ear, "All is well, Forelia. Everything is going to be fine."

Then she was down, sliding across the ground in a great thundering crash and all was silent. Though the battle raged around them, Vukel heard nothing. Though his leg was still impaled upon the arrow, he felt nothing.

Ripping his leg free of the arrow without thought to the damage it might cause, he stumbled off her back and fell at her side. He crawled to her head where she labored for breath.

"Forelia," he whispered. "Forelia."

Dragging her head onto his lap, he stroked her snout. "Please, Forelia, fight."

Staring into her eyes, he saw what she saw.

He heard from her mind to his, the mind-song of her mate.

She lifted her head toward the sky, her eyes on the great nargnet bearing down upon them.

Vukel had one moment to share her thoughts – he was so beautiful, the one who had come, come to take her home. Home to the nesting grounds – and then she was gone.

"No, no, no! Forelia…" and there in the midst of battle and blood and great waging war, he wept and he grieved.

PRESENT DAY

ENSHROUDED

SAMANTHA'S EYES SNAPPED open. Gasping for breath, she touched her face and was shocked to feel tears upon her cheeks. This was the second time she'd seen Forelia in her visions. Forelia, a nargnet whose life she had not written. What she had just witnessed was neither her story nor Jonathan's, but something entirely new, somehow a mix of their ideas together – the Battle of Shorel she had written meshed with Jonathan's vision, along with elements that belonged to neither of them, including a nargnet they did not know.

At that moment, she felt a touch on her shoulder, a caressing hand of comfort. Glancing behind her, expecting no less than Jonathan at her back, she was stunned to find another Shrouded One. Its trunk supported her back and its vines twined around her shoulders, a gentle and soothing embrace. Once more, she sat within the cool and comforting haven of a weeping willow. Turning so that her entire body leaned into the tree, resting her cheek upon its rough and rugged bark, she whispered, "Hwanon," and imagined the tree whispered back, "Sehmah."

CARCASS OF DREAMS

JENNIFER STOOD THERE and stared at the spot where the willow tree had once stood. It was only a stump now, a terrible, awful stump. There had been a lightning storm, the young couple now living in the house had told her. A lightning storm and a horrendous fire, and by the time it was done, the willow tree and three others on the bordering lands had perished. The tree had died, though its carcass still stood in the aftermath of the storm.

Jennifer sank to her knees by the tree's stump, feeling completely ravaged by grief. The scent of death surrounded her, acrid and smoky. Leaning forward and touching her forehead to its surface, Jennifer finally broke down and wept, whispering to the tree, "Is this the way it's supposed to be? Jonathan gone, Samantha gone, this tree, this precious tree…" She moaned softly, crying, "I'm sorry, I'm so sorry, I'm sorry."

It seemed as if she were losing Jonathan all over again, as if the tree served as an omen that she would lose Samantha too. If Jennifer could have, she would have taken the tree with them when they moved to the city, if only to bring that one tangible link to Jonathan with them.

Those last hours in the house, when she was packing the final items they would take with them, Samantha had retreated to this tree. She was gone for hours and Jennifer hoped to allow her as much time as she needed, but finally, when she could wait no longer, she journeyed outside to their backyard, to check on

Samantha, to make sure she was all right. She found Samantha beneath the willow tree, her entire body turned into the tree, rocking against it, her knees up to her chest, her arms wrapped around her knees, her head tipped back toward the canopy above, her cheek resting against its bark. At her side lay a spiral book and pen, both long forgotten.

A helpless witness to Samantha's rage and grief, Jennifer desperately wanted to go to her niece, to wrap her in her arms, to rock her and cry with her, but she didn't. Instead, she became paralyzed with grief. Every single silent scream, every thump of Samantha's fist against the tree trunk, every rocking motion of her body, every single rasping gasp of air reached deep inside Jennifer, to that place she had yet to face, to that place of unfathomable grief, to that empty place inside where her own voice was wailing its own silent scream of abject misery. Locked in her own struggle against debilitating grief, Jennifer felt incapable of moving forward to help Samantha.

This, she knew, was where she had made her first fatal mistake.

Every night since then, when Samantha retreated to her bedroom and closed the door, effectively blocking Jennifer from her world, she was left to wonder if her niece was lying in bed, rocking herself to sleep with her silent screaming, unable to voice or express all the grief that tore her up from the inside out.

Every single night when Samantha closed that door and Jennifer failed to intrude upon her silent weeping. *Every single night* when she had been such a fool.

Jennifer sobbed out all her pain and anguish against the remains of the same tree that once had sheltered and comforted Samantha when she had not.

*

Finally, when the storm of emotion had passed, Jennifer raised her head and looked around the backyard. There was nothing else she could do but wait, either here or at the cemetery, or back home. Samantha had the ability to reach her if she wanted, no matter her location, and so Jennifer decided that here at this tree was the best place to wait, at least for now. If Samantha planned to travel here, at least she would not be alone when she discovered this new tragedy.

With this decision made, Jennifer reached shaking fingers toward Samantha's willow tree box, which still waited patiently for her attention. Setting aside the one story she had already read, she reverently reached for the one beneath it.

KEEPER OF SOULS

TAKEEM PACED HIS way around the tree. His head felt like it was going to explode and nausea roiled inside him. Every single one of his attempts to join Samantha beneath the tree had failed. He had tried spirit walking, but the Shrouded One had slammed his spirit back into his body every single time, in a fierce rejection of the attempt. When his final effort the night before had left him retching and shivering, too weak even to stand, he knew it was time to stop. He and Hulak had made camp there, alongside the Shrouded One. They had kept a vigil all night, keeping a lookout for the spinner armies and the Tekhlan. None of their enemies had arrived nor had Samantha emerged from beneath the tree.

The sun was now high in the sky and he had circled the tree thirty-seven times since waking, but he didn't know what else to do. There was no gap in the leaves and he knew any attempts to break through the clear barrier set forth by the Shrouded One would be met with resistance. He wanted Samantha safely away from that thing, but he also knew it was an honor to be chosen. He should not feel resentful of a tree, particularly one so sacred and highly revered. He could not help it though. This tree had stolen his Samantha, and he didn't know how to get her back. What if she never emerged? Others had chosen to stay. Those with sorrow in their hearts often preferred the Shrouded Ones to real life.

With these thoughts swirling in his head, Takeem began his

thirty-eighth circuit around the tree, wondering what he would do when he reached fifty or a hundred or even a thousand.

Growling in frustration, he stalked away from the tree, only to stop a few moments later, unable to leave Samantha behind.

Thirty-nine circuits were not yet too many.

Swinging around, he was headed back to the tree when the vines before him lifted away, like a curtain being raised by an unseen hand, and Samantha walked out, seemingly unscathed.

Takeem raced toward her. "Are you all right?" he exclaimed.

"I'm fine," she said. "What about you? I know you were upset earlier and I really am sorry, Takeem."

"Never mind that! It is you – you know that, right?"

"What's me?"

"You're the one bringing the Shrouded Ones back to the world."

"I -" Samantha glanced back at the tree. "Well, maybe, but I'm not doing it on purpose."

"It doesn't matter how it's happening, just that it is. The Shrouded Ones are almost extinct and this one's appearance here is a great honor to those who died on these lands."

"Marin said the same thing, that the tree in her village honored her family's passing. What does that mean, Takeem?"

"Beneath the Shrouded Ones lie the worlds of the dead. The trees are soul-keepers. Here, sit down." He fixed a plate of food for her. "They only grow in places that have experienced the entire cycle of life and death." He sat at her side, setting the plate of food on the ground in front of them. "I should have known. I mean, they were growing in the Sky villages, where my mother apparently traveled with Brenin all those years ago. By visiting those villages, Brenin marked them for the Tekhlan and for death. We should have stopped at Volya and Lieria to allow Shrouded Ones to grow there as well."

"I don't understand, Takeem."

"By appearing here, the tree has made a pledge. It will hold the souls of those who died here in its keeping, until it is time for them to move on. They will not be required to wander the Path of Solitude, waiting for their next life. They will be held in tranquility, until they are needed again."

Staring at the Shrouded One, Takeem contemplated what Samantha's arrival had done for those who had died on the battlefield of Shorel. He owed her an apology. Catching her right hand in his left, he linked their fingers together. "I shouldn't have yelled at you, Samantha." He spoke softly. "I don't know how you did it, but I am forever in your debt."

"No," Samantha shook her head. "Takeem-"

"Yes. You brought the Shrouded One here, Samantha, to this place. You brought it here for Forelia and the nargnets, for my father and my uncle, for the Skies and the spinners, for everyone who perished here. You brought them peace."

*

Samantha held onto Takeem's hand and stared at the willow tree. Was he right? Had she brought the willow here? Or was it Jonathan? And where was he anyway? She just wanted him back.

"Here." With one last squeeze of her hand, Takeem picked up the plate of food and handed it to her. "Eat," he commanded.

Murmuring a soft, "Thank you," Samantha picked at her food. The weeping willow had brought her to Lutia, to their Willow Tree World for a reason. She was convinced it would eventually lead her to Jonathan. It was her link to him, her path toward finding her lost family, toward finding her twin. If the tree was also a keeper of souls, that could mean –

No.

She refused to think it. She could *feel* Jonathan here. She *knew* he lived. He wasn't a soul waiting to be reborn. He was *alive* and she *would* find him.

"Did the Shrouded One share any more stories with you?" Takeem looked at her closely. "Did you see what happened here?"

"I did. It was horrible. I saw Forelia's fall."

"Hulak's mate."

Samantha nodded. It made her heart break. She'd written Hulak alone, but he'd had a mate and he'd lost her to war.

"My father was Forelia's companion. Did you see him?"

"I did. He was grief-stricken over Forelia's death. It was weird because he was such a monster, killing all those Skies, but I forgot all of that when Forelia fell. He truly loved her and he mourned her passing. I was surprised. I didn't think him capable of love."

"Of course he was capable of it – he loved my mother."

"No, he didn't," Samantha said. "She was just a possession, Takeem. The way he thought of her, as belonging to him, as if she were something stolen that he had to regain. He didn't worry about her well-being or fear for her life. He wanted revenge because of his ego and his pride. If he loved her at all, it was a selfish, possessive love."

Takeem was silent for a while, then said, "I hadn't thought about it like that, but you're right. He wasn't acting like he loved her. Maybe that changed when he found her though. I mean, he was upset because she'd been taken. Maybe -"

"He didn't act like he cared about Forelia at all when she was mourning the Skies he'd just killed and he ordered her to take him to the next village. But then when she died, he was completely devastated, so I suppose it's possible. Maybe he did love Alatore."

Takeem was quiet for a minute, then changed the subject. "Did you see the fires of Shorel? Where they came from?"

"I didn't see any fires. The vision ended with Forelia's death."

Takeem stood and began moving around the camp, packing up their things. "She must have died before the fires began. If the tree showed you the battle of Shorel, then it shared with you the souls it's taken into its keeping. That means *you* are their keeper now, just as the Shrouded One is."

"What does that mean?"

Takeem swung their packs across Hulak's broad shoulders, patted Hulak's side then looked around the camp. After a moment, he returned to where Samantha sat. Settling upon the ground once more, he leaned back and stared at her. "Sometimes the Shrouded Ones keep their companions for centuries or longer. The companion becomes another soul the Shrouded One holds in its keeping. It's very rare for them to send their companions back out into the world, as a living soul-keeper, as the link between the worlds of the living and the dead."

Samantha shivered. "I'm not a soul-keeper or a link. I can't be. The Shrouded One is *my* link. It's my gateway to Jonathan."

"Jonathan?"

"My brother, Hwanon."

"The Shrouded One shows you Hwanon? Is he dead then?"

"No. I told you. He's here, somewhere in Lutia. I have to find him." She stood and walked toward Hulak. "Shouldn't we be off then? At the rate we're going, we'll never make it to the Shrine."

Takeem joined her and vaulted aboard the nargnet, then helped Samantha do the same.

With a great flick of his wings and a powerful leap forward, Hulak raced across the land, then hurtled through the sky, crossing beyond the forests of Bipin, heading toward the Lixorian Mountain Range, upon whose highest peak rested the Holy Shrine of Vanadevi.

The Next King of Lutia

By Jonathan Whittier

I am Huk, the last of the nargnets. We were once the greatest of warrior companions. We ruled alongside our brothers and sisters, scorching the world with the flames of our justice. We and the Lorki flew the night skies without fear, patrolling the unnamed lands of our world. But then the dark came and the Lorki were devoured by hatred and by fear and they became as nothing; mere ghosts wandering the lands of their death, forever seeking the nesting grounds of their salvation.

Today, the Lorki are gone. In their place, mere shadows of men. Shadows incapable of the mind-speech they once knew. Divided where once they were one, trapped where once they were free, the humans are Lorki no more. As they have diminished, so too have we. We nargnets, once so many, fierce and proud, a nation like no other, have dwindled to one.

I am Huk. I am the last. With no one to hear the whisperings of my mind, no one with whom to embrace the mind-songs of my nation, I am alone in all things. I carry the human king into battle and await the day that I too will wander the lands of my death.

*

The horns of war sound. The king and I must ride again. We fly.

There is nothing but war and the whistling sound of the brekzor we battle. I see its breath steaming out, the whistle it makes between its gnashing teeth a grating sound that boils my blood.

The brekzor roars and rakes at my wings with his massive claws. I take offense and use my own forbidden claws to burn his wretched wings to cinders. I watch in triumph as they turn to dust and the brekzor spirals downward, bearing his rider with him. I am Huk, the last of the nargnets, and I will not betray my kind by falling now.

As I weave in and out of battles, the king on my back, I try to ignore the call for flames. I have already used my forbidden claws in anger this day. I cannot be trusted to fight, but I have no choice. War rages across the world and I must do my part to protect the human king.

*

Endless battles later, the king and I arrive at the palace and are greeted by Arioan, my king's nine-year old nephew. One day soon, I will bear the next king into battle, but it will not be this young man, so compassionate, so infinitely wise. Instead, it will be his younger brother, still nestled safe in his mother's womb.

*

Jennifer's breath caught as she turned the page and found a handwritten letter on its back. She had assumed Samantha wrote all the stories in the box. However, the note was in *Jonathan's* handwriting. Had Samantha seen this, she wondered, tears burning her eyes. Had she seen this wonderful gift Jonathan had left for her?

Dear Sehmah,

It makes me laugh, that I'm able to slip these stories into your box and you never seem to notice. Are you really not paying attention or are you just ignoring me? I know you don't like it when I change the story without talking to you about it first, but I can't help it. I felt that Huk needed to share his story, plus it gave me a chance to make Takeem and Arioan royalty. I know you wanted the two of them to be regular people, but how can Queen Sehmah ever hook up with Takeem, if he's just some regular guy? He's got to be royalty too. Can you see the grin on my face right now? Because I can see the face you're probably making and it doesn't fool me at all. I know you like

Takeem and I'm going to make sure you get him, even if it is only in a story. So here's to Takeem, the next king of Lutia.

Your loyal twin (who is always right),

Hwanon

JUDGMENT

HULAK FLEW THEM as far as he could. Still, it was late afternoon by the time they reached the Trail of Truth, about two-thirds of the way up the highest peak of the Lixorian Mountain Range.

Samantha was horrified, staring up the steep trail that led around the mountain. "That looks dangerous."

"The trail itself is safe," Takeem said. "It's the journey that will be perilous."

"What does that mean? Can't Hulak just fly us the rest of the way?"

"Petitioners are required to walk the Trail of Truth. The mountain will judge the purity of our intentions. Should we fail, we will not be allowed entry to the Holy Shrine."

"How do we prove the purity of our intentions?" If Takeem was right and she *was* a living soul-keeper, would the mountain judge her more leniently or less? "I mean, do we know what our intentions are?"

"You simply concentrate on your goals in coming here. Ponder what questions you have as you walk along the Trail of Truth."

"I don't have to speak them out loud? All I have to do is think them and my thoughts will be heard?"

"Of course."

"Who will hear them?"

"What do you mean?"

"Who will hear my thoughts?"

"Vanadevi, of course."

Samantha didn't know if she believed him, but she walked toward the path, clutching her mother's locket. She rubbed the flower with her thumb, back and forth, aware of Takeem following silently in her wake.

She had so many questions – about the Tekhlan, about the nargnets, about her brother and the world they created together.

She wanted to know why the Tekhlan had targeted her.

She was curious about Forelia – had she made it to the nesting grounds?

She worried about the fires that burned that day, wondering whether she was the cause of that scorched battlefield and whether the fate she had written had been averted somehow, or if they were all still destined to burn.

She wanted to know where Jonathan was. She wanted to find her Hwanon.

With all these questions in her mind, Samantha stepped onto the Trail of Truth.

*

Takeem followed Samantha silently. They were here to ask why the Tekhlan were pursuing them, but he had so many more questions than this. He had questions about his own existence, about his family and their treatment of him. His mother ignored him in favor of his Royal brother. So why not execute him when he was born? Why allow him to live?

As if he had conjured him, a Royal-Blue man appeared on the path. He was dressed all in black, with the red sash of the Tekhlan around his waist. Both ends had a blue striped feline woven upon them. The sash was tied so the two felines appeared to be lunging from the man's waist toward the ground. This man, marked by the beasts on his sash, was the leader of the Tekhlan. But he was not Yezyr.

"Son," the man spoke, his voice harsh and angry. "Blood of my blood, spinner-born, how is it that you live?"

*

Samantha moved swiftly, almost at a run, when a woman stepped onto the path. Samantha skidded to a stop.

"You do not belong here," Alatore said, her voice echoing along the trail. "You are not Blue. You need to leave this place."

"I'm sorry," Samantha said, her heart pounding. "I know you don't like me. I know I'm not Blue, but I have to go to the Shrine." She stepped toward Alatore. It was like walking through water. Glancing down, she saw that a fog had risen, obscuring her feet. She continued walking, though it seemed the fog was trying to push her back.

Samantha reached Alatore and cringed as she stepped forward, anticipating a physical confrontation if Alatore refused to move.

The moment Samantha stepped into Alatore's space, the queen disappeared. Samantha whirled around. She was alone on the Trail. Takeem had been behind her, but now she couldn't see anything. She was surrounded in fog. "Takeem?" she called out. Her voice echoed back, but there was no reply.

*

"Father?" Takeem gasped, staring at the man he had spun endless childhood dreams about. *If his father had lived, he would be loved.*

"You are not worthy of this place," Vukel growled. "Leave and do not return, spinner filth." He rushed toward Takeem, who cringed in anticipation of a physical confrontation with the father he had never known.

Nothing happened. He opened his eyes. His father was gone. Takeem whirled around. He was alone on the mountain.

"Samantha!" he called. There was no answer. The silence was oppressive, as was the fog slowly creeping toward his waist, obscuring the path he followed.

Taking a deep breath, Takeem muttered, "The Mountain is testing me. That's all this is. It's just a test. That wasn't my father. It wasn't." He moved through the fog, though his legs felt heavy and exhaustion pressed upon him.

Another man stepped onto the path. He wore the crown of

Lutia. "Nephew," he growled. "You do not belong here. Alatore should have executed you at birth. Leave this place, abomination!"

"Not there," Takeem gritted, moving forward. "You are not there." He pushed through the image of his uncle Sorelion and kept walking.

*

Samantha stood in the fog, alone, terrified. She was afraid to move, afraid to stay. Had Alatore really been there? Were the Tekhlan on the mountain as well? She couldn't see the path she followed and was terrified a misstep would send her tumbling off a cliff.

She carefully tucked her mother's locket back into her shirt and reached out to the side, hoping to feel the mountain's surface, hoping to use it as a guide, but there was nothing within her hand's reach. Was she even facing the right direction? She couldn't stay there forever. Clenching her fists, Samantha forced herself to inch forward. She had only taken a few steps when Vukel appeared on the path.

"Vukel!" Samantha gasped. He'd died at Shorel, with everyone else on that battlefield. How had Takeem's father come to be here, on the mountain? Was Takeem right? Had she become a living soul-keeper? A shiver raced down Samantha's spine.

If he was a ghost, he wasn't really there. She inched toward him.

"Abomination," Vukel accused. His voice echoed around the mountain. "You are not worthy of my son."

He was right. Takeem deserved better.

"You are not worthy of this place."

She and Jonathan had created this world though. Maybe not the Shrine specifically, but it was of their world.

"You need to leave this place."

"No." Samantha said, finding strength in the idea that the Shrine belonged to their world. "I don't." She forced herself to take a step, then to keep moving, one foot in front of the other, until she finally reached Vukel.

Leaning over, he shouted in her face, "Leave!"

Just one more step.

Samantha took it, heart pounding.

*

Takeem kept moving forward, head down so he would not see anyone else sent to confront him, desperate to escape the fog before more family members arrived to test him.

"Takeem."

He froze in place.

"Takeem, look at me."

Takeem looked up.

Alatore stood on the path directly ahead.

"Mother."

"What are you doing, Takeem?"

"What I must."

"You must not enter this Shrine. You know that. You must leave this place."

"I am worthy, Mother. I am." Takeem walked toward her.

"Takeem." Alatore's voice was filled with sorrow. "You cannot change what you are. You are spinner-born. You are the only Royal-spinner in this world. You must not waste that gift on impossible dreams. You do not belong here."

"Then where do I belong, Mother? There is nowhere in Blue territory that I am welcome. If I am such an abomination, why did you let me live?"

"You are my son."

"That's not an answer. You have never treated me like a son. You might as well have delivered me to the mountains, left me for the Mozkola to raise or to kill." He stood in front of Alatore. He should push through her and continue on his way. Force her to disappear, but he couldn't. He had to know. "Why did you let me live?"

"Takeem." Alatore took a step forward, her image disintegrating as it moved through him. "You are the Royal-spinner." Her voice whispered in the air around them.

"Descended from a long line of kings and queens. You are my son."

*

Samantha stood alone on the mountain once more. Vukel was gone. The world was silent, the fog oppressive.

Trusting she was moving in the right direction, she continued walking forward slowly.

Would this fog never end? A few steps and she jerked to a stop.

An entire line of Royal Tekhlan stood ahead, blocking the path.

One stepped forward. It was Yezyr, the man Takeem had said was the leader of the Tekhlan. As he moved, the blue tigers on his red sash moved with him, their bodies stretching and undulating, their heads turning, their blue eyes staring into hers.

Yezyr circled her form, his eyes prowling over her body, contempt pouring from him. "You do not belong here. You will not survive this path you take."

Samantha's breath caught in her throat, frozen silent as Yezyr continued to circle.

"We will pursue you. We will find you." Yezyr completed his circuit to stand in front of her, eyes staring into hers. "This path leads to death." He stepped back, moving slowly until he once more reached the center of the line of Tekhlan.

The sashes around his waist rippled and the two blue tigers lunged forward, leaping from the sash to the ground. As they leapt, their forms grew to massive sizes. The Tekhlan on either side of Yezyr hurtled forward, their bodies morphing into royal-blue tigers. They raced down the path, toward Samantha, the two sash-tigers in the lead.

At the last minute, Samantha flung her arms up over her face, trying to protect what she could. A harsh wind blew past, the breath of a thousand angry tigers rushing by and then silence fell. She slowly pulled her arms from her face.

The Tekhlan and the tigers were gone. The fog was fading.

She moved forward again. She could see the end of the Trail, the peak of the mountain, just ahead.

Someone stood there, right at the peak, waiting.

*

Takeem moved forward, his mother's words echoing in his ears. She had sounded so adamant, so strong when she claimed him as her son. Why would she claim him here, on this mountain, but not back in the real world? His mother had always ignored him. That wasn't true though. There had been a time – but that time was long gone, ten years in the past. Why now, in a vision that wasn't true, did she claim him, did she sound almost tender when she spoke to him? Why now did the love she never bore him shadow her voice?

He was so intent upon his thoughts, he walked through the Tekhlan before he even realized they were there. They parted for him, but then reappeared further up the Trail. Takeem stopped and gauged the distance between them. Did they intend to attack?

Yezyr stepped forward. "You will not pass." His voice echoed down the Trail toward Takeem. "This Shrine is a holy place. It is for Blues, not the spinner-born."

Takeem's thoughts were still so much with Alatore that he was speaking before he realized what he was going to say. "I am my mother's son. I am the Royal-spinner. This Shrine is for me as much as it is for you, assassin."

"You will not pass."

Takeem met Yezyr's eyes with his own, set his jaw in determination and ran for the line of the Tekhlan. When the beasts on Yezyr's sash lunged forward and the Tekhlan transformed as well, Takeem didn't falter. The beasts poured over him in the waves of a harsh wind, but he kept moving forward, his feet pounding the ground, faster and faster, until he burst from the Trail onto the flattened peak, the entrance to the Shrine straight ahead.

Standing in front of the entrance barring the way, stood Arioan.

*

At first Samantha thought Takeem was waiting for her at the top of the Trail. However, as she drew closer, she realized it was someone she did not know. His head was shaved completely bald and his sky-blue skin was covered in the markings of a Shrouded One. Royal-blue vines of leaves trailed from the top of his head, down his forehead, face and neck to disappear beneath his clothes. The vines reappeared at his hands, trailing down across his fingers. His eyes were black pools of darkness and they tracked her progress as she slowly approached the peak where he stood.

He seemed to Samantha to be a living Shrouded One, a being filled with magick.

She came to a stop before him, just below him on the Trail. "Who are you?"

"We are the Mozkola." His voice was a thousand voices, echoing down the mountain. "If you continue down this path, you will be sentenced to the isolation of death."

Goosebumps spread across Samantha's skin. "Why?" she whispered.

"This path you choose is one no other may take. It is for you or it is for no one. If you choose to follow this path, we will carry out your sentence."

"What path? Searching for Jonathan?"

But the Mozkola had disappeared, leaving Samantha alone at the top of the Trail.

It didn't matter. Nothing would stop her from discovering the truth of their world. Nothing would keep her from finding her brother.

Straight ahead stood an open area, a cliff that butted up against the mountain. A giant archway was carved into its rocky surface, providing an entrance into the Shrine. Etched all around the opening were elaborate carvings of a willow tree's branches, giving the illusion that the doorway was the trunk of a massive willow tree.

Between Samantha and the entrance stood Hulak and Forelia, both of them in their smaller forms, heads twined together, bodies leaning into each other, eyes on Samantha.

*

Takeem moved forward, slowly approaching Arioan. The fog had lifted, but he wasn't certain his brother was truly there.

"Arioan?"

"Takeem. You should not be here."

"Why not? This is where I have been sent, by our mother, by the women on her list."

"You should not be here. This is no place for the spinner-born."

"I am as much of our mother's blood as you are, Arioan. I have as much right as you to walk in this place."

Arioan shook his head. "I have less right than you, Takeem. Still, you should go back. This is no path for you to walk."

"What do you mean, you have less right?"

"Go back, Takeem. Go back before it is too late. We cannot protect you from the Tekhlan. No one can."

"No one has protected me since the day I was born." Takeem shoved forward, ready to push Arioan aside, but instead stumbled through him as Arioan disintegrated. Takeem slammed to his knees, the force of his forward movement plummeting him to the ground.

"You have been protected from the moment you were conceived, Takeem." Arioan's voice echoed around them. "No other has been more protected than you."

Silence fell.

Takeem looked up. He was kneeling within the holy Shrine of Vanadevi. Somehow, he had passed the Mountain's test. The chilled air of the shrine felt amazing against his skin, as the peace and serenity of the chamber seeped inside.

Samantha was nowhere to be seen.

*

Samantha walked toward the entrance of the Shrine. When she reached Hulak and Forelia, she stopped.

The light banner of Forelia's golden color mixed with Hulak's deep purple. They stepped apart, their colors separating, so they stood, one on either side of the entrance to the Shrine.

Samantha took a step forward, but stopped when Forelia burst into flames. She did not disintegrate, but instead stood there, a nargnet wrapped in fire. "You wrote this world to burn." Her voice whispered through Samantha's mind, stopping her breath, driving her to her knees.

"I'm sorry," Samantha gasped.

Hulak burst into flames on the other side of the entrance. "You wrote our lives to burn." His voice wrapped through her mind, tangling her thoughts, blazing a truth to the center of her being.

"I'm so sorry." Samantha crawled toward the entrance of the Shrine, tears pouring down her face.

"If you stay," their voices echoed all around, "if you remain on this path, you share our fate."

"I'm sorry, I'm sorry, I'm sorry," Samantha chanted as she crawled across the threshold, as she collapsed upon the ground, the cool air of the holy shrine enveloping her, soothing her, extinguishing the flames of the nargnets' fire.

The Book of Ages

ONE MOMENT TAKEEM was alone in the shrine and the next, Samantha was at his side, collapsed on the ground, whispering over and over again, "I'm sorry."

Takeem dropped to his knees beside her. "Samantha." He touched her arm.

She jerked to a sitting position, gasping.

"Are you okay?"

"I-I think so." She glanced around. "Are we in the shrine?"

"Barely. There's still a journey we must take, here inside the Mountain."

"Oh, no. Not another test. Takeem, I can't."

"No. We've made it inside. There shouldn't be any more tests." He hesitated. "Was it terrible?"

Samantha thought back over everything that had happened – Takeem's parents, the Tekhlan, the Mozkola, even Hulak and Forelia, all of them warning her to turn back. All of them warning this pathway led to death. "It wasn't great. How was your test?"

"The same as yours. Difficult, but manageable."

"Do you want to talk about it?"

Takeem shook his head. "You?"

"Not really. I'd rather do what we came here to do, if that's all right."

"Of course." Takeem helped her stand and stood at her side

as they surveyed the Shrine.

They stood inside the mountain, on the edge of a giant canyon. To their right, carved out along the wall, were stairs leading downward, deep into the mountain, into a giant cavernous space. Above them, the walls stretched upward, forming a hollow peak, through which the bright afternoon sun shone, lighting the walls of the canyon in an eerie orange glow.

"Are we supposed to go down the stairs?" Samantha asked.

"I think so. I think the Book of Ages must be down there." He pointed into the canyon.

"Okay. So let's go." Samantha grabbed his hand and started toward the stairs.

"Wait," Takeem protested, pulling her to a stop. "I don't know if it's safe. I mean–"

"Not safe? Takeem, we've traveled all this way, been judged by the mountain and now you're worried it's not safe? We'll be fine."

"It's just–"

"What?"

"This is considered to be the holiest spot in all of Lutia and I don't think I should be here."

"Of course you should, Takeem."

"You don't understand. I've been told my entire life this place isn't for the spinner-born. It's a holy place for the Blues, not for me, not for people like me."

"You walked the Trail of Truth, didn't you?"

"Yes."

"And the mountain tested you?"

"Yes, but–"

"But nothing. Now you're here, inside the Shrine, so the mountain must have judged you worthy. Look, we'll go together. It's going to be okay. You'll see." Samantha headed for the stairs. They were steep and narrow. There was only room for them to go down single file, so Samantha led and Takeem followed.

Neither spoke, choosing instead to concentrate on where to place their feet. The space demanded their silent reverence, as if they had entered a place where few humans dared trespass.

For a time, there appeared to be no end to the stairs, no floor at the bottom of the cavernous mountain. The farther they walked, the cooler the air became. In the beginning, the stairs were well lit in a continuous spiral, but as they walked, the shadows lengthened and the stairs curved less and less.

When they finally reached the end, the first thing Takeem saw was the Shrouded One. Standing at the center of the mountain, the Soul-Keeper seemed to him to be the oldest Keeper in existence. It had a solemnity and gravity to its presence. Its roots were gnarled and thick and they grew as much atop the ground as beneath it. They stretched out from the tree, all the way to the sides of the mountain, in some places even twining their way up it.

The Shrouded One stood as sentinel, a witness to all of creation, making the space seem all the holier to Takeem. He felt as if he intruded where he should not. He inched back toward the stairs, as if by slowly backing away, he might not gain the attention of this holiest of Shrouded Ones.

Samantha turned to him, a look of radiant joy upon her face.

He had never seen her smile like that.

"Look, Takeem. Another willow tree." She started toward it.

Though he dreaded approaching the Shrouded One, he followed Samantha across the root-laden land.

The thick vines around the tree lifted and parted, revealing the nucleus of the Shrouded One. A pedestal stood at the base of the tree, and upon that pedestal a book of such substance, it appeared to glow.

Samantha stepped forward, but Takeem caught her hand in his. "Wait, Samantha. Be careful. You risk everything in touching such a powerful book – your life, your sanity."

"It's going to be okay, Takeem."

"Maybe I should go with you, maybe we should touch the book together." He shuddered at the thought of walking beneath this Shrouded One, but he couldn't let Samantha take the risk alone. Truly, he shouldn't allow her to take the risk at all. "In fact, m-maybe you should wait here and I'll touch the Book."

Samantha laughed softly. "Don't worry so much, Takeem. I'll

touch it first, see what we can find out. Then if we still need answers, you can try as well." She stepped beneath the green canopy of the Shrouded One.

Takeem feared the Keeper would close her within its sphere, but even so, he could not force himself to step across that invisible threshold. Though he had woken twice now beneath a Shrouded One, he'd not yet been required to walk beneath one willingly. And this Shrouded One, one of the oldest in existence, was not one he wished to begin with. He stayed at the edge of its borders, standing just outside the opening it had revealed for Samantha, and was relieved when the leaves did not close around her, barring her from his sight.

She approached the pedestal and placed her hands upon the Book's pages.

You wish to know the truth. The words echoed in Takeem's mind. *But are you prepared to accept it?*

Was he ready to learn his mother's secrets – why the Skies hated her, why she feared Samantha, how she truly felt about Takeem? Was he ready to learn why she had set the Tekhlan after them?

Perhaps.

A searing white light emanated from the Book of Ages, encompassing Samantha's form, then his. It bathed the entire chamber, and Takeem imagined, the mountain and the world beyond, in light.

He was falling.

*

You wish to know the truth. The words echoed in her mind. *But are you prepared to accept it?*

Samantha wanted to shout yes, but she shivered in fear instead. She was supposed to ask about the Tekhlan, why they were after them, how to defeat them, but these were not the questions burning inside. The world she and Jonathan had written was so much more than she had ever imagined.

Was she ready to face the truth of their world? *Yes.* As she pushed this thought forward, the image of Hulak and Forelia engulfed in flames filled her mind. Was that the truth of their world? The flames she had written to burn them all?

A searing white light blanketed her, bringing with it stabbing pain, and then she was falling.

*

Falling into the path of another's world.

HULAK THROUGH THE AGES

THE ROYAL NARGNET

HULAK SERVED THE Royal Line. This was his destiny, his calling. This was who he was: the Royal Nargnet, born to rule the nargnet race and serve as warrior-companion to the Royal Line of Lutia, born to bear that line into battle. Only an equal could be trusted to serve as brother or sister-in-arms to a king. Only an equal could be trusted to imprint the knowledge of the ages into the Book.

He was the one called to truth, the one called to bear silent witness, and so he did.

He imprinted upon the book that which each of them had done – Torel, Sorelion, even himself. He imprinted everything they had done in giving in to their fears, everything he himself had done in giving in to his rage.

He spared no one the truth, not even himself.

SERVING TOREL

130 YEARS AGO, in the time of the Purge

"I don't know what to do, Hulak," King Torel said. "Things have gotten out of hand. The riots… Why can't people accept the way things are? Why can't the Sky-Blues be happy to serve? Why must the spinners always plot and plan and never simply accept?"

Hulak was weary. Weary of the questions. Weary of the whining. Weary of the Royals' inability to understand the needs of the other classes. Humans were so difficult. They could not simply live and let live. They had to impose, to demand; they had to *strive* for more, never mind that attaining more meant others would live with less.

Torel paced back and forth across the great room. "Who do they think they are? Did you see this list of demands, Hulak? The right to serve on the high council? Ridiculous. They haven't the knowledge or the ability to serve in such a way. Not one of them with even a tiny shred of Royal-Blue blood. Sky-Blues and Sky-spinners, not one of them worthy. The right to vote for their leaders? *We* are their leaders. The right to choose their own occupation? What about tradition? We have lived by this tradition for thousands of years. Chaos would be the result. Can you imagine? Suddenly we would have ten thousand artists and not a single worker for the fields. They should be proud, proud to follow in their father's and their grandfather's footsteps. Proud to be part of a farming family or an artistic one and not worry so much about what they would rather do. It's about tradition, Hulak."

Hulak had heard this all before and so he simply watched Torel as he paced, and waited for the king's fury to abate. At that point, Hulak knew, the king would make decisions about what must be done. Hulak could only hope these decisions would not make things worse than they already were. At least they had a council meeting scheduled for later in the morning. Surely the council would be able to calm the king.

Perhaps not though. The high council, after all, had been appointed by King Torel.

*

"We must do something." Lord Nerys slammed his fist on the table. "They are talking in the streets of rebellion. The Sky-Blues and the spinners are starting to fight amongst themselves. I believe it is the only thing that has kept the palace safe to date. If they ever reach an agreement, my king, we are doomed."

"He's right. Truthfully, I don't even know why the spinners have held off as long as they have," Lord Marel said. "With the way their powers have grown over the last few generations, they could annihilate us before we even managed to prepare a defense."

"Yes, yes," King Torel snapped. "I think we all know the situation is dire. What I need now are suggestions, not more complaints. You are my advisors. Advise me. What should we do? Almost anything we attempt is sure to be seen by their seers. How do we keep them from knowing?"

"We need to bind their powers," Lord Zarkonen, the king's chief advisor and leader of the Tekhlan, stated grimly.

"What?" Shouts rang out through the room as the different council members tried to make their voices heard.

"If we bind their powers, we bind our own as well."

"There are so few of us able to spin the magicks anymore, I

hardly see how that matters."

"We would still have the Book of Ages, which is more than the spinners would have."

"What if it affects the Book though? How do we know that it won't?"

"Or the Royal Line's ability to read it?"

"It could come back upon us in ways we cannot even begin to imagine."

"Silence," the king said. "Lord Zarkonen, even if we wanted to bind their powers, I do not see how we could do so. Yes, we've had to bind the powers of one or two, but to bind the thousands who plague our society now? I do not think it is possible. Even if we managed it, there would be no way to tie the spell to the spinners and them alone. There would surely be some spillover and we would all be affected. What little powers we have would be forfeit as well." He shook his head. "I don't see…"

"My king, these spinners are capable of much more than we are." Lord Zarkonen paced the room, his hands clenched, the red sash around his waist fluttering as he moved. "We have no true magicks to defend ourselves with, not the way they do. Your ability to read the Book and spin the occasional spell is no match for the thousands of magick-wielding spinners we now face. If they decide to attack, what shall we do? Our way of life is at stake here. Our very existence is at stake. It may already be too late. If we wish to preserve our way of life, we have to act now."

"The people would never forgive us." Lord Kessink spoke up for the first time. "They would riot. Even with the unrest in the cities, the Sky-Blues would be horrified to know we bound such power. Doing such a thing would mean the end of us all. In attempting to save our way of life, we would end up destroying it."

"Then we would have to be smarter and more devious than ever," Lord Marel said.

"What do you mean?" King Torel asked.

"We simply come up with an explanation for our actions, one that will appease the people of Lutia. In fact, I suggest we find an explanation that makes us their heroes, their saviors. We must make them *want* us to take the actions that we do."

Hulak, who had sat quietly at King Torel's feet during the entirety of this meeting, shuddered to hear these words. What terrible truths would he be witness to now?

*

It took seven months for the king and his council to create a spell they felt sufficient to bind the powers, not just of those spinners living at the time, but of all spinners yet to be born. They spent endless hours in the Royal library, where their people's ancient tomes of magick were housed. They found the information they needed almost immediately. However, none of them were spinners and though the king had some spinning ability, he had nothing like the endless, dark power required for the spell they wished to spin.

And so they searched for a spell to gain more power.

It was Petryus who found what they needed. He would have hidden the spell, terrified of its dark nature, but before he could, Zarkonen read its potential over his shoulder and congratulated him on his find.

The arguments waged for hours, but in the end, each of them conceded. To save their people, to save their way of life, they would sacrifice anything. They would sacrifice *anyone*. Each of the king's seven advisors stole out into the night, to pursue their dark efforts on their own, seeking to gain power by spilling the blood of a spinner.

While they were committing the darkest of acts, Royal metal workers labored tirelessly, creating seven elaborate gates. Before the metal was poured, Torel spun a spell upon it, one whose effects would not be seen until the binding spell was spun. Once the gates were finished, he sent them out with the Royal guard, who carried the gates to specific spots across the lands of Lutia. The first gate was placed seven hundred seventy-seven kilometers away from the palace, at the very edge of the known territories, right before the barren lands. Each subsequent gate was seventy-seven kilometers closer to the palace, until the inner gate stood exactly three hundred and fifteen kilometers away, along the border between Royal-Blue and Sky-Blue territories.

As dawn approached, each of the seven advisors, eyes deadened with darkened power, gathered at the Holy Shrine of Vanadevi, far from the palace, deep into the mountains of Lixor. And so they were ready.

Hulak arrived in time to witness the end of everything.

*

Zarkonen, the king's chief advisor began. "Into the darkness, we cast our fears." Circling round the trunk of the Shrouded One, he poured the blood of the spinner he had slain earlier that day onto the sacred ground. Seven hundred and seventy-seven kilometers from the palace, yet not too far from where they now stood, a loud clanging sound was heard throughout the land, as the first gate of Lutia latched itself shut. In the next instant, a roaring sound filled the air as the first wall of Lutia burst into existence, exploding from both sides of the gate, reaching deep into the soil to take root, spreading across the land in an ever-increasing circle, slowly enclosing the known territories within a giant stone wall. As the wall crossed through mountain ranges, rivers and forests, it destroyed everything in its path.

"Into the darkness, we cast our hatred." Kessink followed the same path Zarkonen had, adding the blood of the spinner he had slain to the mix. Seven hundred kilometers from the palace, the second gate of Lutia slammed shut and the second wall formed, cleaving the Lixorian mountain range in half and severing contact between its villages.

"Into the darkness, we cast our fury." Marel followed Kessink. Six hundred and twenty-three kilometers from the palace, the third wall exploded into being, dividing the forests of Bipin. Hundreds of trees were annihilated while others were split in two, the wall powering through their massive trunks.

"Into the darkness, we cast our vengeance." Nerys circled with purpose. Five hundred and forty-six kilometers from the palace, the fourth wall journeyed through the lands of Lutia, damming rivers and sending the waters cascading across the lands, flooding farms and homes.

"From the darkness, we gain deliverance." Petryus circled with faltering footsteps, his hand shaking as the blood spilled to the ground. Four hundred and sixty-nine kilometers from the palace, the fifth wall cut across the land, decimating the Sky villages caught in its path.

"From the darkness, we gain salvation." Loxoryon moved swiftly, his voice strong and sure. Three hundred and ninety-two kilometers from the palace, the sixth wall was born, destroying nests and fracturing the Nargnet Nesting Grounds.

"From the darkness, we rise anew, our enemies forsaken." Ferilis delivered his vow with a fierce smile on his face. All the peoples of Lutia felt it when the seventh wall sprang into being, when the seventh gate slammed shut three hundred and fifteen kilometers from the palace. The sound resonated throughout the land. It was the sound of an entire way of life dying.

The walls came into being too quickly for the spinners to formulate an attack. As the first wall went up, the truth came upon them, the terror of what the leaders of Lutia were about to do. The spinners tried desperately to stop it, tried spinning a multitude of spells, but it was already too late. The black magick already had form and substance. It was already on its way, aimed straight for the heart of every spinner in existence.

Torel stepped forward, the final offering in his hand, a cup that held the blood of all seven sacrifices, mixed with the liquid metal used to make the seven gates of Lutia. He stood ready to seal their dark spell forever. "We make this offering to the dark, that it might smite down our enemies, that it might bind their powers into the cold metals of hatred, that such cold hardness shall endure through the ages, an unyielding defense against all who would stand against us." He circled the tree, pouring the dark liquid of hatred. "We offer these sacrifices, welding our magick to the lands of Lutia, sealing the magick of all those who would oppose us, empowering the gates that will stand strong in our defense."

*

Hulak would never forget what he witnessed that day. It was burned into his memory, into his very being. He would never feel clean again. The moment the final drop of that dark brew hit the soil beneath the Shrouded One, the entire tree turned black.

It terrified him. He backed away from the darkening tree, from this thing his companion had done. He reached the stairs and wished to race up them, away from this sacred place they had just defiled, but he could not. He could only stare as the darkened tree shuddered and died. Its roots shriveled back into the ground and the trunk bowed with a great, thunderous crack. The entire tree melted into nothingness.

The snap of the breaking of roots, the horrible sound of the limbs dying, he would hear in his nightmares for the rest of his days.

King Torel and his council backed away from the tree. They raced up the stairs, their panicked shouts dwindling as they ran from the shrine. Hulak was unable to follow them. All he could do was stand and bear witness to the worst thing he had ever seen: the death of a Shrouded One.

When it was done, the entire tree had melted back into the land, and where it had once stood, there was only an oozing, blackened patch of darkness. It reached across the land, breathing darkness everywhere. This Shrouded One, this ancient tree, had always been the place where the Book of Ages was housed. How was he to imprint the events of this day when the Shrouded One was now gone, taking the pedestal and the Book of Ages with it?

As if in response to his question, the pedestal bearing the Book of Ages slowly rose from the black. Hulak was unwilling to wade through the blood of seven spinners and the tainted remains of the Shrouded One to reach the Book of Ages. Faltering at the side of this dark pool, he paced back and forth, unable to venture closer. Finally, seeming to understand his reluctance, the pedestal itself lurched forward, sending the Book sailing across the chamber onto unspoiled ground. Hulak leaned down and prodded it with his snout.

The last time he had visited the Shrine, this book had glowed with vitality and health. Now that glow had been replaced with a dark aura. When he nudged the book, ashes fell from its form.

Where the book traditionally would spring open with joy anytime he touched it, today it shook and trembled before eventually falling open to a dark and smudged empty page. Though he dreaded this task, Hulak slumped forward so that his head rested upon that empty page and with great sadness, imprinted the deeds that had been done that day.

*

Later that afternoon, King Torel and his council of advisors addressed the people.

"I had a vision, my people," Torel said. "A catastrophic vision. I saw the unrest within these cities expanding to new heights. I saw our people dying by the thousands. I saw war breaking out across our lands and all of the blues, Sky-Blue and Royal-Blue, being destroyed by the spinners. I saw their willingness to use their magicks against us all, to kill and to destroy. Therefore, in the interest of saving all Blues everywhere, we have temporarily bound the powers of the spinners. In one year's time, should our conditions be met, their powers will return and they will be free to spin them as they like.

"They will not, however, be allowed to spin them here in our cities. The seven walls of Lutia have been built for the separation of our kinds. So that we do not have to live in fear of those with power, and so that those with power can build their own societies as they see fit, we now declare this a time of transition."

Turning from the crowds, he signaled Lord Zarkonen, who stepped forward with the official proclamation of the Royal palace. Clearing his throat, he read from the parchment:

"All spinners are hereby exiled from the lands of Lutia, to be enforced immediately." When a great roar from the crowd rose, Lord Zarkonen simply raised his voice and continued reading, "All spinners are given exactly three months to vacate these lands, to travel to the seventh wall of Lutia and beyond it. All spinners are forbidden from returning to these lands.

"Any spinner found within any of the seven walls of Lutia after the three months have passed will be executed immediately. This is for the protection of all concerned.

"In twelve months time, if the lands of Lutia are spinner-free, the spell shall be complete and the powers of the spinners shall be returned. In this way was the spell written, in this form was it spun, in this manner only shall it be done." Lowering the parchment, he gazed out across the crowds of stunned and disoriented spinners and Blues.

"We ask the spinners to begin preparations to leave these lands and the Sky-Blues to assist in whatever manner most fitting to their station. Transportation will be provided beginning tomorrow at dawn. May the blessings of Vanadevi be upon you."

Swiftly turning, the council members retreated back into the palace, leaving behind a stunned populace that would riot and rage over the following days before eventually settling down and beginning the difficult task of segregating an entire world.

*

The following months were agonizing for Hulak to witness. His brethren were used as work beasts to carry the bound spinners into exile. They were forced to participate in this separation of those who were different. The nesting grounds of the nargnets had fallen inside the walls of Lutia, which was a mixed blessing. In these sad times, it might have been better for them to have fallen outside the walls. Even worse, many nargnets announced their intention to follow their companions into exile. It was not just the human world being divided. The Nargnet Nation was breaking apart as well.

More horrifying still was the loss of the Shrouded Ones. Those that had survived the initial spinning of the spell sickened and died over the following months. The Shrouded Ones, almost overnight, became extinct. The Royals announced it was the work of the spinners, claiming they had managed to spin a deadly spell before Torel could stop them. With this news spreading across the land, public sentiment turned in favor of Torel's actions. The creation of walls separating the lands and limiting access to many of their holy lands was now considered the necessary price of being safe from the magickal malevolence of the spinners.

The Royal guard worked tirelessly to gather the spinners and ship them out as quickly and quietly as possible. Though there were a few spinners who flaunted the law and who refused to leave, those spinners paid quietly with their lives. The Tekhlan swiftly and silently disappeared them off the streets of Lutia and the story was circulated that they had complied and traveled into exile.

Eventually life returned to a semblance of normalcy and Torel and the members of his council were hailed as heroes by the peoples of Lutia, for they had done the impossible: they had defeated the spinners and made the lands of Lutia safe once more.

Serving Sorelion

Hulak wandered through the nesting grounds of his brethren, Forelia at his side. Her soft presence drifted through his mind like a soothing embrace. All those years without her. All those years, witness to such horrific things, serving as companion to such a dark brother. How much more bearable might those years have been had she been at his side?

Their love was young and he had resisted at first. The idea of sharing his burdens as the Royal companion was a foreign one. How could he ask someone else to live with the memories he held? Though Sorelion was nothing like Torel had been, he still refused to see the truth. He still refused to accept the culpability of his people. To ask someone else to share that burden of knowledge, to share what he had witnessed – he couldn't even imagine.

But Forelia had persisted. She had continually forced her presence into his world. She had dragged him into the light, pushing him toward the young ones, forcing him to see the joys of life all around them, even in the midst of war. She had come to him again and again, between battles and during them, forcing him to acknowledge her existence and her skill.

She was the companion to the king's chief advisor, Vukel, and though he worried about her every time they went to war, he had given up the fight to leave her behind after she pinned him for the first time during a mock battle. Perhaps he had not fought as fiercely as he should have in the beginning – after all, she seemed so fragile (Forelia's gentle mind-snort rolled through his head in response to that thought) – but he had quickly learned not to underestimate her… and still she had pinned him.

This, of course, made him even more frustrated and annoyed at her, which probably hindered rather than helped her cause in the beginning, but Forelia was nothing if not stubborn (*like you're not* her voice mind-whispered) and eventually, through sheer determination, she had won him over. He didn't even realize it was happening until one bright morning when he woke to war with joy in his heart because Forelia would fight by his side.

They had been together eighty years now and he could not imagine returning to his life as it had been before her. He had his bond with Sorelion, of course, but he knew better than most nargnets that one could not depend on having a true companion's bond with a human simply because many were not worthy of a nargnet's esteem. Torel had been such a human, and Hulak had held a bit of himself back from the sacred relationship of a nargnet and his rider ever since. He simply found it impossible to trust humans since the events of Torel's generation. Hulak was always waiting for that moment when his rider would fail to fulfill the promise of the companion oath – to seek enlightenment for all. Because he failed to fully establish the companion bond, he was left with an aching void that could not be filled, though Forelia tried so desperately.

Today, Hulak and Forelia stood together and watched a group of young hatchlings playing a game of fire-tag. Of course, the hatchlings were so young their fire was more like a wisp of smoke, but it was enough to make the game interesting and fun, not to mention entertaining to watch. They were undeniably adorable. Though he and Forelia thought it would be nice to have a family of their own one day, they both agreed: no hatchlings until this war was done.

Hulak did not expect the war to end under Sorelion's reign, for

Sorelion was too influenced by the stories his father had told of
their ancestor Torel. However, one day soon, perhaps in a
hundred years, the unborn king would inherit the throne. No,
that wasn't right. Humans were so fragile in their life-spans. A
hundred years, though barely an instant to him, would be too
long for this particular unborn to wait. If Hulak was right and
Vukel's unborn child was destined to one day rule these lands, he
would do so in a flash of time.

Hulak hoped what he saw would truly come to pass. He hoped
the child the Book had shown him, the man he would become,
was indeed the babe of Alatore's womb. Of all the Royals he had
met through the years, none seemed so utterly right for the
throne as the young unborn soul he had met in his dreams.

*

Hulak and Forelia returned to the warfront days later, with
King Sorelion and Vukel on their backs. The battles were not
going well and even worse, both men were distracted when
racing toward war. Hulak was certain it had something to do
with the king's sister. Alatore was always antagonizing her
brother, the king, and her husband, Vukel. After all these years,
Hulak would have expected her to adjust to her circumstances,
but like all humans, Alatore fought against the currents of her
life, determined to move the river in another direction.

When the horns of war sounded on the seventh morning after
their return, Hulak mind-sung the song of war for Forelia as they
took to the skies.

War has come, my beloved
Do not falter in your fight
My warrior queen, fly strong
Into this darkening dawn

We are one in the madness
We are one at war
Your battle is mine
My combat is yours

Do not falter, my beloved
Fly to war with me
Do not fear, my beloved
Our path is destiny

As they flew, they mind-sung in harmony until the heat of battle ended their song.

*

Hulak hated the brekzors. They were always so ready to tear the wings off a nargnet. They had deadly, rapier-like claws they used quite viciously, ripping massive holes in the wings of unsuspecting nargnets. The brekzors were pitch black, with smoky, translucent wings. At night, they were the worst enemy a nargnet could ever meet. Blending with the night sky, the brekzors could attack and kill their victims before they even realized anything was out there.

The most annoying thing about the brekzors, however, was not their massive claws, nor their vicious teeth, nor even the crest on their heads that felt as hard as a rock when slammed against a nargnet's unsuspecting snout. No, the most annoying thing about the brekzors was the whistling sound they made while gnashing their teeth. The whistling sound filled the air that day, on the battlefield of Shorel, as hundreds of battling brekzors and nargnets filled the skies.

Hulak barely ducked in time as a brekzor aimed for his throat with three fully extended claws. Hulak mind-roared, spewing fire across the brekzor's back, catching the spinner there and sending him burning and screaming to the ground below. The brekzor whipped around and charged Hulak. Opening its mouth, it screeched in rage, the sound like a thousand whistles screaming across the land. Hulak cringed from the sound, even as he braced for impact. The brekzor collided with Hulak with a great crash and the two grappled together mid-air, swiping at each other with claws and teeth and whipping tails. The brekzor managed to clip Hulak's snout with his crest, infuriating him.

Hulak could feel his eyes burning red, his fury turning bright hot. Ripping away from the brekzor, he whirled in mid-air, ready to strike again, when he felt a searing pain across his wings. That vile creature had tried to tear his wings off.

He flung himself forward, pierced the brekzor's chest with the three bright-red claws he never used and watched as the brekzor burned from the inside out.

My wings, he mind-hissed, forcing his thought past the barricade of this stupid creature's brain. *Now die.* And flinging the brekzor away from him, he did not even bother to watch as the brekzor, turning to ashes from the inside out, fell from the sky.

Whirling around, Hulak tried to determine where his king had gone. He had not been on his back for a while, having jumped to a neighboring brekzor some time past. Searching the mid-air battles, he did not see him. Turning his attention to the ground below, he caught sight of the king fighting amidst spinners and skies.

Hulak was headed for the king, he had him in his sights, when the worst came to pass. The soft presence of his *unai*, his beloved, faltered in his mind, just a bit. It flickered, then came back, but not so strong as before.

Forelia! Frantically searching the air around him, he completely forgot his rider, the king. *Where was his Forelia?* And then he saw her. Desperately flapping her wings, she was clearly headed to the ground. And then she was down.

Whipping in and out of battles, under and over lunging nargnets and brekzors, Hulak followed her path to where she lay.

Forelia!

Why wasn't she answering him? Blessed Vanadevi, she was dying, he could feel her going, he could feel her…

As he came upon her dying place, arriving at her side, he saw himself in her loving eyes, in her dying eyes, and then she was gone.

No! Forelia! His cry was echoed by Vukel's. Vukel, who had held her as she died. Vukel who had failed to save his *unai*.

Vukel, the first to burn.

If there were witnesses to the events that followed, they might have said they saw a purple nargnet turn bright red as the sun. Hulak, whose colors had always been black and purple, would thereafter be more red than the other two. He would take some comfort in this, for red had been one of Forelia's colors – red and gold. His red, however, was the red of blood, the red of fire, where hers had been the red of passion and of love.

His red was a burning red that swept across the land.

Hulak flung his form over Forelia's, and in the sacred ways of his kind, embraced her and in that final embrace, burned her to dust. As the wind swept through the land and lifted the remains of Forelia across the battlefields, the red that had come to honor her passing, became a raging red that fired the world.

Murderers! was the scream that lived in his heart, that could not be heard, but that burned across the land.

As he rose into the sky, a burning beacon of light and rage, the Nargnet King's song of fury burst across the minds of the entire Nargnet Nation, sparking flames everywhere it touched.

Spinners and Blues,
Murderers all are you!

The Blues for setting this war into motion,
for not honoring the lies they told.
The spinners for fighting rather than accepting what was,
for launching the spear that pierced my unai.

Forelia, he wept, breaking hearts and minds as he rained ashes upon the world.

Brekzors and nargnets,
Murderers all are you!

The brekzors for bearing the spinners to battle,
for fighting a war that is not theirs.
The Nargnet Nation
for witnessing all that has come to pass

for imprinting the truths upon the Book
for bearing the humans into battle
over and over again
for failing to stop this war.

Murderers.
Murderers all are we.

Everything between the second and third walls of Lutia burned that day. As the world turned to ashes, Hulak's form fell from the sky to impact the bed of cinders with a great thudding crash. Though his form continued to burn and sizzle, as red-hot as any fire, he did not turn to ashes himself.

*

When Hulak became aware again, he found the entire battlefield a scorched wasteland and the holy forests of Bipin towering trees of ash. Struggling to an upright position, he stood in the center of the field, covered in ashes, and he wept. Throwing back his head, his heart screamed to the sky, his mourning so loud it might have shattered the minds of any nargnets close enough to hear. There were none however. There were none because those left behind in the nesting grounds all burned to dust when Hulak's potent fire touched their loved ones' minds and burned a path straight to theirs.

Hulak's endless grief found power and form as it flew across the land. His sorrow beat against the walls that stood for hatred, the walls that led to this, to his Forelia's undoing, and burned them to dust.

PRESENT DAY

TIDAL WAVE

TAKEEM STRUGGLED TO his knees from where he had collapsed at the edge of the Shrouded One.

He couldn't believe what he had just witnessed, what Hulak had done. Takeem had been relieved when the Shrouded One failed to enclose Samantha within its sphere, ensuring he would share in her visions. Now he wished the Shrouded One had locked him out. He wished he had not seen the vision it shared with her. He wished he had been spared that knowledge.

Samantha cried out, catching his attention. She lay collapsed near the trunk of the Shrouded One.

Takeem hesitated for a moment, somehow more terrified than ever at the thought of crossing the threshold.

Samantha whimpered.

She needed him.

He closed his eyes and lunged across the threshold. He waited, trembling, frozen. When nothing happened – when the vines didn't fall, trapping them beneath the Shrouded One – he scrambled across the ground to Samantha's side.

*

Hulak's grief tasted of ashes on Samantha's tongue and she clutched her head, trying desperately to push the visions of all she had seen back to some far corner of her mind. How could this be the world she and Jonathan designed? How could this

Hulak be the Huk they created? Had she caused this?

She whimpered as the vision began again, as Forelia plummeted.

Someone grabbed her shoulders, shook her. "Samantha." It was Takeem, his voice so far away. "You have to leave them now. Come back from the battlefield. Samantha!"

"Hulak," Samantha whispered as his song of fury rang in her ears. "Hulak, no." The fire that had destroyed an entire species coiled, brighter and brighter, flaming through her mind.

"Samantha, wake up. Open your eyes. Open them."

She heard Takeem's voice, but could only shake in the grips of the blazing truth that was Hulak's fire.

*

Takeem didn't want Hulak's help, but Samantha wasn't coming out of the vision on her own. Somehow he'd escaped, but she was stuck there, caught in the web of Hulak's fire. Holding her in his arms, he shouted Hulak's name and tried not to remember that the nargnet he called upon had murdered his father.

Giant paws thudded against the ground outside the tree.

"Thank Vanadevi," Takeem whispered.

Hulak pushed his way under the willow tree, transforming as he moved beneath its branches, arriving at Samantha's side in his smaller form. Hulak pressed his snout to Samantha's cheek and Samantha jerked in Takeem's arms, her eyes flying open.

Takeem caught his breath. The dark pupils expanded outward while the irises darkened from her normal Sky-Blue to a deep and brilliant Royal-Blue. The three distinct areas of her eyes mixed and mingled, swirling within and around each other. The irises overtook the whites of her eyes as the pupils bled their midnight color, forming streaks of black within the darkening shades of blue. They were spinner eyes, but not.

"Samantha?" Takeem whispered, dread filling his voice. He should never have allowed her to touch the book. His mother had warned him nothing good could come of visiting this shrine.

Then Samantha spoke, her voice sending a chill down

Takeem's back. It was deeper than her normal one and resonated with power. "One hundred and thirty years ago," she rasped, "innocent life was spilled upon this holy ground, when the Royal families of Lutia cast blood magick upon these lands. This magick will not be defeated until the blood of those who defiled these lands has been willingly cast here in contrition, to mix with that of the spinners sacrificed for personal gain. In this way the spell was spun, in this way shall it be undone."

Samantha's eyes rolled back and her body went limp.

Takeem carefully lowered her to the mountain floor, gently brushing her hair away from her face. "What does that mean?" he demanded of no one. "How has any of this helped us?"

Hulak gently nudged Takeem with his snout.

Takeem jerked away.

The truth was simply too much. First, he'd witnessed his father's terrible actions thirty years ago, then he'd met his father on the Trail. In both cases, Vukel had not been the man Takeem had always imagined, the one he'd spent his childhood weaving dreams around.

Now he discovered Hulak was responsible for Vukel's death, and though Takeem understood Vukel could never have been the father he'd always hoped for, a thousand childhood dreams held their own form of truth.

If his father had lived, he would have been loved.

"How could you, Hulak?" He surged to his feet. "All this time, we thought the fire was spinner magicks raging out of control, but instead, it was you."

Hulak watched Takeem with ancient eyes.

The grief Takeem saw in them matched his own as he considered all the possibilities Hulak's raging sorrow had ended. Takeem wanted to scream at Hulak, to throw him to the ground, to fight him, but the creature he confronted was not the one who had wreaked havoc on the battlefield of Shorel. This Hulak was a well of sorrow, not the raging monster who set fire to the world.

"Transform. Transform so I can see the one who killed my father, so I can see the nargnet king who burned his world to extinction."

Hulak obediently stepped away from Takeem and shook his body. He leapt forward, twisting mid-air, growing from the smaller black and purple form to his larger, brilliant red one. He hunched down and pushing outward with all his might, launched his giant wings from the two black streaks along his side.

Hulak bowed his head and waited for Takeem's judgment.

"The burning nargnet," Takeem murmured, everything coming clear. "You didn't take Forelia's color to honor her as everyone assumed." He stepped forward and looked up into Hulak's eyes. The knowledge of millennia stared back at him.

Takeem lifted his hand and laid it upon Hulak's snout. "You turned fire-red as a mark of your shame," Takeem whispered. "That's it, isn't it?"

Hulak's eyes closed. When he opened them, fires raged inside them, flames licking across the pools of darkness.

The blazing brightness faded and Forelia flew across the midnight orbs, the nesting grounds rising in the distance. Millennia spun out in a rolling wave across Hulak's eyes. Generations of nargnets being born, launching their wings, taking flight, building nests, bearing the Blues and spinners to war, dying in nargnet flame.

The truth broke over Takeem, crushing his rage, setting afire his grief.

In the end, it wasn't the death of Forelia.

It wasn't the death of Takeem's father.

It wasn't even the thousands that perished on the battlefield that day.

Instead, for the entire world, for every generation yet to come until the end of time, it was the loss of something far greater.

It was the unbearable tragedy of Hulak becoming the last of his kind.

The truth pulled Takeem under, a tidal wave buckling his knees and slamming him to the ground.

The Royal Nargnet collapsed beside him and Takeem pressed his face into Hulak's neck, throwing his arms around him. Their shared grief spun from one to the other until it seemed the entire world was saturated with their sorrow. Though Hulak never made a sound, his cries of grief were no less powerful than Takeem's.

*

Samantha woke weeping. The tidal wave had broken around them, saturating the world with its grief, and she was drowning in it. Thoughts of her parents and of Jonathan lambasted her. She did not often actively think of her parents. Though their faces always hovered at the back of her mind, it was Jonathan's who filled her every waking moment.

Curling into a ball, Samantha cried out against the pain. "Mom," she wept. "Daddy."

Inside, her emotions seethed, roiling and raging, desperate to escape. How was she to live with the grief and the despair and the haunting loss? It required Jonathan.

It had *always* required Jonathan. He was the one who was always there, the one to dry her tears at imagined hurts and painful losses, the one to comfort her when their cat died, when their best friend moved away. It was him. He had always been the one, the only one able to make her feel as if she weren't entirely alone.

And just like that, her thoughts moved from Jonathan to the other person in her life who was as alone and filled with sorrow as she was. Samantha had a vision of her aunt Jenny, sitting all alone in their apartment, clutching Samantha's picture and sobbing. Samantha knew she and Jenny were somehow supposed to help each other through this, but they never had. Instead, Samantha had left Jenny behind, to face the grief on her own, and now to wonder and to worry, to weep over one more lost family member.

It was in that moment of clarity that Samantha recognized the sacrifice required of her. To be here in this world, she'd have to turn her back on the only family she had left. She'd have to leave behind the one person who would never cease to mourn her passing.

*

The sounds of Samantha's weeping penetrated the shared grief of Takeem and Hulak.

Takeem quickly rubbed his face against Hulak's neck, tightening his arms for one brief moment. He then stood and walked to Samantha.

Sinking to his knees beside her, he pulled her up and into his arms. She curled into his embrace, weeping against his shoulder. He rocked her gently, whispering soft words of comfort. "Sweet Sehmah," he murmured, "why do you mourn so?"

Samantha chuckled. "Do you know, those were the first words your brother spoke to me when we met?"

"And did you weep all over him as well?" Takeem asked, surprised to discover he felt a spurt of jealousy at the thought.

"Of course not," Samantha said. "I didn't even know him, not really. I wasn't sure he was Ari and even if I'd known he was—" She fell silent.

"Even if you'd known, what?"

"I still wouldn't."

Takeem was strangely relieved to hear that answer. "And what did you tell Arioan when he asked you the same question I just did? I only ask because I have yet to receive an answer myself."

"What was the question?"

Takeem snorted in exasperation. "Why do you mourn so?"

"Weren't the stories we witnessed enough to make us all mourn?" she asked. She pulled away from Takeem, scrambled to her feet and crossed to Hulak. She threw her arms around his neck and stood there, leaning against his form.

Takeem frowned. He was so angry at Hulak and so sad for him, all at the same time. Hulak's emotions had been clear in the vision – his sorrow over Forelia's death had filled the entire world, but that sorrow was nothing compared to his feelings over the loss of the nargnets.

Though it wasn't fair, Takeem couldn't hold the confusion inside. "How are you able to forgive him so easily?"

"What do you mean?" Samantha pulled away from Hulak and walked back toward Takeem.

Behind her, Hulak settled onto the ground.

"Thousands of people died because of him. All the nargnets perished, even the fledglings in the nesting grounds. Hulak committed genocide, not just of the nargnets, but of many creatures of Lutia, including the brekzors and the garnonens. How can you forgive that?"

"He'll never forgive himself, Takeem. It doesn't matter if I forgive him or not because he will continue to blame himself."

"He is to blame."

"Perhaps. But I won't judge him because I know what it's like to live with that much hatred."

"Who have you ever hated?"

"The man responsible for the deaths of my parents and…" she stopped, shaking her head. "He was drunk and he crossed the center line. They never had a chance."

"I don't understand."

"Never mind. It doesn't matter. It's just that I understand how Hulak must have felt in that moment, but Takeem, when the anger dies, and it always does, what's left behind is grief. Endless grief. Hulak is all alone, but he loves you so much. He would do anything for you."

"He doesn't love me. He's been in the Royal family for generations. He tolerates me because I'm of Royal blood and he's the Royal Nargnet, pledged to protect our lives. He was my uncle's companion, but hasn't bonded with anyone since his death. My mother claims she's bonded with Hulak, but I know the truth. They don't act bonded. They never have. Besides, if they were, he would be with her now."

"Instead he's here with us."

"Exactly."

"Here with you."

"What? No."

"Yes, Takeem. He's here with you. Maybe he's planning to bond with you."

Takeem shook his head. "That's ridiculous. Hulak and my mother bonded before I was born."

"You just said you think that's a lie."

"I–"

"You said that Hulak would stay with the person he's bonded with. He's not with Alatore, Takeem. He's with you."

He hadn't really thought about that. Why *was* Hulak with them? Takeem had simply commanded Hulak to leave Royal territory, and the nargnet had done so, without even hesitating. Takeem should not have been able to commandeer him like that and Hulak should not have obeyed.

Of course, one of the reasons Takeem was certain Hulak hadn't bonded with Alatore was because he never showed any preference for her. Instead, he had always split his time at the palace between Arioan and Takeem. Still, for Hulak to carry them away from the palace grounds against the command of the queen –

Takeem turned and stared at Hulak, who was still lying on the ground, his wings folded at his side, head resting upon his giant paws, eyes focused upon the two of them, never wavering in his melancholy staring. Without looking away from Hulak, Takeem asked, "How old are you, Samantha?"

"I just turned eighteen. Why? How old are you?"

Takeem felt his heart clench in terror. "Nineteen," he murmured distractedly in answer to her question, staring at Hulak in horror. Dear Vanadevi, was it Samantha? Hulak *had* protected her from the moment she arrived in Lutia. And if it was her, how was he to protect her from Alatore, from the Tekhlan? They would never allow Samantha to claim the throne. Alatore was appalled at the idea of Takeem and he had Royal blood and was her son. Samantha, with her pale skin and red hair would never be Royal enough. Alatore would kill them both first.

Takeem approached Hulak, sinking to his knees before him. Reaching out with shaking hands, he lifted Hulak's head from where it rested upon his paws, drawing him forward, so that Takeem could stare into his eyes.

"Why did you come here, Hulak?" he murmured. "Why did you leave Alatore behind? Are you here as companion to Samantha?" And staring into Hulak's amazingly dark eyes, he saw Forelia fly across them, then Hulak blinked and she was gone, replaced by the image of two thrones of Lutia. In a thousand years of recorded history, there had only ever been one throne. One throne for one king or one queen. Even when the king or queen had a mate, that mate had never been given his or her own throne, but had rather stood at the Royal's side. The mates were never chosen to lead. And yet, here they were, the twin thrones, staring out at him, from Hulak's eyes.

The thrones were seated back to back, so that when viewed from the front of either throne, it might appear as if there was only one, but as Takeem was given a side view, he could clearly see there were two, and that they shared one solid stone back. A young man ascended the stairs to the left of the thrones while a young woman ascended from the right. They approached the thrones and settled upon them, so that their backs were to each other and they faced outward. The image moved, showing first the young woman, then the young man. He was not surprised to discover Samantha seated upon the throne, but was stunned and amazed to see his own image seated at her back.

How was this possible? He was spinner-born.

"You cannot possibly believe this, Hulak," he snapped. "It will never happen. You should go back to Queen Alatore before you end up paying for this with your life."

"What are you talking about?" Samantha asked.

"Nothing important. It's time we go." He stalked away.

"Wait. We can't just leave. We have to figure out our next step. And... and I have to ask the Book another question. Two questions. I have to ask it two questions."

Takeem stopped. "What do you mean? What kind of questions do you need to ask now? The last time you asked something, we saw Hulak burn the world. I would think that would be enough answers for one day. We need to—" he hesitated.

"To what? What are we going to do, Takeem? The Tekhlan and your mother still want me dead. And the book has given us no answers."

"No answers? Hulak committed genocide."

"And how does that help solve our problem? How does that

help us escape the Tekhlan?"

Takeem's shoulders slumped. "How should I know? You were the one who touched the Book of Ages. What question did you ask anyway?"

"I – I really don't know. I was thinking about something I saw on the Trail of Truth."

"What?"

"I saw Hulak and Forelia. Together. They were both on fire. I couldn't stop thinking about it, wondering why."

"Well, now we know, though I wish we had been spared that truth."

"We also know about the magicks and the spell Torel spun to purge them," Samantha reminded him. "I didn't ask about that though. I don't know why we were given that vision."

"It might have been me. I was thinking about my mother and why she sent the Tekhlan after us though I'm not certain how understanding why the magicks were purged helps to answer that question. Besides, it's not like we can repair that situation."

"Why not?"

"It happened one hundred and thirty years ago, Samantha. There's no way to change that."

"But – don't you think we should try?"

"What? Are you insane?"

"It's the perfect solution. We break the spell, the spinners get their magicks back, which means you get your magicks back, and then you can use your magicks to protect us from the Tekhlan."

"That's a terrible solution. If we break the spell, the spinners will fall upon us like the avenging sword of Vanadevi. They'll use their magicks to break us in half."

"So… because you're afraid of the spinners, you're not willing to do what's right?"

"No." Takeem jerked in protest. "Well, yes. I mean, I don't know, Samantha."

"Torel destroyed your people, Takeem. *Your* people. Living in Blue territory doesn't make you any less a spinner than those people exiled beyond the walls of Lutia. You are the Royal-spinner, Takeem, and your ancestor, Torel, stole the spinners' way of life forever. He stole the magicks from your people and he bound them out of hatred, using the lifeblood of seven spinners to do it. How can you not want to reverse that?"

"It's not that I don't want to reverse it. It's that there are consequences to ending such a powerful spell."

"Like what?"

"The Tekhlan are already after us. If we release the magicks, they won't hesitate to execute us."

"I doubt they'll hesitate whether we release them or not, Takeem. Besides, are we truly going to allow fear to stop us from doing what's right?"

Takeem stared at Samantha. He finally understood. This. Right here. Dear Vanadevi, this was why the Tekhlan were after them.

"What?" Samantha asked.

Takeem couldn't reply. It was too horrible. Too much.

"What is it, Takeem?"

"I just realized the vision of the purge did answer my question."

"What do you mean?"

"I finally understand why the Tekhlan are after you, and why Alatore wants you dead."

"You do? Why?"

"Because they knew this would happen. They knew you would want to release the magicks." Everything made sense now. The list his mother had given him so many years before. Samantha's unexpected arrival. The Tekhlan. Had his mother known all those years ago how this would progress?

"It's because you're the End Song," he said.

"The what?"

"The End Song. It's been sung for a hundred years in the villages of the Skies. The End Song will bring about the fall of the Royal Line, in waves of red and blue. The Skies believe the red stands for blood. Now I know different." Takeem swung around to stare at Samantha. "It stands for you."

"I'm not the End Song. That doesn't even make sense. I think we should ask the Book a few more questions and somehow release the magicks."

Takeem stood for a moment, thinking. "You said something about using the blood of the ones who defiled these lands to undo the spell."

"I did?"

"Yes, something about mixing the blood with that of the sacrificed."

"When did I say that?" she asked.

"When you first came out of your trance, when the tree released you from the memories."

"I don't remember."

"I think maybe the tree or even Vanadevi was speaking through you, telling us how to end the spell."

"I doubt the blood of the sacrifices is still here. I mean surely it's soaked into the ground by now."

"Maybe it's not a literal mixing," Takeem mused. "I suppose the blood could be poured around the tree, like Torel and his advisors poured the blood of their sacrifices. Theoretically, that would work, blood cast in contrition poured on top of blood spilled for personal gain." Takeem stared at the tree, pondering. "The thing is," he said, "Torel and all of his advisors have long since turned to dust. They died, I don't know, a good hundred years ago."

"What about the blood of their descendants?" Samantha asked.

"That might work, but it would take forever to track them all down. I'm not even sure all of them *have* descendants. Even if we find one or two, maybe we can use their blood to release at least some of the magicks." He paced as he thought out loud. "Of course, my blood would serve for Torel."

"Yes, but he's the last one to pour the blood and I don't think he actually sacrificed anyone. Did he?"

"Probably not," Takeem spoke bitterly. "Nothing like making your advisors commit murder for you. If we want to track down the descendants, we'll need help. One of the names on my mother's list is Nonomay, the keeper of the ancestral trees of Lutia. She's the official Secret-Keeper and knows more about the history of this world than anyone else alive and should be able to help us track the advisors' lines."

"I'm still worried about using Alatore's list," Samantha said. "I know we didn't have a lot of choice when we first left the palace, but your mom wants me dead and she knows the names on that list."

Samantha was right. He didn't know why he was clinging to his mother's list as if it were somehow proof that she cared. "I know I shouldn't trust her," he said, "but I believe she was telling me the truth when she gave me the list, when she said the people on it would protect me from the Tekhlan. More than that, I trust Devix."

"All right." Samantha nodded. "It's just one more name, right?"

"Yes. Nonomay. Though she could refuse to help us." Given the reactions of the others on his mother's list, it was highly probable.

"Maybe she'll surprise us."

"Yeah. Maybe. I guess we'll find out tomorrow."

"Tomorrow? We're not leaving now?"

"It's too dangerous to travel through the mountains of Lixor at night." Takeem hesitated and glanced at the Shrouded one. "Perhaps we should camp up top."

"What? Why?"

"This is a holy site, not for sleeping."

"But I want to stay with the Shrouded One, Takeem. Besides, I don't think there's room up top for another tree to grow."

Takeem scowled, remembering the tight space at the top of the stairs. "Good point." Should they risk trying to hike off the mountain in the dark?

"Besides, you've slept beneath the Shrouded Ones before."

"But not this one." Why didn't she understand this was different? "Besides, they grew while we were sleeping. I didn't know they were there."

Samantha giggled. "Well, they wouldn't have grown in the first place if they didn't like us."

She really didn't understand.

"We'll be fine, Takeem. I promise."

Takeem sighed and began to set up camp, rolling out their bedrolls along the wall at the base of the stairs, as far from the Shrouded One as he could get them.

*

Night fell as they ate and prepared for bed. The inside of the mountain was now bathed in shadows. Moonlight shone through the opening at the top and what looked to be a thousand stars lit the night sky.

"It's beautiful," Samantha said.

"The stars of Nōn are always amazing."

Samantha did not answer. Instead, she stared up at the sky, wondering if these were the same stars she used to gaze at from her backyard in Harrisonville. They seemed so much brighter here, so much closer. Staring at the stars, she could almost imagine Jonathan was moving them into a pattern, a pattern with a message just for her.

She imagined that Jonathan and her mother and father and Aunt Jenny all gazed upon these same stars at this same moment. She imagined they were all connected by this, the simplest of acts.

PATTERNS

JENNIFER HAD SPENT the entire afternoon resting upon the remains of Samantha and Jonathan's willow tree, reading story after story. She'd only left when the sun began to set. The young couple who lived there would not be happy to discover she still lingered in their backyard when they returned home from work.

With nowhere else to go, Jennifer checked into a cheap motel room, but the room was entirely too small, too constricting for all the feelings she had boiling inside. She traveled down to the outside pool, which was empty of water, the gate around it padlocked. She slid the twins' boxes carefully beneath the gate, then climbed the fence, and with boxes in hand, carefully clambered down into the empty depths of the pool.

She stretched out and stared up at the stars, which were exceptionally bright tonight, the stars she was rarely able to see in the city, the stars that called her this night.

She tried to see a pattern within their midst. It seemed they were moving of their own accord, slowly arranging themselves into an image only she could see.

She imagined her brother was up there among the stars somewhere, that Adam and Kate and Jonathan were moving among them, perhaps arranging them into a perfect message, one that was meant to be shared by her and by Samantha. She imagined that Samantha was gazing upon these same stars, that the five of them were connected as if by an invisible string, one that stretched from the stars to each of their souls and back again.

As her eyelids became heavy and drifted shut, Jennifer imagined she saw the stars painted above her, dancing in the darkness. Even as she succumbed to exhaustion, she recognized their patterns as that of a tiger lunging across the sky and a willow tree beckoning from the stars.

COMFORT

SAMANTHA'S HEAD WAS pillowed upon Hulak's back, his soft and even breathing a gentle lullaby that had coaxed her to sleep the night before. She sat up and glanced around. Takeem lay stretched out upon the ground at the base of the stairs, as far from the Shrouded One, and from Hulak, as he could get. She had missed his arms around her in the night, had missed the comfort of his embrace, but could not bear to leave Hulak by himself, not now that she knew how truly alone in the world he was.

Reaching beneath her shirt, she was relieved to discover her mother's locket still hung around her neck. After carefully extracting it, she gently popped it open. Ashes sprinkled down, landing in her lap. Turning the locket back and forth, she was dismayed to see there were no baby pictures inside.

Blinking back tears, she unhooked the chain from around her neck and carefully tried to scrape as many of the ashes back into the locket as she could. Mostly though, the ashes clung to her jeans in blackened streaks. A single tear slid down her cheek and fell onto her jeans, to mix with the ashes of the past. She gently closed the locket and hooked the chain around her neck once more.

Heart aching, eyes burning with unshed tears, Samantha looked up and caught sight of the Shrouded One. It stood at the center of the chamber, its solemn beauty beckoning her. She stood and walked toward the tree. The vines parted as she approached, forming a gateway. She walked beneath their branches, headed for the trunk she loved.

There was no sign of the pedestal with its Book of Ages this morning, but that was fine. Samantha had another reason for approaching today. She needed the comfort of an old friend.

Sinking to her knees before the tree, Samantha leaned into its embrace. Resting her right cheek against its trunk, she raised her left hand and settled it palm-forward against the rough bark. Listening with all her heart, she whispered as quietly as she could, "Hwanon," and imagined she heard the world whispering back, "Sehmah."

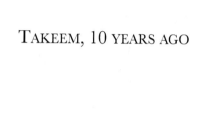

TAKEEM, 10 YEARS AGO

THE MARK OF THE THRONE

THE ROYAL-BLUE Palace, Year 120 AP

Takeem came awake with a cry. He flung himself from the bed, landing on the floor with a thud. "Mama!"

The blankets were tangled around him, holding him down. He writhed beneath them, whimpering and fighting against the sheets and the pain.

His back was on fire!

He reached back, trying to pat out the flames, but there was nothing there, just pain that went on forever.

He gasped for breath, clutching at the floor and crying out for his mother again. Where was she?

He tried to crawl to the door, but his arms weren't working. Nothing was working. He lay there in the dark, crying and wishing for his mom, for Arioan, for Hulak, for Devix. Where were they?

Finally the pain eased, leaving a deep throb in its place.

Takeem struggled for the energy to move, to climb back into his bed, but instead fell asleep, exhausted from the ordeal.

Into his dreams came a boy and a girl, twins with red hair that burned like the sun. They were nothing of Lutia, neither sky nor royal, but a strange other shade – pink yet not.

The three of them rode Hulak into war, fighting long into the night against the spinners and dark beings of magick.

"Sehmah," Takeem whispered in his sleep as he wielded his father's sword. "Hwanon."

*

"Takeem? Takeem?"

Takeem opened his eyes.

His mother was leaning over him, her soft royal hair brushing against his cheek.

He sat up and launched himself into her arms. "Mama," he whimpered, a couple tears escaping.

"What is it, baby? What are you doing on the floor?" Alatore hugged him close.

Takeem cried out and pulled away.

"What's wrong?"

"My back hurts."

Alatore turned him and lifted his nightshirt. She gasped.

Takeem looked back. "What is it?"

"The mark of the throne."

"I got the mark?" He jumped up, pulled off his shirt and went to check in the mirror. He stared over his shoulder at his back.

The mark belonged to the throne. Only those who were true heirs, who might one day inherit it, received the mark. Even though his mother had told him he was an heir and even though Hulak had shown him sitting on the throne, Takeem understood enough to know it wasn't possible. No spinner would ever inherit.

Yet the mark lay upon his back, the biggest mark he'd ever seen. The thick trunk of the Shrouded One marched up his spine and its vines covered every inch of his shoulders, arms and back. The roots of the Shrouded One wrapped around his hips and disappeared beneath his pants. Takeem peeked and was horrified to realize the roots continued across his bottom.

"The mark's wrong, Mama."

"What do you mean, Takeem?"

"It's too big. And it's the wrong color."

Alatore turned Takeem so to face the mirror.

He looked down so he wouldn't have to see his eyes. His scary, beastly eyes.

Alatore wrapped her arms around him and rested her chin on his head. "No color is ever wrong, Takeem. You should know that. The Skies are as much a part of this world as the Royals and the spinners. You're a beautiful blend of all of us."

"What do you mean?"

"Your skin may be Royal, but your eyes are what I love the most about you for they are a blend of both Royal and Sky. Do you think I like your sky stripes less than your royal ones? I do not, my son. I love them equally." She stroked a finger along one of his sky stripes at the edge of his right eye. "And now you have a Sky-Blue mark of the throne. You truly are the best of all of us."

Takeem stared into the mirror. His mother was wrong. His eyes weren't beautiful. None of the Royals liked him and now that he had a sky-blue Shrouded One on his back – "Will Kirosko hate me more now?"

"What do you mean? Kirosko doesn't hate you, sweetheart."

"Yes, he does. And Stilel calls me 'bomination. They won't like it that I received the mark, will they?"

"No, they won't. So we're not going to tell them, do you understand?"

"Not at all?"

"If they ask, you must tell them the truth, Takeem. Never lie to the Council. But if they do not ask, we will not say a word. Understood?"

Takeem nodded. "Yes, Mama."

PRESENT DAY

The Thrones of Lutia

Takeem woke with a jerk.

Hulak was pacing in a circle around the Shrouded One.

"Where's Samantha?" Takeem demanded, leaping to his feet.

Hulak nodded his head toward the tree and continued to pace.

"Again? We don't have time for this. We should have already left." He glared at the tree.

The vines were completely closed, trapping him outside and Samantha within, keeping him from seeing whatever visions the tree chose to share with her.

He wanted to try to force his way beneath the tree, but remembering the horrendous headache he'd achieved the last time he tried that, he decided to focus on packing up the camp and preparing their breakfast instead.

He had just finished eating when the branches of the Shrouded One lifted and parted, revealing Samantha as she approached the outer world.

"Finally." Takeem jumped to his feet. "What were you doing in there again? Did the Book of Ages tell you anything more?"

"The Book wasn't around when I entered," Samantha said.

"Well, then, what was the point?"

"I like the tree, that's all. We should go, right?"

"Yes, but first you need to eat." He thrust a plate at Samantha. "Here. Eat while I finish packing."

"Where does the Secret-Keeper live?"

"Nonomay? She lives in the village of Soryn, between the third and fourth rings of Lutia," Takeem said. "She's closer to the fourth than the third, so it will take us a little while to get there."

"We're between the second and third rings, right?"

"Actually, we're between the first and second, closer to the second."

"So we have to make it across two rings before we reach Nonomay's home."

"Yes. We're deep in the War Zone now, and even worse, we're in Mozkola territory. I never should have allowed us to linger yesterday, and we definitely should not have stayed the night. It was reckless. I should have kept a closer eye on the waning sun." He sighed. "Of course, we were probably safer here than the night before when we camped on the battlegrounds themselves."

"Have you been getting any sleep at all?" Samantha asked.

"A little."

"You should have asked, I could have taken a shift to keep watch."

Takeem grabbed the bundle he had just finished packing. "It was no big deal," he snapped, wishing with all his might that he didn't know what he now knew, that he didn't see Hulak differently now. He felt so much anger and sorrow, all mixed up inside, so deep and desperate, that he wanted to avoid even looking at him. Gritting his teeth, he forced his feet to carry him forward, toward the Royal Nargnet.

Hulak quickly transformed as he approached.

Takeem avoided looking at Hulak's face as he strapped the pack to his back. As soon as the pack was secure, Takeem grabbed Samantha's hand and pulled her toward him. Grasping her around the waist, he flung her up onto Hulak's back, then without giving himself a chance to think, he vaulted up after her.

Wrapping an arm around Samantha's waist, Takeem leaned forward and commanded, "Let's go, Hulak. To Soryn."

*

Samantha held her breath as Hulak lunged forward, racing

across the root-laden interior, headed straight for the far wall. The wind whistled past and Samantha flung herself forward, squeezing her arms around Hulak's neck, a scream bubbling in her throat. The wall approached closer and closer.

"Hold on," Takeem roared, leaning forward and sheltering her body with his own as he latched onto Hulak's neck with a fierce grip.

Suddenly Hulak launched his body into the air and just when they would have smacked straight into the mountain face, he turned his body so that he now raced straight up the side of the mountain, hurtling toward the sky. Samantha thought they would tumble off his back as they took a gravity-defying lunge straight upward, but somehow Takeem maintained his seat, holding them both tight to Hulak's back. Just when Samantha was certain Takeem would not be able to hold on any longer, they exploded from the interior of the mountain, racing toward the sun, then suddenly leveling out before plummeting back toward the land.

Samantha gasped for breath, her entire body aching from the tension of this ride, so grateful for the feel of Takeem pressed against her back, his arms wrapped protectively around her as he grasped Hulak's fur. Certain Hulak was doing this on purpose, she opened her mouth, intending to shout at him to stop showing off, but she couldn't find the breath to do so. Just when they would have plunged straight into the lake at the bottom of the mountain, Hulak leveled out again so that they hurtled across the surface of the water.

Takeem sat up and reaching down, gently unclenched Samantha's hands from Hulak's neck. He then pulled her to an upright position and settled her back against his chest, his arms around her waist. Samantha couldn't stop trembling. She wanted to kick Hulak for his insane flying, but was afraid she might dislodge herself in the process.

Takeem rubbed his chin across the top of Samantha's head. When she glanced up at him, she saw that he had a huge grin on his face. It seemed the death-defying antics of Hulak had mellowed him out and much improved his mood. "Wasn't that amazing?" he exclaimed.

"Amazing? Not what I would call it *at all*," she muttered, watching as the scenery quickly flashed by.

"What did the Shrouded One tell you today?" Takeem asked.

"What makes you think it told me anything at all?" She didn't want to tell him what she'd seen. She felt as if she'd invaded his privacy, observing things from his childhood he hadn't chosen to share.

Takeem leaned down and murmured into her ear, "Because you are its companion, its soul-keeper. Of course, it shared more truths with you."

Samantha shivered as his breath streamed across her neck and ear. She wanted to turn completely around so they were facing each other, so she could see his eyes when they talked, but she was afraid. What if she fell off the nargnet? Even worse, she would not be able to see where they were headed, to anticipate Hulak's movements.

"Are you sure you want to know?" she asked, pulling forward tentatively and looking over her shoulder, trying to see his face. She wasn't certain what to reveal.

"Of course I do."

"I asked it a question."

"What did you ask?" Takeem tightened his arms around her waist and pulled her toward him, nudging her head around to face forward again, settling his chin back on top of her head.

"I asked whether you were meant to be king."

Takeem didn't speak for a moment.

The silence was terrible. She didn't know what to say.

"What did it show you?" His voice was quiet, a murmur she almost didn't hear.

Did he really want to know?

"Samantha, tell me please."

"It showed me your mark of the throne."

"You mean—"

"Your mother was right, Takeem. You are the best of them all and that is why you will make a wondrous king."

Takeem was silent for several moments.

She hated that he knew she'd seen that moment between him

and his mother, that she'd spied on his fear and his feelings about his status as a spinner.

"That was a long time ago, Samantha. And almost immediately after telling me I was the best of all of them, she had me removed from the family quarters. I'm pretty sure she was lying."

"Oh, Takeem." Samantha tried to pull away to look up at him, but he tightened his arms around her, holding her still.

"It was my mother's way of announcing I wasn't good enough for the throne."

"Takeem, no. You're her son. I saw how she felt about you."

"You saw an illusion, Samantha. One she got tired of when I turned ten. Once the other Royals saw how she treated me, they made my life miserable."

"Don't you think -"

"No, Samantha. I am not destined to be king. Even if Hulak were to choose me as his companion, my mother and the Royals would ensure it never came to pass."

"I'm sorry, Takeem," Samantha whispered. "I didn't mean to bring up bad memories."

"Don't worry about it. Just do me the favor of not pretending that the impossible is possible."

"All right."

Though Takeem sounded angry and bitter, he did not loosen his hold of Samantha. Instead, he held her close the entire way to Nonomay's village.

The End Song

IT WAS LATE afternoon by the time Hulak's flying brought them to the outskirts of a small farming community. They flew over fields of crops, toward several buildings that stood in the distance. People working in the fields glanced up, shouted and pointed, then ran in their wake.

"They're following us," she reported to Takeem. "Why do they always do that?"

"Hulak is the last remaining nargnet and they know he bears the Royal line. They will be curious and anxious to meet us."

They now raced across the land, paws pounding the terrain, until Hulak slowed, then with a thudding jolt, came to a halt right outside a small cabin.

Takeem immediately leapt off the nargnet. He caught Samantha about the waist as she slid to the ground. Samantha stumbled forward a little when he let her go, her legs almost refusing to hold her after so many hours seated upon the nargnet. Takeem gently steadied her, then with his arm still around her waist, faced the many people who had gathered.

"Good afternoon," Takeem greeted them.

No one in the crowds answered him.

Samantha shifted uneasily at Takeem's side. As in the previous villages they had visited, the skin of everyone there were the lightest of blues and their sky-blue eyes were full of suspicion.

Finally, a voice broke the silence. "Well, let me through then!"

As soon as the words were spoken, the crowds in front of Takeem and Samantha parted, making a path for the tiny, elderly woman who approached. Her hair was snow white and piled atop her head. What made Samantha's eyes widen, though, were her eyes. Though the elderly woman's wrinkled skin was the lightest of sky-blue, her eyes were deeply, darkly royal.

Coming to a stop a few feet in front of them, she announced, "So. Takeem, the Royal-spinner heir. You finally deign to visit the lands of the Skies."

Pulling his arm from Samantha's waist, Takeem stepped forward and bowed his head to the woman. "Hello," he murmured, "I apologize for not visiting sooner. I was uncertain of my welcome."

"The heirs to the throne are always welcome in my home. I am Nonomay and you are Alatore's youngest child."

"I am." He held out his arm to Samantha. "Nonomay, this is Samantha."

"Welcome, Samantha. Welcome to you both. We were about to sit down to our mid-day meal. You will join us, of course."

"Thank you."

"Yes, ma'am, thank you for the invitation," Samantha whispered.

"Now, none of that. You will both call me Nonomay. Yes?"

Samantha smiled. "Yes, ma'am – Nonomay."

Nonomay led them through the crowds toward one of the buildings.

A Sky-Blue man stood waiting on the porch. Quickly stepping forward, he helped Nonomay up the two stairs leading to the front door.

"Thank you, Marconen," Nonomay said.

As Marconen led Nonomay into the cabin, he threw a suspicious glance over his shoulder at Takeem and Samantha. His glare clearly promised retribution should they upset the elderly woman in his care.

Samantha offered him a smile, hoping to reassure him, but his eyes simply narrowed in response.

Hulak shrank to his smaller form and followed Samantha and

Takeem into the cabin.

Nonomay led them through a small front room to a larger room at the back. A huge, scarred wooden table took up much of the floor space. She made her way to the wooden chair at the head of this table. As soon as she was seated, she began giving orders.

People of all ages appeared from nowhere, jumping to meet her demands. While the Skies bustled about, bringing trays of food and drinks to the table, Nonomay waved Takeem and Samantha to the chairs on either side of her.

"Come," she commanded. "You will sit by my side and we will talk."

Takeem led Samantha to the table, gently squeezing her hand in reassurance as they went.

"So how are your mother and brother?" Nonomay asked. "Are they doing well?"

"Better than us, I'm sure," Takeem muttered.

"So it's still that way, is it? I'm afraid Alatore has never made the best of decisions, when it comes to the ones she loves."

"She has a funny way of showing her love," Samantha burst out. "moving Takeem from the family quarters, convincing him he's not worthy of the throne."

Silence fell throughout the room in response to Samantha's words.

"Perhaps," Nonomay agreed. "However, it is easy to judge, young Samantha, when we do not see."

Samantha swallowed and looked down at her plate. Was Nonomay right? Was she judging Alatore too harshly? After all, the woman she'd seen in her vision that morning had seemed to love Takeem very much.

"We've consulted with the Book of Ages, Nonomay," Takeem announced from across the way. "It has brought us here, to you."

"The Book of Ages," Nonomay said. "It answered your questions?"

"It answered Samantha's," Takeem replied.

"This is an unexpected and wonderful surprise. I have long felt the winds of change approaching. And now, finally, it appears the time has come." Smiling in anticipation, Nonomay decreed, "But first, we must eat!" Glancing around, seeing the rest of the young people in the room standing still, listening to their conversation, she snapped, "Well, sit down then!"

The frozen paralysis that had gripped the room since Samantha's outburst was finally broken and all the young people who had set the table and served the food quickly approached and found their places.

Soon the room was filled with happy chatter and laughing voices.

There was a time when Samantha's family had filled their house with joy and laughter like this one. Closing her eyes, she could almost imagine Jonathan was at the table with her, along with her parents and her Aunt Jenny, all of them sitting at this table and sharing one last meal together.

"Samantha."

Blinking her eyes to push back the tears that had gathered there, Samantha glanced at Takeem. "What is it?"

"Nonomay was asking you a question."

"I'm sorry. I was—"

"Lost in your memories," Nonomay said.

Samantha caught her breath. "Yes. Yes, I was."

"I have oft had that same look upon my face, I've been told. That same look that remembers the ones we've lost and can never find again. Why do you mourn so, child? Whom have you lost?"

Samantha answered quietly, "My parents."

"And another," Nonomay said.

"No, I will find him. I have not lost him, not like the others."

Nonomay watched her with sad eyes. "I hope you are right, child. I will pray for you and for him."

"So, you're the End Song." Marconen interrupted, glaring across the table at Samantha. "You do know the Song, don't you? The one they say you began on the battlefields of Shorel a few days back?"

Samantha glanced at Takeem. "Um, not really," she admitted. "I mean, Takeem mentioned it, but I don't really understand.

How can a person be a song? That doesn't even make sense."

"It does make sense," Nonomay said, "if you're the person who can bring the melody, chords and lyrics together, if you are the Song the peoples of Lutia have been failing to sing for thousands of years."

"I'm not the End Song," Samantha said.

"Not alone, you're not," Nonomay agreed. "But you are the piece that brings the whole together. The piece they call Sehmah."

Samantha inhaled sharply, to hear that name spoken again, the name that was Jonathan and Samantha and their Willow Tree World.

"Sehmah?" Marconen spoke sharply. "I've not heard that name before."

"It is an ancient name, one that has not been given in millennia. It is a name unspoken until the End Song is upon us, gifted to the one who needs it the most. It is the half of the whole that is our creator; it is the sorrow of love."

A tapestry hanging on the wall behind Takeem caught Samantha's attention. The willow tree as its center beckoned and she imagined she saw Jonathan's brilliant blue eyes winking through the leaves at its top.

"The sorrow of love," she whispered.

"Very well, then, if you're the End Song, tell us how you intend to fulfill your prophecy," Marconen demanded. "Tell us how you plan to repair this broken world?"

Fix their world? She was still trying to understand it. "Why don't you tell me what you need? Then I'll tell you if I can get it for you."

Nonomay chuckled. "A good answer, my dear, a good answer. Well, Marconen? What is it you think we need to solve our many problems?"

"We need a leader who understands a person's value is not determined by the color of their skin. We need someone who will give our people a voice, who won't incite the spinners but won't condemn them either, who will seek peace instead of war and will strive to bring the peoples of Lutia back together again!"

Samantha couldn't believe what she was hearing. "Back together? You want to bring the spinners out of exile?"

"Of course."

"But – the Blues are at war with the spinners!"

"Not all Blues. The *Royals* are at war with the spinners and as usual, the Skies are caught in the middle, suffering the most."

"But I thought the Skies were on the frontlines, constantly under attack from the spinners, fighting to keep them back."

Marconen smiled. It wasn't a nice smile. "That was certainly true twenty years ago. Then the walls fell and thousands on both sides burned on the fields of Shorel. The spinners and Skies who were not there that day met in the War Zone and we negotiated our own peace, without the Royals." He glanced toward Takeem. "You're far from the palace now, boy. The rules are different out here close to the War Zone, far different from when your father walked these lands and your uncle brought them to ruin with his wars."

"So, the Skies and spinners aren't at war?" Takeem asked.

"We are not."

"But we hear of Blues dying all the time, killed in sneak attacks by the spinners."

"Because those are the stories we cycle – that Skies and Royals are dying at the warfront, but really, how many Royals do they send to fight anymore?" Without pausing, Marconen answered his own question. "Very few, that's how many. Since Sorelion and Vukel died, Alatore shows no interest in the war. She's backed away, stopped sending Royals to defend Sky territories. Once or twice a year, she sends out the Tekhlan to check on the status at the warfront. We receive word from the Sky villages that the Tekhlan are on the move and we station our men where the walls once stood to convince her we still engage the enemy. When the Tekhlan arrive, we pare them down a bit, then send the survivors back with stories of the spinners attacking in the dead of night and our men falling to protect Blue territories. We even show them the House of the Dead, where the names of those fallen in the war are engraved. We point to a few names and share some sad stories and they are appeased. They return to Royal territory, content to let the Skies continue dying for their freedom."

"I saw the men along the walls," Samantha said. "Several days ago, when Arioan and Hulak found me and we were flying to the palace."

"King Arioan flies to the War Zone several times every week," Marconen said, "to mourn those we have lost. He keeps our secrets well."

Takeem stiffened. "King?" he asked.

Marconen sniffed. "Alatore will never be Queen in the eyes of the Skies. We do not recognize the Mendacious One. Arioan is our true King."

"But I thought–" Samantha glanced at Takeem, then back at Marconen. "Hulak hasn't chosen Arioan."

"Why should that matter? The Royal Nargnet was companion to King Torel and is now companion to the Mendacious Queen. Perhaps he is no longer worthy of choosing our next ruler."

"But he's not Alatore's companion," Samantha protested. "He's Takeem's."

Gasps resounded around the room.

"Takeem's?" Marconen exclaimed. "Are you insane? Even if the Royal Nargnet did choose a spinner for the throne, the people would never stand for it."

"He's the son of Royals," Samantha said, "descended from a long line of kings and queens, dating all the way back to Torel."

"He's still spinner-born. No Royal will look past that. Truthfully, the Skies will also object. They won't like a spinner obtaining the throne before a Sky-Blue does."

"Why not?" Samantha asked. "You said you wanted a leader who doesn't judge others by the color of their skin. What other leader will understand what Takeem does? What other king will know what it is like to be an outcast? Takeem will stand for all the peoples of Lutia."

"Samantha." Takeem spoke quietly. "Enough."

"But, Takeem–"

"He's right, Samantha. We've already discussed this. Besides, we have more important things to worry about."

"The magicks," she whispered.

"What about the magicks?" Marconen asked sharply.

Takeem ignored his question. "Nonomay, we came because we were hoping you would be able to help us identify the descendants of King Torel's advisors."

Nonomay pushed herself to her feet. "Come," she spoke. "I will share with you the genealogical records of our people." Glancing toward those still seated at the table, she said, "The rest of you may return to your duties. What happens next does not concern you."

There came a general shuffling as most of those seated at the table rose and exited the cabin. Finally, only Marconen was left behind. "Nonomay," he spoke.

"No, Marconen. You will trust me to know what I am doing. We will speak later. Now go."

Marconen obediently climbed to his feet. Before exiting, he cast one last suspicious look upon Takeem and Samantha, then warned in a grim voice, "Do not hurt her or I will break you." He stalked from the room.

"I apologize for my grandson. He is often angry and finds it difficult to trust anyone. The majority of his family died in battle before he was born and he has grown up an orphan, belonging to everyone, yet no one. Now come. Let us see what the trees of Lutia have to tell."

THE DEEP END

JENNIFER WOKE, SHAKING from the cold that had seeped into her very bones. With a loud groan, she pushed to her feet, dismayed to discover herself standing in the deep end of an empty swimming pool.

What had she been thinking? At least she hadn't been drinking. Checking her pockets, she found her cell phone. No missed calls or texts. What was she going to do if she couldn't find her?

Carefully climbing out of the pool using the side stairs, she picked up the boxes, then slid them under the security gate. Climbing the fence this morning after a night sleeping on the hard ground of the pool was more difficult than it had been the night before, but she managed.

Heading back toward the motel room, she wondered whether she'd been wrong about why Samantha had disappeared. What if it wasn't about Samantha's emotional state, but rather about one of the terrible things that could happen to young teenaged women in the city?

Clenching her fists tight, Jennifer vowed she would find Samantha, no matter the cost. She would. She had to, for she could not possibly survive another loss.

THE TREES OF LUTIA

LEADING SAMANTHA AND Takeem through the kitchen to a door
at the back of the house, Nonomay walked outside and strode
across the grass toward a dense collection of trees. The sun had
set while they were eating and it was only by its waning light that
they were able to see anything at all. The trees they approached
were not willow trees, and yet their branches swayed in the
breeze, pulling apart to form a narrow passage, so the three were
able to enter beneath their dense canopy. Takeem entered last,
and the moment he stepped upon the path that had formed for
them, the passage closed behind him.

Following Nonomay, Samantha could not help but nervously
eye the shadowed trees around her. They had formed a narrow
tunnel, forcing the three of them to walk single file. Hardly any
light filtered through, leaving them cocooned in a sphere of
darkness. Samantha could barely make out Nonomay's shape
moving in front of her and she feared the trees could easily
divide the three of them, leaving them each lost forever within
the forest's maze.

Finally, though, the passageway broadened and they arrived in
a small clearing. At the center of this clearing there stood a
ramshackle building covered in vines and foliage. The building
looked as if one stiff wind could knock it over. Samantha
wondered if it could possibly hold and protect the genealogical
records of an entire people.

Nodding to the covered doorway at the front, Nonomay commanded, "Open the door for us, Takeem. It's been quite some time since I have entered here."

And so Takeem, with Samantha's help, quickly pulled down the vines growing across the doorway. Though the door had clearly not been used in quite some time, it opened easily and without any noise, revealing a darkened interior.

"Help me inside," Nonomay said.

Taking her arm, Samantha gently led the woman across the threshold into the dark.

"I don't know about this, Nonomay," Takeem said. "We can't see a thing."

"Hm. That is easily changed, young Takeem." With these cryptic words, Nonomay slammed her cane to the floor, causing it to light up beneath them, sparked to life from the spot her cane first touched. The glowing embers stretched across the space, filling in the image etched there, until finally, the entire floor was ablaze in lights, the trunk of a huge willow tree beginning at their feet and stretching forward. The leaves and vines exploded from the trunk at the center of the room to the walls all around. The entire image was ablaze in golden light.

"That is wondrous, Nonomay," Takeem murmured.

"Amazing," Samantha agreed.

"Come." Nonomay beckoned Samantha and Takeem to follow.

The door swung shut behind them. The walls shimmered and words flared to life, all of them lit in a golden hue.

Samantha approached one particularly bright phrase. It said Queen Sehmah. She reached to touch those glowing words, but they faded from sight.

Turning, she asked Nonomay, "Did you see that?"

"Oh, yes, my dear. That is your own family tree, but you are not meant to see it, not yet. For it has not yet been written, not clearly. It is spinning in place, waiting the events that will allow it to have form."

Samantha glanced back toward the wall where her name had been, then gazed around the room, wondering if somewhere in this vast place of glowing words burned the name Hwanon.

"So," Nonomay spoke, "you wish to know the descendants of Torel's advisors?"

"Yes," Takeem said.

"May I ask why?"

Samantha spoke up. "If we are to release the magicks of Lutia, we must first find the descendants of those who spun the spell that contained them."

"Very well. First though, you need to understand the nature of our family trees." Nonomay addressed the wall opposite the door. "Lord Zarkonen, please, leader of the Tekhlan and chief advisor to the throne of Torel."

The words glowing upon the wall faded away, leaving nothing in their wake. A few moments later, a tree blazed into being. The roots of the tree bore the names Zarconen Ryvar and Soraya Meloren.

"That is so cool," Samantha whispered, stepping forward. She wrinkled her brow in confusion. "I – I don't understand."

The branches of the tree, and there were many, were mostly empty with only the words "records removed" to indicate a name had once resided there.

"What is this?" Takeem said. "What's going on?"

"I'm afraid, Takeem, you will discover this world has been censoring its information for quite some time. The records are, at best, incomplete."

"But, Nonomay, you're the Secret-Keeper. How were the names removed without your consent?"

"We keepers have never had any say in how the records are written, Takeem. We simply serve as witness and that is all."

"But how did this happen?"

"It is the end result of Torel's spell. It took a while for the ramifications to reach the family trees, but eventually they did. Torel's spell divided us in two. We were once all of Lutia, but now many of us are beyond Lutia's walls, and are no longer considered to be a part of the whole. Those living beyond the walls no longer appear on our family trees."

"But those beyond the walls are spinners, right?" Samantha

asked.

"Most of them."

"So all of the descendants of Zarkonen were spinners?"

"Not at all. I'm not a spinner, yet my name is not on that wall."

"Wait. You're a descendent of Zarkonen?" Takeem asked.

"Yes. Zarkonen had one child, a daughter, Xelia. She married a Sky-spinner and they had six children. Their youngest was my grandmother. I'm certain Zarkonen was quite furious she did not marry a Royal like him."

"If she was his only child and she married a spinner, then all of his descendants should be spinners, right?" Samantha asked.

"No, dear. The ability to spin is not an inherited trait. It is a blessing from Vanadevi, a mark of greatness, that a Blue child was chosen to spin the ancestral magicks of Lutia."

"So why isn't your name on the tree?" Takeem asked.

"Because the world was not segregated one hundred and thirty years ago the way it is today. When the world divided, my great-grandparents' names disappeared from the records. Even though my grandmother stayed behind, how could her name remain on the trees, when there were no ancestors to hold her place? She became cut off, adrift, and the trees no longer recognized her, nor her children, nor her children's children.

"The truth is, this happened to almost every family in Lutia. No family was unaffected by the exile. We were too much a blended society by then. Skies and Royals had been mixing and marrying for decades, their children born with royal, spinner and sky traits. The more the races mixed, the more spinners were born.

"My grandmother's baby brother was one. All six of my great-grandparents' children were beautiful. One was Royal-Blue from his hair to the tip of his toes, one was completely Sky and three of them were a beautiful combination of the two." She paused and stared at her empty family tree. "The last, though, the youngest. He was the Royal-spinner-Sky." Her voice was heavy with sorrow.

"So what happened?" Samantha asked.

"It was a dark time. If you truly wish to know the truth, the trees hold the answers."

"You mean the Shrouded Ones?" Takeem asked.

"I mean the trees." Nonomay nodded toward the tree that still glowed upon the wall. "The Trees of Lutia have always held the answers. Though the names of our ancestors may be lost, the truth of their lives is still embedded deep within the roots of our world."

Reaching out a trembling hand, she traced a single branch of the tree upward. "My grandmother Lorena's name should be here. She was their oldest and the only one of the six born purely Royal-Blue. And here," she traced a line outward along the bulk of the tree toward its very edge. "Here should be Morgel's name, the only one of the six marked by Vanadevi with spinner eyes. He was so young, just a babe when everything went wrong." She stopped there, finger gently touching the edge of the tree, lightly tracing a branch that hung there, as if she could bring his name back into the fold of her family's history. "Right here," she whispered. "Right here. Poor Morgel."

Though Samantha felt a strong sense of foreboding and preferred not to know the answers to her questions, she still asked, "What happened to him?"

Nonomay grabbed Samantha's hand and dragged her forward with surprising strength.

"Here, my dear," she spoke softly. "Come and know the truth of our world's history." Keeping a firm grip on Samantha's wrist, she forced her hand to connect with the family tree, with that very spot where Morgel's name should have resided.

The moment her hand touched the wall, Samantha's knees buckled. Nonomay refused to allow Samantha to fall to the floor. Instead, she kept Samantha's hand pinned to the wall with one hand upon her wrist and with the other arm, she tried to brace her form.

*

"Nonomay, what have you done?" Takeem raced forward to pull Samantha away.

"Leave her!"

"But, Nonomay–"

"If you wish to help our world, if you wish to rule it, then there are certain things you absolutely must know."

"Then share them with me! Why does the world show Samantha what it will not show me?" Takeem wrapped his arms around Samantha's waist, holding her tight, supporting her weight.

"Because, Takeem, this is Sehmah's role, to stand between you and our world, to provide you with the distance you need to become an effective ruler."

Samantha cried out in anguish and flung herself away from the wall, breaking his hold on her as she stumbled away.

Takeem lunged forward, but was unable to break her fall.

MORGEL, 130 YEARS AGO

SACRIFICE

Morgel loved to play in the fields of Soryn. These were the ones left to grow wild during the planting season, the lands left to recover, untouched by the community. In these fields, he found hundreds of bugs, wild flowers and strange prickly plants. He loved these fields for there was no place he could not walk, no growing plants he had to watch out for. He could simply run and play and chase the flutterbies and not worry if he happened to stomp on a growing morbu stalk.

Here he was free. He had managed to sneak away from his sister Lorena. She was giggling with her friends over a Royal-spinner who visited the village yesterday and she hadn't noticed when he skipped away. He crouched on the ground, the wild plants around him providing the perfect hiding place. If she looked for him here, all she would see were the swaying stems of thousands of wild flowers. He giggled softly to himself. She would never find him.

Staring at the ground, he saw the tip of a shiny stone or maybe it was a hala gem. Lorena would be so excited if he brought her a hala gem, she might even forget to yell at him for running away again. She would stand with her hands on her hips, a frown on her face, and then she would come to find him. She would call his name and he would hide and giggle so that she would hear him and find him, and then she would hug him and snap at him, then tickle him for making her worry.

Morgel dug in the dirt with his stick, trying to pry loose the stone. He had managed to clear the path around it to reveal the perfect yellow color of a true hala gem when he heard the sound of a brekzor's wings beating the sky. The brekzor approached so swiftly, its whistling sound was a screech that filled the air. Morgel dug his fingers into the dirt, clutched his precious hala gem and jerked with all his might. He toppled over with it clutched in his hand. Scrambling to his feet, he ran through the wildflowers, headed back toward his family's cabin, back toward Lorena.

He could hear the brekzor behind him as it approached closer and closer. Terrified, he flung himself toward the ground, hoping the brekzor would swoop over him, but instead found himself suddenly jerked upward. He cried out as he watched his hala gem, his beautiful shining gem, spin through the air and fall down toward the field of flowers. It disappeared between thousands of blooms.

Slammed face down upon the brekzor, a hand planted firmly upon his back, Morgel gasped for breath. "Lorena," he cried out. "Mama, Papa, Lorena."

"Be silent, you," a harsh voice snarled as a large hand slapped down hard upon his bottom, making him cry out in pain.

"Let me go," he wailed.

Another swat broke him into tears. Sobbing, he looked back toward the farmhouse they flew away from. He stared until it was a tiny pinprick in the distance, until it was no longer there, until he had to close his eyes if he wanted to picture it at all.

At some point, lulled by the movement of the brekzor beneath him and the waning sun at their back, Morgel's sobs fell quiet, his breathing evened out and he fell into an exhausted sleep.

*

Morgel woke to the sound of chanting. He was in a darkened cavern, the walls covered in strange symbols drawn in red, a campfire making these symbols glow and dance upon the walls. The chanting he heard was at his back. Morgel shivered and faced his captor.

His eyes widened when he saw the man who stood at his back.

"Grandfather?" he whispered.

His grandfather ignored him and continued to chant.

Morgel had only met this man three or four times, but he was certain it was his grandfather Zarkonen. Zarkonen, chief advisor to his king, his mother's father, his blood.

"Grandfather Zarkonen," he whispered, "where are we?"

His grandfather ignored him and continued his chanting. Morgel swallowed hard, trembling even more, as the relief he felt at seeing this man he knew drained away. Carefully stepping backward away from this familiar stranger, Morgel turned to flee, only to find the back of his shirt captured again, much the way it had been when he was taken earlier that day.

A strong arm lifted him from the ground. Pinned to the front of his grandfather, staring at the fire, Morgel kicked his feet and cried out in fear.

"Mama," he screamed, certain something bad was about to happen. "Papa!" Squirming and kicking, fighting with all his might, his efforts were for naught.

His grandfather simply grunted, and held him tighter as he continued to chant, the sound of his voice escalating Morgel's terror.

"This blood I spill is mine own, this blood I offer a sacrifice for the safety of all my Royal-Blue kin. May this tainted, spinner blood I spill cleanse our world of its shame."

Not understanding the words so much as their intent, Morgel bellowed out one final scream of rage and innocence, his fear and his life echoing throughout his tomb as he saw in his final moments a flash of silver and then burning red.

PRESENT DAY

THE BLOOD OF TOREL

CROUCHED UPON THE floor, on her hands and knees, Samantha trembled in horror at what she had seen.

Jonathan, Jonathan, Jonathan, her mind was one blank slate, with only one word that trembled in its every corner. *Jonathan,* her mind screamed, *not true, not true, Jonathan!*

"Samantha." Takeem tried to help her up from the floor, but she jerked away from him, crying out in pain at his touch.

Covering her head with her arms, she rocked back and forth, her mind wailing.

Not our world, Jonathan, not our world.

She could hear Takeem's voice, but all she could see was Morgel's body, all she could think was *Not our world.*

Thud! Thud! Thud! Takeem said something and stood. *Jonathan. Crash!*

The door exploded inward and Hulak lunged across the threshold.

Not our world.

Hulak skidded to a stop directly in front of her, nudged her head and captured her eyes with his.

Jonathan.

Forelia.

Jonathan.

Forelia. Forelia. Forelia.

Samantha blinked, slowly registering Hulak's presence. *I am not*

Forelia.

And I am not Jonathan.

Samantha gave a watery chuckle. "Huk," she whispered, "what would we do without you?" Flinging her arms around his neck, she buried her face in his fur and wept.

*

Takeem didn't know what to do. He wanted to comfort Samantha, but clearly Hulak was accomplishing what he could not.

How ridiculous. Jealous of a nargnet.

Wondering how Hulak had managed to get past the forest of trees outside, Takeem simply stroked his hand up and down Samantha's back, hoping this was enough to indicate his concern.

A few moments later, Samantha raised her head and asked, voice choked with tears, "How old was he? When they killed him, I mean."

"Seven," Nonomay said.

"Were there other children sacrificed?"

"There were seven children who went missing that day, though no bodies were ever found. My grandmother told me the truth was easy to deduce. Morgel disappeared, along with six other spinner children, then the magicks disappeared and the Shrouded Ones died. In the aftermath, King Torel announced all spinners were to be exiled.

"My great-great grandparents packed everyone up that very day. They wanted the rest of their children safe. But my grandmother Lorena refused to leave. She could not bear to go without Morgel, without at least knowing he was truly gone."

"So Lorena was the only one of Zarkonen's descendants who stayed in Blue territory?" Takeem helped Samantha stand.

"The only one."

"Does that make you the last of her descendants?" Samantha asked.

If Nonomay was the last, he didn't know what they would do. He couldn't ask this of her.

"There are two others – my grandsons, Marconen, whom you met inside, and young Lourx."

Marconen. Takeem winced. He couldn't imagine the angry Sky would ever agree to help them. Perhaps this Lourx –

"What troubles you now?" Nonomay demanded.

"We were hoping to bring each advisor's descendant to the Holy Shrine of Vanadevi," Takeem said. "We thought to start with Zarkonen's descendants, but I'm not certain Marconen will agree. How old is this Lourx?"

"Too young for whatever you're thinking," she admonished them. "Do you truly need a descendant of Zarkonen?"

"Well, the exact words were the blood of those who cast the spell," Samantha said. "We interpreted that to mean a descendant."

"While I would be happy to serve as the blood needed–"

"No, we couldn't," Samantha said.

Nonomay smiled. "I do not think that will be necessary." She faced the wall one final time and stated, "One more tree, if you will. King Malcor's, in its entirety."

Zarkonen's tree disappeared and was replaced with one that filled the entire wall, easily three times the size of Zarkonen's. Packed with names and the words "records removed", this tree was overwhelming in the sheer depth of the information it provided.

"Look, Takeem. Your name and Arioan's are at the top of the tree." Samantha pointed toward where Takeem and Arioan's names stood out in brilliant golden light, perched on two branches that stretched upward from a larger branch with Alatore's name.

Nonomay stepped back, to allow the two of them space to examine the tree in its entirety.

"And my uncle." Takeem pointed to Sorelion's name perched on a branch across from Alatore's. "He has a star."

"All the rulers of Lutia have stars by their names," Nonomay explained. "One day your name shall have a star too."

"No," Takeem murmured. "Not mine."

"Alatore's name doesn't have a star," Samantha whispered.

"I knew it. I knew they weren't bonded in truth," Takeem said. "But how is that even possible? She bears the mark of the throne and the mark of companionship."

"What does that mean?" Samantha asked.

"Every eligible heir to the throne receives the mark at the age of ten, but only the one chosen by the Royal Nargnet will actually ascend to the throne. When Hulak chooses his companion, the mark of the throne is outlined in red to represent a nargnet's flames," Takeem said. "It cannot be faked and must be displayed for ascendancy. Alatore had to show her mark to receive the crown of Lutia – it's on her palm with Hulak's flames clear to see. So I don't understand why she doesn't have a star by her name."

"The star only appears when the companion-bond has been fulfilled," Nonomay explained. "The Royal Nargnet and his companion must accept the bond, with all of the responsibilities that accompany the throne."

"If she has the mark—"

"Hulak accepted the bond," Takeem said.

"So Alatore refused to accept it?" Samantha asked.

"Perhaps," Nonomay said. "The ascendency, the truth of the rightful king or queen of Lutia, is for the two of you to discover on your own."

Takeem was tired of this talk of rulers. His mother had always been a mystery to him. Her ascendancy to the throne should be no different. "What about those branches there?" he interrupted, pointing toward the middle of the tree. "Those branches where all the records have been removed? Are those all people who went outside the walls? Are they all spinners?"

"I'm afraid so, yes," Nonomay answered. "Many of the names removed would have been simple Blues, no spinner traits at all, but somewhere along that line was a spinner who was exiled. The records removed may only include that one individual, or they may include his or her family members, regardless of spinner status, who accompanied him or her into exile. In some cases, like my own, they may even include those descendants who did not go into exile, but found their names were never added to the trees simply because their ancestors had been purged from them."

"That's so sad," Samantha murmured as she studied the tree from the middle of the room. "All those families torn apart."

"Except for mine," Takeem said, turning his back to the wall to face Nonomay. "Why wasn't I immediately exiled or executed when I was born?"

"There was no possibility of that, Takeem. You were protected the moment you were born beneath the willow."

Samantha swung around to stare at them. "The willow?"

"Another name for the Shrouded One," Nonomay said. "You were born into the embrace of a Shrouded One, Takeem. No one would dare reject the child Vanadevi herself embraced."

Samantha smiled and studied the tree once more.

"Every moment of my life has been about rejection, Nonomay."

"You are wrong, Takeem. Every moment of your life has been about love."

"Takeem," Samantha interrupted their conversation. "Come here." She beckoned him toward her spot at the center of the room.

Takeem and Nonomay walked over to stand on either side of Samantha. "What is it?" he asked.

"Look." Samantha pointed to the far corner of the tree.

"What am I looking at?" he asked.

"Stay here," Samantha commanded, then rushed to the wall. She headed for the far corner, where she reached out a finger and traced the words "records removed" at the bottom left branch of the tree. Looking back toward Takeem, she said, "Now watch." She then walked along the wall, tracing her finger in a line, all along the bottom branches of the tree, gently touching each of the names etched upon them: Kessink, Loxoryon, Nerys, Torel, Zarkonen, Marel, Ferilis, Petryus.

"The advisors were all brothers to the king?" Takeem couldn't believe it.

"Every last one," Nonomay said.

"It's you, Takeem." Samantha walked toward him.

"Me what?"

"You're the descendant, the blood that we need. You're the blood of all eight of them, of Torel *and* his seven advisors. You, the great-great-great-grandchild of King Torel, the great-great-great-grandnephew of all the rest."

Takeem shook his head, unable to speak.

"You have your part in the End Song as well, Takeem." Nonomay spoke quietly. "You are the piece that sheds blood for the world."

He stared at his family tree, watching as his name and Arioan's blinked in place, a golden glow at the very top of the tree. "Maybe it's not me. Maybe it's Arioan."

"Maybe it is Arioan," Nonomay agreed, "or maybe it's you. Arioan was not born beneath the willow, though he is no less worthy than you. What do you feel inside, Takeem? Is this what you are meant to do?"

Was this what his entire life had been building toward? To return the ancestral magicks of Lutia, to reverse his ancestor's devastating spell? "I think so," he said slowly, staring at Torel's name winking on the center branch, just above the trunk of the tree. "This must be my path, to finally right Torel's wrongs."

Samantha smiled. "You really are going to make a wonderful king, Takeem."

"I'm not agreeing to that, at least not yet. I'll try to release the magicks, but I won't commit to the throne."

Nonomay reached up a wrinkled hand and cupped Takeem's cheek. "When you are ready, Takeem. The world will wait until then, I promise."

"I suppose we should leave for the shrine then."

"Yes," Samantha agreed.

"Nonomay," Takeem said, reaching out toward her.

Nonomay smiled and grasped his hands. "Samantha is right, Takeem. You will truly make a wondrous king. Now, off you go, both of you." She guided them across the floor toward the door, Hulak following.

They had reached the doors when they heard a commotion outside. It was Marconen's voice. "Nonomay," he hissed. "Come quick. The Tekhlan are marching through the village. They seek Takeem and his companion."

Takeem froze. "The Tekhlan," he whispered. He met Samantha's eyes. His mother had betrayed him after all. She had sent the Tekhlan to the villages she had claimed would shelter him.

Samantha stepped closer. She leaned into him and took his hand in hers. "I'm sorry, Takeem," she whispered.

"You two stay here with Hulak." Nonomay pushed past them. "The trees will hide you until it is safe to come out. I'll send these murderers on their way and return as soon as I can."

She pushed through the door and was gone.

*

"Maybe – maybe the Tekhlan are only after me," Samantha said. "I mean, you're her son. She probably told them to kill me, but protect you. I bet they're here to get you away from me, maybe even protect you from me."

"No." Takeem stared into space. "Maybe when she gave me the list, she intended to protect me, but we're way past that now. I'm her Royal-spinner son, the one she could not execute because I was born beneath the Shrouded One; not the one she loves, but the one she was not allowed to kill. It explains so much."

"It's not right." In that moment, Samantha had never wished so fiercely for her parents to still be alive. She wanted them with her so that she could share them with Takeem, so that he would know love. She had heard what he told Nonomay – that his life was about rejection. He meant his mother, of course, and his brother, too, maybe even the father he'd never known. She wanted him to have her memories of her mother, her memories of her father, of Jonathan, of her Aunt Jenny, because in that moment, Samantha understood something she had never understood before. Her life, even after her family's deaths, truly had been all about love.

"You don't need to come with me, Samantha." Takeem spoke quietly, interrupting her thoughts. "Nonomay will hide you while Hulak and I journey back to the shrine. When we have finished releasing the magicks, we'll come back for you."

"No. I go where you go, Takeem." She pulled away to stare up into his eyes. "We stay together."

Takeem searched her eyes for a moment. "Very well," he said. "But the Tekhlan have caught up with us, Samantha. We may get away from here, we may lose them for a while, but they will continue to pursue us. They will continue to find us." He hesitated, then spoke firmly, "Samantha, the next portion of this journey could get very dangerous. I don't want you hurt."

"I don't want you hurt either. We stay together, Takeem. I need you and you need me." She hugged him tight. He had become so important to her in such a short amount of time. Takeem, this young man she had written, but never thought to meet.

*

Takeem closed his arms around Samantha and held her close. He was terrified to leave her behind and terrified to take her with them. He was very much afraid she was right and the Tekhlan were not after him so much as they were after her – the one who had spun the ashes to life, as the End Song predicted; the one who pushed for the magicks to be awakened; the one who could potentially displace his mother from the throne.

"Maybe we should touch Alatore's name," Samantha said. Or Jonathan's. Would Jonathan's name be somewhere hidden in these trees?

"What?"

"We have so many questions about her choices, about what she's doing. When I touched Morgel's name, I learned a lot. Maybe we should touch hers." If Jonathan's name was there, would touching it reveal where he had gone?

"I'm not sure that's a good idea."

"Don't you want to know why so many Skies hate her?" If Jonathan's name wasn't there, would that mean he was truly gone? "We might as well get some answers while we're waiting, right?" She caught his hand and dragged him toward King Torel's family tree, where Alatore's name shone in golden light toward the top.

"I may be taller than you, Samantha, but even I can't reach a name nine feet in the air."

Jonathan's story felt even further out of reach.

Dragging in a deep breath, Samantha made the request. "Please show us Queen Alatore's family tree."

King Torel's tree faded, then was replaced with a much smaller one.

"Holy crap," Samantha gasped.

"Blessed Vanadevi," Takeem said. "It's true. I didn't believe it, but it's true."

They stared at the tree, which showed the name Alatore Moriena upon a center root, with two additional roots branching off to either side. The root on the left was labeled Brenin Ryvar and the one to the right Vukel Balil. Leading up from these roots, the tree split into two separate entities, the trunk forging to the left bearing the name Arioan Ryvar and the trunk to the right Takeem Balil.

"No wonder the Skies call him King Arioan," Takeem whispered.

"Okay," Samantha said. "No more secrets." She laced their fingers together and touched both their fingertips to Alatore's name.

ALATORE, 20 YEARS AGO

PILGRIMAGE

When Alatore entered the council chambers, Kirosko turned from the window overlooking the courtyard and gestured to one of the chairs. She knew what he was going to ask before he spoke. He'd requested this meeting here, just the two of them, and the moment she saw his face, she knew.

She'd been dreading this moment since she realized the full ramifications of Shorel: that most of the Royal Council had perished in the fires, their seats to be inherited by their angry firstborns.

Alatore and Kirosko sat across from each other, the long table in between them, the additional chairs empty of the other council members. Did he know she would refuse? Why else would he ask in private?

"You know what has to be done, Alatore."

She shook her head. "I won't do it." Kirosko wanted vengeance. It was the only reason any Blue would ever ask for this.

"You must. It is time, past time for you to call the Mozkola. Your brother should have done it years ago."

"Even Sorelion knew the Mozkola should not be called," Alatore said. "I won't do it."

"You're the only one who can. We must use them to destroy our enemies."

"The Mozkola are never to be unleashed. You know this. They are banished to the mountains for a reason. I cannot call them."

"You must."

"They are darkness, Kirosko. There is no controlling them. They choose no sides, see no colors, feel no emotions. If we let them loose, if we call them to war, they will wage war against us all. That is fact. It has happened before."

"Because your ancestor was a fool. Joryn sent the Mozkola into Blue territory with orders to destroy the invaders and the Mozkola did just that. They slaughtered anyone they came across, including the Blues. I'm not suggesting we send the Mozkola into Blue territory. The spinners have retreated back to their lands and I suggest we send the Mozkola after them. No Blues are there. We'd be safe."

"You're suggesting genocide."

"Of course, I am. They deserve it."

"If the spinners were responsible for Shorel, why did they retreat? Why not attack while the battlefield burned?"

Silence.

"I'll tell you why," Alatore said. "Their forces burned too, which means the spinners weren't responsible for the fires or if they were, it was an accident."

"It was dark magicks. It had to be, and of course it wasn't an accident. They managed to tear down the walls keeping them out while our forces burned on the battlefields. We must destroy them before they invade and use their magicks against us further."

"The magicks haven't returned, Kirosko. You and I both know Torel lied when he promised the spinners their magicks would be returned a year after their exile was complete. Those magicks are gone forever. It's why they fight. It's why this war will never be done. Because a hundred and ten years ago, the king of Lutia stole their birthright."

"Their birthright? Their birthright was to serve the Blues. Instead they demanded equality, to lead. They demanded the throne and they plotted to use their magicks to gain it."

"You're right," Alatore said. "All I'm saying is they'll never forgive us and that's why they fight. Right or wrong. That's why they hate us. Whatever happened at Shorel, whatever happened to those walls, it wasn't because of any magicks they spun. They don't have any magicks, Kirosko. "

"The Mozkola exist. They are the dark magicks that couldn't be purged, rolled into dark beings. Who's to say there aren't other dark magicks around? Maybe the spinners found those magicks and used them to start the fire and destroy the walls."

"Perhaps they did, but why not invade then? They retreated, Kirosko. There have been no battles, no spinner invasions, no spinners sighted since the burning of Shorel six weeks ago."

"Which is why we should unleash the Mozkola. Now, while it's quiet. While they're unsuspecting."

"No. I'm the only one who can call the Mozkola and I won't do it."

"You're not the only one, Alatore. Hulak has not yet bonded with you, and Arioan has the blood of Torel, just as you do. We'll use him if we must."

"He's too young for what you want."

"Ten is old enough to go to war, to lead a country. He'll serve if you won't."

"Stay away from my son."

"Or what?"

"Or I will call the Mozkola, and I'll send them after you." Alatore used the table for leverage to stand and left the room. She walked slowly down the hallway and turned the corner. She wanted to run, but at nearly nine months pregnant, a brisk waddle was all she could manage.

She needed Hulak. He would be with Arioan and Devix, the Tekhlan assigned to guard Arioan months ago. She'd tried to dismiss him after her brother's death, but Devix had threatened to involve the Council. Sorelion had no doubt told him she was a threat to Arioan or perhaps Devix suspected the truth. Whichever it was, he watched her with suspicious eyes.

With Kirosko's threats, though, she couldn't afford to wait any longer. Devix or no, it was time for another pilgrimage.

*

Night had fallen.

Alatore would not leave Arioan behind, which meant she had to allow Devix to accompany them.

She led the way toward the gardens of Xilat at the center of the palace courtyards. Hulak padded at her side and Devix followed, carrying a sleeping Arioan.

When they arrived at the gardens, Hulak stretched out at the edge of the lake. He rested his head upon his paws and closed his eyes. He still refused to forge the bond.

Devix settled Arioan on the ground at the base of a tree and stood guard, watching Alatore's every move.

Alatore strode to the edge of the lake and stared at the Shrouded One growing at its center. The tree was the only life that truly flourished in the royal gardens, which had lain barren since the purge of magicks so long ago. The tree's trunk exploded from the center of the lake, a towering structure whose vines fell below the water, twining deep.

This Shrouded One was the oldest in existence, the only one she knew of that had survived the purge of magicks one hundred ten years before. Of all those that had died, only the one at the Holy Shrine had come back. Two in a world that once housed thousands.

Legend claimed the vines of all Shrouded Ones used to lift for the kings and queens of Lutia, inviting them to walk beneath their canopies. At the time of the purge, the tree at the Holy Shrine of Vanadevi was the only one permitting access. This Shrouded One, and all others like it, had been closed to those seeking wisdom for centuries before the purge.

Perhaps if this Shrouded One accepted her, Hulak would finally agree to the bond.

Alatore stripped down to her undergarments, kicked off her shoes and walked into the lake. The waters were soothing and cool, instantly relieving the tension and pressure in her lower back. When it became too deep for walking, she ducked beneath the water's surface and swam toward the tree.

When she reached the tree's vines, she glanced back toward Hulak. She could see him standing at the edge of the lake, watching. Knowing he was there, serving as witness, gave her the courage to face the trailing vines.

She reached out a hesitant hand and touched one.

"Please, Vanadevi, allow me entry."

The babe inside her kicked suddenly, a rush of movement, as if he were doing gymnastics. She lowered her hand and stroked her belly. "It's all right, sweet Takeem. It's all right."

A splash sounded behind her.

Hulak no longer stood on the edge of the lake.

Ripples raced across the water's surface.

Something nudged Alatore. It pushed against the small of her back, shoving her forward just a little. Her belly brushed against the vines and they lifted away.

Hulak surfaced at Alatore's side. He swam forward, leading the way beneath the Shrouded One.

Alatore followed, hands cradling her belly.

Her feet touched something. It was slippery and rough, wide and curved and sloping upward.

The roots of the Shrouded One.

Settling a hand upon one of the roots, Alatore cradled her belly with the other and awkwardly crawled her way along the root, following it upward, until she was no longer in the water.

It was dark beneath the Shrouded One. Too dark to see where Hulak had gone. Too dark to see anything at all.

She continued to climb.

Her face brushed against something rough. It was huge. Tall and wide. Rough and gnarled.

Alatore pushed to her feet, bracing herself against the trunk of the Shrouded One. She stood upon its roots, so wide and strong they lay below the water and above it.

She inched her way around the trunk, walking on its roots, feeling the Shrouded One beneath her feet, at her fingertips, brushing against her soul.

Takeem kicked again and Alatore knew it was time to rest. She carefully settled on a wide root and set her back against the trunk, exhaustion weighing her down.

Fur brushed against her and Hulak settled beside her.

He nudged her with his snout.

"What is it, Hulak?" she asked.

He blinked and a rush of images raced across his darkened eyes.

Forelia flying, Vukel on her back. A spear tearing through her, launched from below, lodging deep.

The two of them falling.

Forelia on the ground, dying, Vukel holding her head, staring into her eyes.

Hulak landing at their side. Embracing Forelia. Burning her.

Hulak, red as fire, rising high.

Flames everywhere.

The burning forests of Bipin.

The fires of Shorel consuming the battlefield.

Hulak at the center of the nargnet nesting grounds, nothing but ashes in every direction.

Dear Vanadevi, how could one spear have brought about such devastating results?

Hulak blinked and the images were gone. He leaned his head against Alatore's rounded belly, sighed and closed his eyes.

"Oh, Hulak," Alatore whispered, digging her fingers into his fur. She didn't know how he bore the grief and regret, when her own were so vast. She leaned her head against the trunk of the Shrouded One.

Takeem kicked and she rubbed her belly. "I had no choice," she whispered.

She'd conspired against the throne, yet danger still surrounded her sons. Unless she found a way to protect them, her unborn spinner child would be executed and Kirosko would use Arioan to unleash the darkest magicks ever spun into existence.

If the Mozkola went to war, the world as they knew it would burn.

Alatore stared at the canopy above her, imagining she could see the Mozkola marching within its writhing vines. Her eyes slid closed and as she slept, the Shrouded One shared with her visions from eighty years before.

*

Royal-Blue Palace, Year 30 AP

"How did they breach the walls?" Joryn demanded.

"We have no idea, sire," Livaro said. "It shouldn't have been possible."

"Those walls were built with the last of the magicks this world has ever seen. Has the spell been broken then? Have the magicks been released?"

"We don't believe so, sire. If the magicks were released, the spinners would have done much worse than simply breach a couple walls. They haven't reached the third wall yet, but it's chaos, full-out war. The Tekhlan are in command of the Blue armies, and Skies and Royals alike are defending the territories, but the spinners are pushing forward. Word is they'll reach the third wall in another day."

"Unacceptable," Joryn said. "How are they breaking through the spell? Those gates are protected, locked against all spinners. They shouldn't be able to even touch the gate or wall, let alone breach them."

"Word has it one of the spinner commanders is capable of unlocking the gates. Whatever he does when he reaches them unspins the spell all along that wall, and then the spinners are like a tidal wave of vengeance. We lost every Sky village between the first and second walls before we managed to put together any kind of defense force. Now we're fighting for every village between the second and third. At this rate, the spinners will reclaim the territories in a week's time."

"Declare the Rule of Mozkola."

"Sire?"

"Declare it."

"King Torel advised -"

"I know what my father advised, but he's not here, is he? Now the spinners he exiled are breaching the walls he created. Do you think my father would stand by and not use every resource, every tool, every weapon at his disposal to fight them back?"

"No, sir. I'm sure he would call upon the Mozkola as well."

"Exactly. Declare it."

"Yes, sire."

*

One hour later, Joryn stood on the palace balconies, with his council members at his back, and faced the Royals gathered below.

"To ensure the safety of all Blues everywhere, we call upon the Mozkola." A soft rumbling of confusion spread through the crowd. Joryn unrolled the parchment, muttered the command upon it and fed it to the fire of Lutia burning from the torch at his side.

He turned and nodded to his chief advisor, Livaro, who stepped forward and unrolled the official proclamation of the palace.

"The Rule of Mozkola is hereby declared," he read. "The Mozkola rule in the name of the king; they are to be obeyed in all things. Those who are spinner-born are not considered to be of Lutia and are thus invaders of these lands. All invaders between the first and third walls of Lutia are subject to immediate execution by the Mozkola. All Sky-Blues are subject to conscription and may be called into service by the Mozkola at any time and for any reason. Those who would defy the Mozkola are subject to the penalty of death, to be administered without delay." Livaro lowered the parchment. "May the blessings of Vanadevi be upon you."

*

Deep in the mountains of Lixor, the Mozkola stirred. They emerged from their caves and gathered in straight lines. They took one step forward and disappeared.

For the first time since banished there, the Mozkola left their mountain homes.

*

The first line of Mozkola appeared between the third wall of Lutia and the Blues who stood with their backs to the wall in its defense. The Mozkola stepped forward, drew long blades from the sheaths at their backs and struck before the Blues realized they were there.

The Mozkola stepped forward, rolling mercilessly over the fallen, and a second line of Mozkola appeared at their backs.

To Blues standing further away, with time to turn and see the enemy they engaged, the Mozkola were terrifying in appearance. They were Sky-Blue in skin tones, but their shaven heads were painted with the royal-blue markings of a Shrouded One. Royal vines trailed down their sky faces and necks to disappear beneath their black clothing. Those same markings reappeared, marching across their hands and fingers.

These two lines of Mozkola rolled forward, a third line appearing at their backs. They mercilessly engaged the Blues, striking them down and walking over their fallen forms.

At the same time this was happening at the third wall of Lutia, several lines of Mozkola appeared at the first. The land before them was empty. They began an inexorable march forward, in search of intruders.

The Mozkola had been given their purpose – to execute all invaders between the first and third walls of Lutia – and they did so. The separate lines of Mozkola met at the second wall, swiftly and silently executing everyone they found along the way.

The spinner intruders fell, as Joryn intended, but because the Mozkola did not register skin tones, eye color or sides, so too, did all the Sky-Blues: the soldiers and their families, the settlers with innocent children, all of them fell beneath the unending tide of Mozkola.

BINDING

Alatore came out of the vision nauseated. This was why the Mozkola were never to be called.

"Kirosko's planning to use Arioan to call forth the Mozkola," she told Hulak. "And if the Shrouded Ones are right and Takeem will be spinner-born, the Blues will execute him unless I gain the power to stop them. They're both going to die if we don't do something. Worse, the world will come to ruin at the hands of the Mozkola."

Hulak lay there, unmoving. Was he even listening?

"We have no choice, Hulak," she said. "Our people need a leader, and Arioan's too young."

The Skies would view her actions as a betrayal, but it was the only way she knew to protect her unborn son. She would keep to the rest of their bargain. She would tell Arioan the truth and send him to Nonomay every six weeks as promised. Hopefully, that would be enough to appease the Skies.

"Hulak, please. You must perform the bonding ceremony if we are to save them."

Still he ignored her.

She understood why he resisted. Once bonded, the bonding held until death. The Royal Nargnet could only claim one human warrior-companion at a time. When their father died, Alatore had been just a girl, barely six years old, and Sorelion nineteen. Hulak had bonded with Sorelion, rather than wait for Alatore to reach the age of ascension. The results had been disastrous.

Alatore wasn't the perfect choice to rule the world, but she would have been a thousand times better than Sorelion, who dragged them deeper and deeper into an endless war. For Hulak to bond with Alatore now, though, was to risk never bonding with one of her sons or bonding with him too late.

"Is there a way to bond with me that isn't permanent?" she asked. "A way to fool the rest of the world into believing we've bonded true?"

Hulak slowly raised his head and looked at Alatore. He pushed to his feet, shook out his fur, lunged forward and exploded into his larger form. He grew to five times his original size, the purples of his smaller form receding and the reds bursting forth onto his larger one. His fur grew shaggier at the front of his face, but seemed to recede a bit in back, and from the two black streaks along his side, his red and black wings launched free. Turning toward Alatore, Hulak hunkered down so that his belly brushed the ground. Alatore approached his left side, but then was uncertain how to go about mounting him. Normally, she would simply launch herself upward, but being nearly nine months pregnant –

One of Hulak's wings scooped Alatore up and settled her onto his back. The wing then snapped away and down, the vines of the Shrouded One rustling from the surge of air the movement caused.

Hulak launched himself forward.

Alatore clenched her thighs around his sides and grasped handfuls of fur at his neck. She wanted to lean forward and throw her arms around him, but her belly was in the way. She'd never manage this. She already felt unbalanced.

Hulak plunged from beneath the Shrouded One, the vines lifting seconds before he reached them and then he was airborne.

The lunge jolted her forward and when she settled again, her feet and thighs planted themselves in the perfect spots.

Hulak angled his body so they flew up in a sheer vertical flight that made her ears ring. Her thighs and hands were clamped so tight, plastered to Hulak, it was as if they were becoming one being.

The world rushed by in a roar of sound and she was no longer on Hulak's back.

She stood in the middle of a field, facing two young men. Though one of hers sons was not yet born and the other only ten, she recognized their older selves immediately. Her beautiful sons, Arioan and Takeem.

They were not alone. A woman with red hair and pale skin stood between them. She didn't have the look of anyone born of Lutia. She had neither royal skin nor sky, though it was covered in royal-blue spots. Her red hair was tipped royal-blue and had one long, royal-blue streak in it.

The background filled in behind them with an army of Royals and Skies, thousands strong.

Alatore turned. Thousands of spinners stood at her back.

Dear Vanadevi. Her precious sons were about to engage the armies of the exiled.

The spinners were a mix of Royal and Sky, their eyes banded in blue stripes. At the front of their lines stood another woman not of Lutia, whose hair was striped royal and red, and whose skin was pale, with royal stripes and sky spots. She stood beside a man with similar stripes. The two looked fierce and wild.

The sight of them sparked a distant memory, of a legend long dead to the world.

Had the Lorki returned?

Movement caught her attention.

Arioan and the striped spinner walked toward each other. They spoke to each other and though she was quite close to where they stood, she could not hear their words.

The spinner and Arioan clasped arms in the traditional warrior's greeting.

Takeem held hands with the woman at his side.

Who had orchestrated this? Arioan? Takeem? This woman?

Peace between the races. Her sons had managed peace. She had this one thought, then the nightmare of all the races was upon the fields with them.

The Mozkola were everywhere. Their sky-blue skin covered in the royal vines of the Shrouded Ones, they marched through and over the endless fields of Blues and spinners.

Dear Vanadevi. Which of her sons had called forth the Mozkola?

It had to be one of them, for only the blood of Torel could call the Mozkola from their mountains.

Arioan and Takeem fought fiercely against the onslaught of Mozkola.

Spinners and Blues battled side by side, against the common enemy of the races.

Takeem disappeared in a mass of Mozkola.

Arioan, fighting to reach his side, was caught from behind, his body falling beneath the black boots of a never-ending wave of Mozkola.

The wind was shrieking in Alatore's ears and her hands let loose from Hulak's fur.

Hulak leveled out and her hands caught in his fur once more, her legs clenching tight again.

They were still flying the Flight of Truth.

Was this her truth then? The fate of her two sons?

Hulak's paws connected with the land, drumming the ground in rhythmic thuds, headed straight for the lake where Devix stood guard by Arioan's sleeping form.

Hulak soared across the lake toward the Shrouded One, flying so close to the surface, his wings sprayed water with each upward glide.

The vines of the Shrouded One lifted and Hulak hurtled beneath its canopy.

He slowed to a stop, settled his feet upon the wide roots of the tree and stood, head hung low, panting softly as Alatore slowly slid to the ground.

She leaned against Hulak's side for a moment, waiting for her legs to stop shaking. After a moment, she walked to stand beneath Hulak's head and staring up at him, gently stroked his chest. "Was that truth, Hulak?" she whispered. "The Mozkola?"

Hulak stared at her.

"Did you not see the Mozkola, Hulak?" she asked.

He turned his head away.

"Do we only see our own truths in flight, not necessarily each other's?" she wondered.

Hulak's only answer was to stretch his wings out as far as they would go, then in one quick movement, snap them back into the folds along his side.

"Did it work, Hulak? Are we bonded?"

Hulak shook his fur, stepped away from Alatore and slowly shrank down to his smaller size. He then stepped forward and nuzzled her belly.

"Hulak?"

The Flight of Truth raced across his eyes, Hulak hurtling upward, Alatore on his back. A golden thread wove itself around them, around her, holding her to Hulak's back. It threaded around her and around him, back and forth, then suddenly arrowed into him. It lit him from the inside out, then left him and sank deep into Alatore, into her belly, where it lit her womb from the inside out.

She gasped. "Oh, Vanadevi, no. You bonded with Takeem? You can do that? If the Council finds out, they'll kill him. Hulak—"

Hulak nudged her left hand.

Alatore opened it and pain blazed searing hot. Her vision went black. When she could see again, she was kneeling on the ground, leaning into Hulak's form. Her hand felt as if it was on fire.

This was the hand where the mark of the throne, a royal Shrouded One, had appeared twenty years before when she reached the Age of Ascension. She stared at the palm where the Shrouded One now glowed a fiery red, as if Hulak's fire lived within that hand. The burning was intense.

A small price to pay for the safety of her sons.

The glow subsided until the tree was royal-blue once more, but now ringed in the red of a nargnet's fire. He had marked them as if they were bonded.

She searched for the golden thread, the one she'd seen that connected her to Hulak, but there was nothing there. The thread was buried deep inside, with Takeem, and she could not access it. The reddened Shrouded One was a false mark, but it would convince the Council, and that was all she needed it to do.

Alatore flung her arms around Hulak's neck and whispered, "Thank you, Hulak. Thank you so much for protecting my son."

She pulled away and climbed to her feet. "Let's go get Arioan. I—" she gasped and clutched her belly. "Oh."

Hulak stared at her with his dark eyes, a thousand mysteries buried in their depths.

"Oh, Hulak. I'm afraid Arioan is going to have to wait a bit more." Heart pounding, she used the trunk for support as she lowered herself to the ground.

Settling between two enormous roots, she lay back and stared at the canopy above her. As she labored to bring Hulak's bonded companion into the world, the light of a new day penetrated the canopy, filtering through its dense leaves, and brightened the world around her.

THE BIRTH OF A KING

HULAK STOOD GUARD as the mother of a king labored to bring him into the world.

The Shrouded One that sheltered them performed the duties of midwife. Its trunk taking the form of a woman, she leaned over Alatore, braids and vines brushing her form, soothing her pains away.

The Shrouded One whispered secrets, to Alatore and to Hulak, secrets he once bore witness to, imprinted upon the Book of Ages and tried to purge from his soul's memory. Secrets he could no longer bear.

Forelia was gone. His light, his shining anchor, the one beauty that made all the darkness bearable, was gone.

And the Shrouded One mourned with him.

The vines that twined round the laboring mother wove round him as well. Binding them together, binding their lives for the sake of the infant king who would change the world.

The Shrouded One whispered tales of the nargnets' flight bearing the spinners into exile, fracturing the world, and of the Mozkola's march so long ago, their destiny to march again.

Their role in everything that had come to pass lay bare before him.

Trying to save the human world, they were instead destroyed by it. And his Forelia, the gnettis in the nesting grounds, every last one of his kind had paid the price for his role as warrior-companion to the kings and queens of Lutia.

The flames of his fury igniting the world.

The soft mewling cry of a newborn broke through the sounds of a thousand memories and the vines holding Hulak in place unraveled.

The Shrouded One lifted the spinner child high – so tiny, fists waving, eyes open, blinking at the world around him.

The curtain shielding them lifted and the vines cradling the child carried him out to the waters, where they bathed him with gentle movements of love and care.

In the distance, the human guard stood upon the bank, watching as his future king was bathed by the most ancient of Shrouded Ones. A witness to the holiest of moments.

More vines writhed beneath Alatore and lifting her, carried her out to her child. They settled her upon a root, where the water lapped at her gently and the vines caressed and supported her back.

Alatore reached for her child and the Shrouded One settled him into her arms.

*

Arioan was surprised when he woke outside.

"Your brother or sister was born this night," Devix said, "across the lake, beneath the Shrouded One."

"Really?"

Devix didn't answer, just walked back and forth at the edge of the water.

Arioan clasped his hands behind his back like Devix and started to walk beside him. "Do you think it's a boy or a girl? Devix, do you think I'll get to hold the baby? I'm going to be the best big brother ever. Devix, do you think the baby will look like me? Do you think the baby'll want to play with me? How big do you think it is? Not as big as me, right? Devix, what do you think?"

Devix stopped and let out a huge sigh. "I don't know, Arioan. You're going to be a great big brother though."

Arioan stood up straighter. "I am. I'll protect the baby from the spinners and the Tekhlan and anyone else who's mean."

Devix turned and stared down at him. "Arioan, the Tekhlan are not mean."

Arioan shrugged and stared at his feet. They were, no matter what Devix said. They were scary too.

"They keep order and help make the territories safe for all Blues. Your father was their leader."

Arioan shrugged again. His father was the scariest of them all.

"Come now, your father wasn't a mean man."

Arioan didn't answer.

"Was he?"

Arioan peeked up at Devix. Would he be mad if he told the truth? "He wasn't nice. He didn't like me. He didn't like Mama either. He made her cry. Every time he came home. Every time he went away. She always cried."

Devix nodded. "She missed him."

If she missed him, why was she so sad whenever she was with him? Movement across the lake caught Arioan's eye.

"Devix, look, look! Mama, Mama!" He jumped up and down and waved.

Hulak was swimming across the lake with his mama on his back. She had something in her arms. Was it his baby brother or sister?

Arioan waited impatiently as his mother slid from Hulak's back and carefully walked up the bank toward him.

"Did my baby get born, Mama?"

"He did, my darling." His mother sank to the ground beside him. She had vines wrapped around her back forming a cocoon at the front. The cocoon moved.

Alatore gently pulled away some of the leaves and vines, revealing a tiny face.

Arioan gasped. The baby didn't look like him at all. He was bald and had sky-blue lines all around his eyes, like rays bursting from the sun. Blue sunbursts. "Mama."

"His name is Takeem. He's a very special child who needs our protection, Arioan."

"But, Mama, he's got spinner-eyes. No one likes the spinners,"

Arioan whispered.

"I know."

"What are we going to do, Mama? Spinners aren't allowed in Blue territory."

Takeem opened his eyes.

"Wow," Arioan whispered.

Tiny streaks ran across the whites of Takeem's eyes, striping them royal-blue, making them wild.

"Mama, they'll send him away. My brother, Mama."

"No one's sending your brother away, my darling. People don't like the spinners because they used to spin magicks, but the magicks are long gone from this world. Takeem cannot spin that which is not there to be spun."

The sleeve moved and a tiny fist waved in the air.

Arioan reached out and touched his brother's hand. "But what about the Tekhlan, Mama? They kill spinners."

Alatore didn't answer.

Arioan looked up at his mother. She was staring at Devix.

Devix looked like the stablemaster had when a krutesk kicked him in the stomach.

"Mama?"

It was Devix who answered. "The Tekhlan will not touch your brother," he said.

*

Though Alatore was exhausted and wished nothing more than to retreat to her quarters to spend time with her sons, she knew there was nothing to be gained by delay and much to lose.

She led the way inside the palace, keeping Takeem's body completely swaddled in the sleeve Hulak had woven from the vines the Shrouded One had willingly given. It was imperative she control the revelation of Takeem's markings. She could not risk anyone seeing them before she was ready.

She stopped the first staff member she saw. "Would you please find Kirosko for me? Request he call a council meeting immediately."

"But, My Lady, they're already in session."

"What?"

"They're in session, My Lady. The meeting began about 30 minutes ago."

"Why was I not informed of a meeting?"

"I'm sorry, My Lady, I do not know."

"Please be certain that everyone on the staff understands there will be no meetings without my approval and presence. Is that understood?"

"Yes, My Lady."

Alatore moved past the man and headed for the stairs that led to the Council chambers.

The man raced around her and blocked the stairs. "My Lady, the meeting has already begun. You cannot enter now."

"As this meeting was called without my approval, it cannot be an official one, now can it? You will step aside and let me pass."

"The chief advisor called the meeting, My Lady. Kirosko specifically requested no one be allowed to interrupt."

Unbelievable. "You're still arguing with me. What is your name?"

"Geron, My Lady."

"Well, Geron. You may be assured that Kirosko's orders do not supersede mine." Even if she weren't about to claim the throne, Kirosko overstepped his bounds. "Now stand aside."

Geron hesitated then slowly edged to the side, allowing Alatore to move past him. She walked up the stairs with Hulak, Arioan and Devix following.

The Council chambers were at the end of a long hallway that led toward the back of the palace. The windows within the chambers overlooked the Gardens of Xilat.

Geron had said they'd been in session for thirty minutes. It took approximately fifteen to walk from the lake to the entrance of the palace. Had they seen her from the windows? Did they know about Takeem?

Two palace guards stood on either side of the doors to the Council chambers.

Alatore sighed in anticipation of another confrontation. Before she could speak, Devix swept in front of her, nodded to the two men standing guard and opened the door for her.

Unexpected.

Straightening her back, gathering control, Alatore walked into the meeting and headed for the front of the room.

"Alatore, you cannot just barge in here," Kirosko said. "The Council is in session."

"The Council does not meet without its Queen."

"What?"

"Hulak has bonded with me." Alatore held her palm up, displaying the mark of the throne with its reddened aura. "This is my Council and it does not meet without my approval." She stared at Kirosko. "You're in my place."

A muscle in Kirosko's jaw twitched, the only evidence of emotion Alatore could see.

"Of course, My Lady." Kirosko stepped away from his position at the front of the table and made his way around it, headed for the seat at the opposite end.

Alatore stepped forward into the space he had vacated, drew in a deep breath and announced, heart pounding, blood rushing so loudly in her ears, she almost couldn't hear her own voice, "My second son has been born, another proud heir to the throne of Lutia." She lifted Takeem and allowed the woven sleeve to fall apart just enough to reveal his spinner markings.

For a moment there was stunned silence in the room. Then, as one entity, the Council members leapt to their feet and began shouting.

"Spinner."

"Abomination."

"What is it doing here? Why is it here?"

"Get rid of it. How could you bring that thing here?"

"We're doomed."

"Enough," Kirosko said, his voice slicing through the chaos. "This is a simple matter. The child is spinner-born. It will be executed immediately."

Hulak lunged forward, his body pushing Alatore's back.

He released his fire in one massive wave.

The Council members cried out and leapt away from the table

as it crumbled to ash.

Dead silence filled the room.

Alatore stepped forward to stand beside Hulak. "The Royal Nargnet will defend my spinner son to the death. You will not touch him."

"He's an abomination," Stilel shouted.

"Silence! Do you think I will not order your death simply because I'm a woman?" Alatore shook with fear and rage, in equal parts. "I'm your Queen and as such, though few of the Tekhlan remain, they are mine to command, as are the Mozkola, as is this Council, as are these lands."

"You're a mother," Kirosko said. "Of course, you're not thinking straight. We understand, Alatore, but please think on this a moment."

"Queen Alatore," Devix said.

"What?" Kirosko stared blankly.

"I am your queen now. Devix simply reminds you to address me appropriately."

"Yes, yes." Kirosko waved a dismissive hand in the air. "Queen Alatore. Still you must understand, he's a spinner, an abom—one of the enemy. He will never be trusted, never inherit the throne. He should be executed. If not, it's exile. You may go with him, of course, but—"

"No!" Arioan cried out, lunging forward. "You can't send my brother away. You can't."

"Arioan, it's going to be all right." Alatore settled her arm around him and hugged him close. "This is not your decision to make, Kirosko. It's not the Council's decision either. My son will not be executed nor will he be exiled. This is his home."

"It *is* our decision to make," Selka spoke up. She was a soft-spoken woman who wielded significant power on the Council. She never made demands. She simply stated her opinion with reason and calm detachment and the others usually followed her lead. "Spinners were purged from Blue society for a reason. We will not make an exception simply because—"

"The child was born beneath the Shrouded One." Devix spoke up, surprising Alatore.

"What do you mean?" Kirosko asked. "The one at the Holy Shrine?"

"No," Devix said. "The one here on the grounds."

"The one in the gardens?" Heriell asked.

"Yes."

"But that tree's been closed for centuries," Kirosko said.

"Exactly," Devix said. "And yet it opened for Queen Alatore. I watched her walk beneath it. Hulak flew the Flight of Truth with her and the tree welcomed them both beneath its canopy. They remained there for much of the night. This morning as the sun rose, the vines of the Shrouded One bathed the child in the waters of Xilat. I witnessed this myself. The Shrouded One cared for the child as if it were its own."

Silence.

Alatore stared at the Council and realized this was the argument she should have made immediately. For the first time, she was grateful Sorelion had assigned Devix as Arioan's guard. He served as witness. His account could very well save Takeem's life.

"Are you certain, Devix?" Selka asked.

"I am."

"Why would the Shrouded One allow a spinner to be born beneath its canopy? It makes no sense," Selka said. "Did Vanadevi truly serve as midwife, Alatore?"

Alatore hadn't thought of it that way, but she supposed– "Yes, she did. She helped deliver Takeem, then bathed him with the vines of her Shrouded One."

"Then the child is truly blessed," Selka said. "To execute or even exile him would be to anger the gods."

"She's right, Kirosko," Heriell muttered.

Kirosko shook his head. "No spinner will sit upon the throne of Lutia. It is unacceptable."

"He's an heir only, Kirosko," Alatore said. "It's unlikely he would be chosen. And even if he were, the magicks are long gone from this world. The spinners are impotent, incapable of using their power to spin what is no longer available to them."

"I still say we should execute him. Worry about the gods later.

That abomination does not belong in this palace," Stilel said.

"What if the magicks are released?" Heriell asked. "We'll have an enemy this side of the walls, capable of spinning destruction all around us."

Alatore shook her head. "You know Torel's spell has no end. The magicks will never be released."

"But if they are?"

"Very well." Kirosko spoke up. "Here's what I suggest. Alatore agrees that her spinner son—"

"Takeem," Alatore interrupted.

"That Takeem will never inherit the throne of Lutia nor spin any magicks. In return, he may live in the palace without fear for his life. If at any point, however, the magicks are released, he will be considered an immediate threat and will be executed as a result. As for the throne, so long as Alatore is bonded with Hulak and serves as our queen, Takeem has no ability to ascend. However, should you die, Alatore, all agreements are off. We will not risk that thing ever becoming king of these lands. Understood?"

"I will agree to all of that, with one exception. My child is not a thing. You will treat him with respect, as if he were in fact heir to this throne. So long as you do so, I will do everything in my power to ensure the magicks are never released, and when the time comes, the throne passes to Vukel's first-born son."

"Though it will be difficult to treat any spinner with respect, even a child, I will do my best. I agree to this pact," Stilel said.

"I agree as well," Selka said.

"And I." The remaining Council members voted one by one, until all seven had agreed.

Kirosko nodded. "Very well. Alatore, your spinner-child may live so long as you adhere to your side of this accord."

"Understood. Now if that is all, this Council is adjourned."

After a moment's hesitation, each of the members filed out.

Alatore waited several moments before crossing to the window. She watched the courtyards below until she saw Kirosko cross the courtyard headed toward the lake of Xilat. He was alone which let her know the Council had broken up, each of them heading to their separate offices or homes.

Kirosko, of course, would be the one who had to check, who would have to see if the Shrouded One would allow him entry. She was tempted to stand there and watch, but any trip to a holy site was a deeply personal one. She did not have the right to intrude upon Kirosko's pilgrimage.

Turning from the window, she held her hand out to Arioan. "Come, my darling, let's go home."

"Takeem's safe, Mama?"

"He is. The Council has agreed that he may live."

"But what if the magicks are released, Mama?"

Alatore sighed. At one time, she had believed releasing the magicks would be the best thing for this world. Release the magicks and perhaps the spinners would forgive the Royals their arrogance and this war would be done. For Takeem's sake, though, she would ensure that future never came to pass.

"Mama?"

"We'll just have to make certain the magicks are never released, sweetheart. It shouldn't be that hard. After all, they've been gone a hundred and ten years now."

She led the way from the Council chambers, down one set of stairs and up another, into the royal suite. The moment the doors had shut behind them, she turned to Devix.

"Devix, thank you so very much. Your words in there made all the difference."

"Your son was born beneath the Shrouded One, my Queen. There is no greater honor. The gods do not care about skin color or magicks; they care about the purity of one's soul. I spoke up because it was the right thing to do, because Counselor Selka was right. Takeem is blessed. Which is why I'm disturbed at your accord with the Council. Even I'm aware that when Vanadevi blesses a child as she did this one, it means he's meant for great things. Why would you deny him the ascendency?"

"He's already been denied, Devix. Hulak bonded with me. I hope to live long enough to see both my sons reach adulthood. By then, I hope they are strong enough to defend their own lives against the Council if need be."

"So you're still planning for Takeem to inherit the throne."

"Not necessarily. I don't know if that's his path, Devix. All I know is he's been blessed by the gods, by Vanadevi herself, and I will defend his right to live, his right to see out his destiny, whatever that destiny may be, to my dying breath."

"I understand. My Queen, I pledge myself to your cause." He bowed low.

"Devix—"

"I am one of only three remaining Tekhlan, My Lady. The Council will build their ranks again, but I do not believe the other two or any other Royals they find to serve will see beyond the markings on your son's skin. Had I not been there to witness the Shrouded One's actions, I do not believe I would either. Allow me to stand for both your sons, Queen Alatore. Your brother assigned me to protect Arioan. Allow me the privilege of protecting them both."

"Very well, Devix. Thank you."

LOSS

"If that's all for today," Alatore said, "why don't we—"

"One last thing." Kirosko nodded to Yezur, who turned and opened the doors to the chamber.

"Bring the boy in." Yezyr stepped back and two additional Tekhlan appeared in the doorway, Takeem and Hulak in his smaller form between them. Devix and Arioan stood behind Takeem, furious scowls on both their faces.

Alatore surged to her feet. "What is the meaning of this?" she demanded.

"This is the boy's tenth birthday, is it not?" Kirosko asked.

"Yes, but—"

"The boy will be examined," Selka said. "We will know whether the child has received the mark of the throne or not, whether this child stands to potentially inherit the throne."

"What does it matter?" Alatore asked. "The agreement is still in place. So long as I live, he cannot inherit and the magicks will never be released, so he poses no threat."

"It matters because we say it matters," Stilel said.

"If he has no mark, then he has nothing to fear from us," Kirosko said.

"And if he does have the mark?" Alatore asked.

"Enough," Selka said. "We will know the truth." She stood and faced Takeem. "Tell us the truth, boy."

Takeem glanced toward Alatore and she nodded to him, praying he would remember not to lie to the Council.

Takeem turned his back to the room and pulled up his tunic.

Gasps and exclamations filled the room as everyone saw the Sky-Blue mark for the first time.

Takeem lowered the tunic.

Alatore strode toward him. She hugged him and turned him to face Devix. "Devix, would you please take Takeem back to the Royal quarters? I charge you with his safety."

Devix bowed low. "Of course, My Queen. Come." He held out his hand and Takeem took it. Devix led the way out of the room.

At the last minute, right before the door shut behind them, Takeem looked back toward Alatore, his bright shining eyes full of faith in her ability to keep him safe.

The moment the door closed, Alatore swung to face the Council. "That was completely unnecessary. Had you only asked, I would have told you about the mark. There was no need to bring my son here."

"There was every need," Selka said. "If only to see how you handle the spinner-child who might one day inherit the throne."

"Arioan will inherit the throne upon my death," Alatore said. "He knows it and I know it. A spinner-heir will never be chosen."

"If that were true, the mark of the throne would not be on the child's back," Kirosko said.

"He must be executed," Stilel said. "We should have done it immediately when he was first born."

Hulak shifted forward and all the Council members pushed away from the table in swift movements.

"The mark is not Royal, no matter that Takeem is," Alatore said. "That fact alone should prove he is not a true heir to the throne. The kings and queens of Lutia have always had marks in a shade of royal, either slightly lighter or slightly darker than their royal skin, but never so light as to be considered sky."

"Just because it's never happened before doesn't mean it won't," Heriell said, "especially given how large the mark was. It covered his entire back. That we've never seen a Sky-Blue mark or one so large only emphasizes the significance of it."

"Of course it's significant," Alatore said. "It doesn't mean he's destined to inherit the throne though. Takeem was born beneath the Shrouded One, his birth attended by Vanadevi herself. The mark only reminds us he's been blessed."

"Blessed, born beneath the Shrouded One, marked by the throne, all valid reasons to believe the child may one day inherit it," Morna said. "This is madness. We cannot allow a spinner to ascend."

"What if this is the beginning of the End Song?" Rienke asked the question none of them had considered.

Alatore's protests froze in her throat. Dear Vanadevi, she'd never considered her sons might play a part in the End Song. This truly was madness. Shaking off the fear, she said, "The End Song's nothing more than legend and superstition. Are we making our decisions based on shadows and myth now?"

The Council members began to speak at once, arguing about the End Song and whether this was the beginning of the fall of the Royal line.

"The End Song is not a myth." Selka's quiet voice cut through the chaos. "Many of its truths are unknown, lost to millennia, but some we do know, including that its prelude began with the fires of Shorel ten years ago. The End Song approaches and nothing will stop its journey. We might sculpt its path, but the melody will remain the same."

"That's not possible," Stilel said. "The End Song requires magicks to be sung."

"The End Song *is* magick, Stilel. Just one of the many magicks still in this world," Selka said.

"The magicks have been gone for over a hundred years," Alatore protested. "Takeem cannot wield them for they are not there to be spun."

"Certainly there are no magicks left for spinning," Selka agreed. "However, the magicks spun into existence millennia ago still exist today – the nargnets, of whom Hulak is the last; the Shrouded One at the Shrine and the one at Xilat; the Mozkola, spun into existence at the purge."

"You're saying the End Song is upon us," Heriell said.

"I'm saying its preludes are already being sung."

"It matters not," Alatore said. "My sons are not the End-Makers."

"Perhaps not, but Skies, Royals and spinners all have verses to play in the Song. How interesting that your spinner child should have both Royal blood and a Sky mark of the throne," Selka said.

"Even if that's true, Takeem is no threat," Alatore said.

"Of course, he is," Stilel said. "The child is the biggest threat we face. We cannot afford to wait. He must be–"

"The reasons for not executing Takeem are the same today as they were ten years ago. " Arioan spoke for the first time since entering the room.

The Council fell silent.

"My brother was blessed by Vanadevi, born beneath the Shrouded One, bathed in the waters of Xilat. The magicks are not available to him and my mother is still bonded with Hulak. Thus, the accord holds." Arioan paced to the front of the room so that he stood at the end of the table, at his mother's side, facing the Council members.

"Not so long as he is treated as a potential heir," Kirosko said. "The accord is clear – if the boy is deemed a threat, he will be executed."

"No one treats him as a potential heir," Alatore said.

"You do, Alatore, as does Arioan. The child has free run of the palace. He follows his older brother everywhere. Arioan takes him flying on the Royal Nargnet, for Vanadevi's sake. The child has no reason to believe he might not inherit the throne. Many of the Royals in the palace believe the same – that the child is a legitimate heir. This is unacceptable. So long as the people believe he might inherit, the child is a threat."

"You wish Takeem to believe he has no chance of inheriting?"

"Not just Takeem. It must be clear to everyone in or around

the palace, to the Royals and the Skies in the villages far from here. No spinner will ever inherit the throne of Lutia, not even a child born to our queen."

"How am I to do this?" Alatore asked. "I've never told Takeem or anyone else that he might inherit. I've always treated Arioan as the heir. What more can I do?"

"You will make it clear to the child and to anyone who witnesses your interactions with him that he is not in line for the throne. You will limit his access within the palace. He may have run of the servant quarters and kitchens, but not the throne room, not the Royal quarters, not the Royal bathing chambers or dining rooms."

"You would have me remove my own son from his home?"

"If you wish to save his life, yes."

"He's of Royal blood, no matter his spinner markings. He does not deserve this, to be shuttled to the servant quarters so young."

"In addition," Kirosko ignored Alatore's protests, "Arioan will no longer provide the child with the opportunity to ride the Royal Nargnet. The child is not worthy of such a privilege in any case."

"He's worthier than any of you," Arioan burst out. "He has the mark of the throne."

"Finally," Kirosko continued, "both of you will make it clear to everyone, including the child, that his spinner eyes make him undesirable as a leader."

"He's my son. I won't make him feel inferior."

"Then we have no choice but to execute him. You treat him as though he were a potential heir. This is unacceptable. We've made it clear he will never inherit the throne. Now you need to make that clear, both to the masses and to him."

Alatore clenched her fists. She could see on the Council members' faces they would not yield on this matter. She was going to lose her son.

"Devix will go with him." She could barely speak past the lump in her throat. "He will continue as my son's guard because your decisions here do not change the fact that Takeem is a

Royal who has been blessed by Vanadevi herself. As such, he deserves our respect and our protection."

Kirosko shook his head, frowning. He wasn't going to agree. What was she going to do?

"Very well," Selka said. Kirosko glared at Selka, but she ignored him. "This truly is for the best, Alatore. By the time your son reaches the age of ascension, no one will consider him a potential heir. That fact will protect him into adulthood."

Alatore wanted to protest some more, to beg and plead for them to allow her to keep Takeem with her. Instead, she turned her back on the Council and walked out.

Arioan followed.

They walked in silence to the Royal quarters, Hulak at their side.

"We should tell him why," Alatore said. "I can't let him think I don't love him anymore. I can't—"

"If we tell him why, no one will believe we've abandoned him. They won't believe it because he won't believe it. Mother—" Arioan stopped in the middle of the hallway and turned to face Alatore. "We have to do this to protect him, to keep him safe. If we fail here, they will execute him."

Alatore nodded. Unable to respond, she strode forward, demanding three servants they encountered along the way accompany them.

Alatore flung open the doors to the Royal quarters and walked inside.

"Mama!" Takeem jumped up from the floor where he and Devix were playing a board game. "I missed you. Come play with us."

Blinking back tears, Alatore stared at the wall above Takeem's head. She could do this. She would do this. She had done much worse to protect her sons. This was nothing. "You three, I need you to pack Takeem's things. Devix, you'll need to pack your own."

Devix stood. "What's going on?"

"You and Takeem are moving this night," Arioan said. "You're being relocated to the servant quarters."

Arioan followed Devix to his room, their voices fading into the background.

Alatore ignored them, heart pounding as the servants bustled around, packing Takeem's toys and clothes, stacking everything at the door to be moved later.

She was losing her son.

"Mama?" Takeem stood in front of her. "Where am I going? You're coming too, right?"

Alatore drew in a deep breath and looked down at Takeem. Aware the servants had slowed their pace and were listening, that this conversation would be repeated throughout the palace, that what she said here might determine the Council's actions for or against her son in the future, Alatore chose her words with care.

"You're ten years old now, Takeem. You're old enough to understand your place in this world. You're spinner-born which means you cannot inherit the throne."

The look on Takeem's face was one of confusion and dawning pain.

Hardening her heart, refusing to acknowledge his pain or her own, Alatore continued, "Truthfully you have no place in the world of Blues. Spinners do not belong this side of the rings." Alatore's voice trembled, then grew strong. "The Council is well within its rights to exile you. Instead, you're simply being moved."

"Where? I don't want to go."

"You have no choice. Devix will accompany you. If you need anything, you're to go to him."

"What about you? What about Arioan?"

"We're very busy people, Takeem. I'm the queen and Arioan is in training. Should I die, he needs to be prepared to take my place. We don't have time to waste."

"But what about me?"

"You'll be fine, Takeem."

"My Lady, the Tekhlan are here."

Alatore whirled to face the door. Yezyr stood there, the red sash of leadership with two royal-blue beasts lunging down it around his waist. Behind him stood three other members of the

Tekhlan.

Before she could speak, Arioan and Devix appeared, each carrying a box. "Why are you here?" Arioan asked.

"We're here to escort the child with his things to his new living quarters," Yezyr said. He glanced at the boxes stacked by the door. "The child does not need any toys or books. And he won't have the space for all of this. Just the necessities. Understood?"

Alatore wanted to protest, but she knew everyone was watching to see how she reacted to this order. "He's correct. Leave what the boy won't need or be able to store."

The servants quickly sorted what was in the boxes until only two remained to carry with them.

"Come, Takeem." Arioan held out his hand. "I will accompany you to your new quarters."

Takeem didn't move.

Alatore drew in a deep breath, settled her hand on his shoulder and slid it down his back, prolonging the moment as long as she could. She then gave him a little push, causing him to stumble forward. "Go on, Takeem," she said, infusing her voice with a sharp coldness. "It's time for you to leave now."

Takeem slowly walked toward Arioan, who stood waiting with the Tekhlan.

Alatore turned away, unable to watch as her son was taken from her. She stood there as the room emptied of people, until the door had closed behind the last servant, until silence fell.

She had failed. Takeem was so young, the same age Arioan had been when Vukel wanted to take him to war. She'd protected Arioan, kept him safe.

Why couldn't she do the same for Takeem?

A textbook Takeem had been studying with his tutor caught her eye. *A History of the Spinner Wars.*

She grabbed the book. It fell open to a page Takeem must have bookmarked. There was a painting of the Mozkola marching through Sky territory, slaughtering both spinners and Skies. The caption read, "When spinners invaded, breaching the first two walls of Lutia and marching toward the third, King Joryn unleashed the Mozkola. The Skies who lived between the first and third walls of Lutia died alongside the spinners, sacrificed beneath the swords of the dark ones. Despite their efforts, no spinner breached the third wall in that invasion, nor has any spinner since."

Takeem had written three words beneath the caption in his neat, tiny print.

Except for me.

Alatore's legs buckled and she fell to her knees. What if his tutor had seen this? What if *anyone* had seen this?

The Council was right. If Takeem believed he might one day inherit, others would believe it too. And if others believed it, he'd be executed.

It wasn't important that Takeem was the true heir to the throne, that he was their rightful king. What was important was convincing everyone of the opposite and somehow protecting him long enough that he might live to the age of ascendency, so that one day, he might claim the throne or choose to walk away from it.

All she'd ever wanted for both her sons was the chance to choose their own destinies.

Alatore turned her hand over and stared at her palm.

Takeem was their king, no matter what her palm said, no matter that his mark was Sky-Blue. He was the true heir and all it would take was one small act on her part to reveal that truth.

And then he'd die. He was too young to defend himself, to stand strong against his enemies.

So Alatore, Arioan and Devix would have to stand strong for him.

By convincing him he had no worth in the world of Blues.

*

Arioan led the way down into the old Sky quarters.

Takeem walked behind him in silence.

The Tekhlan surrounded them on all sides.

Arioan wanted to hold Takeem's hand, to reassure him, but the Tekhlan were watching everything.

They arrived at a room and an argument ensued over its

suitability.

Arioan ended the argument. The room was completely unacceptable. He might be willing to allow Takeem to be moved to servant quarters to save his life, but Takeem would be protected while there. He would be safe.

They made their way to the next room, Takeem protesting as they went.

It broke Arioan's heart, but he did what must be done.

"Takeem." Arioan faced his brother, steeled himself for what he was about to say, for what he was about to do. "You do not belong with us any longer. You are spinner-born. We are Royals. You will find your place, but it is not with us."

He turned away from the pain on Takeem's face. This was madness.

The second room was as unacceptable as the first, but at least it offered more protection. Still he wanted to protest.

What could he say though? That his brother was meant to be king? That he deserved better than this? The Council had made their terms clear. Anything less than compliance would end in Takeem's death. It wasn't worth the risk.

Furniture was moved into the room and all too soon, it was time for Arioan to leave his brother behind.

"Be good for Devix, Takeem."

The Tekhlan moved into the hallway.

Arioan waited until they were far enough away, then quickly pulled from the folds of his tunic his favorite childhood book. He'd planned to give it to Takeem as a birthday gift. Instead, it had become a gift of goodbye.

He handed it to Takeem. "Keep this hidden. Follow Devix's orders and you'll be fine." Resisting the urge to hug his brother one last time, Arioan walked out.

"Arioan, wait!" Takeem barreled into him, flinging his arms around his waist and hugging him tight. "Don't leave me here. Why can't I stay with you? Please don't leave me alone."

Arioan closed his eyes in pain. Surely this was the worst thing he'd ever endured. He lifted a hand, unable to resist, desperate to hug Takeem back, to lift him into his arms, to -

Takeem was gone.

Arioan opened his eyes.

Devix had pulled Takeem away and had his arms wrapped around him, though Takeem struggled and fought.

Devix lifted him up, nodded to Arioan and carried Takeem back to their rooms.

The last glimpse Arioan had of his brother was of Takeem struggling for freedom and crying out his name.

Arioan turned and walked away. Though Takeem's cries rang in his ears and he could barely breathe for the pain, he never looked back.

Long moments later, Arioan reached the quarters he'd always shared with Takeem, his mother and Devix, the quarters he now shared with his mother alone.

Alatore sat on the divan, clutching a book in her arms, weeping softly.

Arioan settled beside her, wrapped an arm around her shoulders and pulled her close.

She buried her face in his shoulder and cried.

Arioan closed his eyes and tried not to think at all, but all he could picture was the look on Takeem's face as Devix lifted him away, as Takeem begged Arioan not to leave him.

PRESENT DAY

SEEKING THE TRUTH

TAKEEM CAME OUT of the vision to find himself standing in the same position as before, fingers twined with Samantha's, tips touching his mother's name. He slowly pulled their hands down and stared at the wall.

"Takeem?" Samantha spoke his name quietly.

"I can't believe it. All this time. All this time I've hated her and she was protecting me. She was protecting me from everyone. From the Council, from the Royals, from the Tekhlan."

"She loves you so much, Takeem."

"Does she?" Takeem pulled away and began to pace around the room, examining his memories. "She never seeks me out, never speaks to me unless she has to. And when she does, she never looks at me."

"It must be horrible for her, Takeem. You're the rightful king and she's serving in your place, to guard the throne for you, but she can't acknowledge any of that – not her love for you, not your rightful place, none of it – because if she does, they'll kill you."

"She negotiated for my life the day I was born, then once more when I received the mark of the throne. Nonomay was right." Takeem came to a stop and stared at the floor. "Every moment of my life has been about love."

"Nonomay – oh, Takeem, we told her we were planning to release the magicks, but we can't."

"Of course, we can, Samantha. We will."

"They'll order your execution, Takeem. We'll destroy everything your mother worked for."

"Let them." So much was finally clear to him. Arioan and his mother, a thousand memories of each pressed upon him. And Hulak. Samantha was right. Hulak had joined them because it was him. All along, it was him, not Alatore.

"Takeem–"

"Hulak chose *me*, Samantha, before I was even born."

"I know."

"I don't even know how to deal with that, but it changes everything."

"I know."

"Samantha–" Takeem shook his head. He couldn't quite grasp it. "What am I going to do?"

Samantha smiled. "You're going to claim your birthright, Takeem. And then you are going to be a truly great king."

Takeem drew in a deep breath. "Mine may be the shortest reign in history, but I intend for it to change the world."

The door burst open.

Takeem whirled and drew his sword.

Marconen stood in the doorway. "Come. Nonomay has sent the Tekhlan in the opposite direction from the shrine. She will meet us in the holding area."

Takeem hesitated, uncertain whether they could trust Marconen.

"I know what you're thinking, but Nonomay told me you intend to release the ancestral magicks of Lutia. Is this true?"

"It is," Takeem said.

"The spinners and Skies have searched for a way to release the magicks for years. The lands are dying without the magicks to nourish them and the people are dying with them. We Skies living so close to the War Zone have pledged our lives to the quest for the magicks. If you intend to release them, we will help you."

"Then we welcome your assistance, Marconen, with our thanks." Takeem gave a small bow.

"Follow me." Marconen led them through the dark woods. The trees parted with each step they took, revealing a path before them. "There are a few places where the magicks still live. These woods that house the Trees of Lutia is one such place. The trees recognize the End Song walks the land once more."

"How far do these woods stretch?" Takeem asked.

"A week ago, not very far at all. Today, however, the trees of Bipin on the fields of Shorel stand strong in life once more. These woods now stretch all the way to them and beyond. We'll not go that far, however. Here." He stopped. "We'll need to cross a barren patch of land to the holding area where the village's krutesks are housed."

"Krutesks – like the beasts the Tekhlan ride?" Samantha asked.

"Yes. They will carry us to the Holy Shrine. Come." Marconen stepped forward and the branches before him parted, allowing moonlight to drift into the darkened forest.

Takeem grabbed Samantha's hand and they hesitantly stepped out into the night.

"We're headed there." Marconen pointed to a large structure about a hundred feet from where they stood. "It would be best if Hulak stays in his smaller form, in case the Tekhlan are still around. He's too noticeable in his larger one." Without waiting for a response, Marconen took off running toward the building.

Takeem and Samantha followed. As they neared the structure, two Sky men stepped out and ushered them through a small entrance. The men shut the door behind them.

The inside was lit with lanterns and there were two rows of stalls, one on each of the long walls. The stalls were empty, their beasts standing in the center of the cavernous room, Sky-Blues mounted upon them.

Samantha had known the krutesks were tall, but now that she was on the ground with them, she was amazed at how they towered over her. Their legs alone were at least seven feet tall. They had sleek torsos and narrow heads with pointed ears that moved independently of one another, swiveling and tilting toward the sounds around them.

"Takeem." Nonomay stepped forward from the shadows. "These men will accompany you to the Shrine."

"Nonomay, we would make better time on our own," Takeem protested.

"Yes, but the Tekhlan are already at the Shrine."

"What?" Samantha gasped.

"One of our men overheard them. They've already been to the shrine. They left half their men there, guarding its entrance."

"You need protection," Marconen spoke up. "We are here to offer it. You cannot win this battle on your own."

"You should not involve yourselves," Takeem said. "You risk everything by participating. The Tekhlan are ruthless. Nonomay, your entire village will be in danger from these actions."

"This is our battle as much as it is yours, Takeem." A Sky-Blue they had not met before spoke up. "We need those magicks returned. Our people aren't starving, not yet, but in another ten years, they will be. The lands are dying, riverbeds drying up." He scowled. "The River of Lutia runs free again and the fields of Shorel are blooming, but they will die once more without the magicks to feed them. We have pledged our lives to this cause and we will not walk away, not now that there is hope."

"I understand. I had not realized the full consequences of the loss of magicks, the long-term effects on the lands and the peoples of Lutia. Now that I know, though, I will not rest until the magicks are released. My heartfelt pledge to each of you." Takeem made eye contact with each person standing there. "You need not risk your lives. This duty is mine to bear."

"And ours is to shield and protect you along the way," Marconen said firmly.

Murmurs of agreement filled the room.

The faces around Takeem were filled with stubborn determination. Nothing he said would convince any of them to stay behind. "Very well," he reluctantly agreed. "In that case, I am most sincerely grateful for your help."

"All of you need to go now," Nonomay spoke up. "I do not know how long it will take for the Tekhlan to realize they have lost your trail and turn back. Travel fast, through the night if you can. Get to the Shrine as quickly as possible. Protect Takeem and Samantha, protect the End Song, at all costs."

"We ride." Marconen leapt upon his krutesk.

Two men brought two krutesks forward for Takeem and Samantha. Takeem shook his head. "We'll ride together on Hulak." The nargnet shimmered into his larger form.

"We cannot protect you if you fly," Marconen protested.

Takeem smiled. "Hulak may have wings, but he also has four legs. We'll do fine on his back."

"We refilled your packs," one of the men stated. He quickly pulled one down from each of the krutesks and tossed them to Takeem, who slung them across Hulak's shoulders.

A few moments later, the group exploded from the structure and raced out across the lands. Takeem and Samantha, on Hulak, were at the center of the group. All around them, Skies were mounted on krutesks, racing in a protective formation, keeping the three of them at their center.

"It's gotten so dark," Samantha murmured. "How will we see?"

"The krutesks have amazing night vision," Takeem told her. "As does Hulak. They'll take us where we need to go. Try to rest now. At this speed, it will take us all night and much of the morning to arrive at the Shrine."

*

Samantha dozed off and on throughout the night, listening to the sounds of the men talking and the drumming hooves of the krutesks they rode. She kept her eyes closed, so she could imagine Jonathan riding at their side. He'd be on his own krutesk, thrilled at the adventure of riding a creature neither had imagined, but that their world had somehow created for itself.

How rich and wondrous our world is, Jonathan, she whispered to him in the quiet of her mind. What a gift we gave ourselves.

While she dreamed of Jonathan, Takeem spent the evening getting to know the Skies around them, learning their names and their stories. Samantha overheard one of those conversations when laughter jarred her awake.

She sat in Takeem's arms. At some point, he had lifted and turned her so that she sat sideways in front of him, his arms wrapped around her, her head tucked beneath his chin, the beat of his heart lulling her to sleep.

"And you, Marconen?" Takeem's voice rumbled above her. "Nonomay mentioned your parents were dead?"

"Yes." Marconen's voice was cold. "My father was killed by yours and my mother died giving birth to me shortly thereafter."

"I'm sorry, Marconen. It seems my father killed many in his time. Do you have no siblings?"

"I do not. I have a younger cousin and that is all."

"Lourx?"

"How do you know that name?"

"Nonomay mentioned his name, that the two of you were her grandsons."

"Lourx is her great-grandson, my cousin's only child. He's nine. We're the last of the Ryvar family."

"Ryvar? I know that name. The Ryvars of Soryn."

"You should know it. It was my entire family your father slaughtered in his quest to reunite with your mother."

"The Ryvars – you're the ones who kidnapped my mother!" The shock in Takeem's voice was palpable.

Marconen snorted. "Right. Well, never fear, young Takeem. All the evil kidnappers are dead now and the Mendacious Queen has been returned to her rightful place, far from Sky territory, completely protected from the reality of her lies."

"What's that supposed to mean?"

"It means, boy, that you know nothing of what happened in the Sky villages thirty years ago and until you do, you should not judge any Sky as being less honorable than the very best of the Royal race. When it comes to honor, the Royals have none." With that statement, Marconen urged his krutesk away.

Samantha pulled away from Takeem's chest. The dark of the night was receding in anticipation of the coming dawn, allowing her to see the tight line of his jaw. "Are you all right, Takeem?" she asked, lifting a hand to his cheek.

Takeem nodded jerkily.

"I heard what Marconen said. He's right. We don't know what happened thirty years ago. Which means we shouldn't judge the Skies or your mother too harshly. She was pregnant and then a new mother. She would have been desperate to protect Arioan."

"Truer words were never spoken." The voice was harsh, making the words that seemed an agreement sound mocking instead. Samantha glanced over and saw the Sky-Blue who had defended the Skies' right to accompany them riding in Marconen's spot.

"I'm sorry, what was your name?"

"I am Revik, my lady."

"Revik, I'm Samantha and this is Takeem."

Revik smiled. "I know, my lady."

"What did you mean? About what I said?"

"Alatore was very frightened thirty years ago and she was very much in fear for her life and for the life of Arioan. What you have to ask yourself, young Takeem, is whether she feared the Skies she was with or the Tekhlan who were pursuing them." Revik yanked on his reigns and guided the krutesk away. Another Sky rode forward and took his spot.

Takeem's jaw was still clenched, now with a muscle flexing.

"Takeem?"

"Let me be, Samantha. We can talk later."

*

The sun was just peeking over the horizon when they came to a halt by the river of Lutia. They needed to rest the krutesks before journeying on.

Samantha and Takeem ate a snack, then stretched out on the ground for a short rest.

Samantha settled her cheek upon Takeem's chest and her hand over his heart and waited.

A few moments passed in silence before he spoke. "I've never doubted the story my mother told because it wasn't only told by her. It's in the history books. The king's sister, Alatore, was kidnapped, shot in a confrontation between the Tekhlan and the Skies who held her, believed dead and left in Sky territory for almost a year. She gave birth to the son of Vukel, her Royal fiancé, in Sky territory and that child, Arioan, was already six weeks old when the Tekhlan finally caught up to them. Thousands of Skies died in the pursuit and rescue of her." He fell silent as he and Samantha reflected on this recitation of facts.

"The Skies are implying the history books are wrong, that my mother's story is nothing but lies. Was she even a victim at all?"

"Vukel was vicious in his treatment of the Skies, Takeem. Maybe she wasn't kidnapped at all. Maybe she was running from him."

"Yes, but if she was afraid of the Tekhlan, if she was running from my father, how did she end up with him? And why do so many Skies in so many different villages call her the Mendacious Queen? I don't understand, Samantha."

"I know." She reached up a hand and caressed his face.

"Why didn't the trees share the rest of the story of what happened between my mother and Vukel? Why all that stupid stuff from the past, making me question everything I've always known?"

"I don't know, Takeem. Try to rest, okay? We've only got a little time before we have to leave."

"Rest. Right. What if a Shrouded One grows while we're resting, Samantha? We don't have time to rest. The Tekhlan could catch up with us at any moment."

"We're not going to be here long enough for a tree to grow around us. Just enjoy the peace and quiet."

Takeem tightened his arms around her. She was probably right. He drew in a deep breath and allowed his body to relax.

ALATORE, 30 YEARS AGO

KILLING THOUSANDS

Sky-Blue Village of Lieria, Year 100 AP

Vukel had found out. Somehow he knew and was chasing them again. After everything Brenin had done, after all he had sacrificed for them to be safe, Vukel had discovered the truth.

Alatore wished Brenin was there, to help her, to give her strength. He was the bravest man she'd ever known, but he'd been gone for seven months now. It seemed a lifetime ago.

She knew what had to be done. She simply had to find the courage to do it. Studying the last note Brenin had left for her, Alatore tried to read his blessing in the message.

"Be safe, my love. Protect our child, by any means necessary. Survive, Alatore. I love you. We will be together again. I am yours, always, Brenin."

Protect our child, by any means necessary. That was like a blessing, wasn't it?

She'd come so close to dying from that arrow. It had been a miracle she hadn't lost the child, that she hadn't bled to death before they reached a healer.

Once Brenin was certain she and their unborn child would live, he'd been desperate to protect them both. He'd built a false trail away, leading Vukel far from where she lay recovering. To sacrifice his life for hers.

Three weeks after they had parted, word had come that Vukel had caught up to Brenin in a village thirty kilometers to the south.

Brenin's body went home to Soryn for purification, but Alatore had been too afraid to attend the ceremony. What if Vukel came and discovered she was alive?

Brenin's family, his five remaining brothers, had protected her. They'd traveled with her, from Sky village to Sky village, never staying in one place for too long, always moving to keep from being discovered. Now she had to wonder if all of the movement was what had given them away. The more villages they visited, the more people knew of her continued survival. And now the Tekhlan were on their trail again and she had to make a decision.

In those first months on the run, she and Brenin had discussed their options. If the child was born a Sky-Royal, with skin as light as his father's, he would be easier to hide in the villages – just one more Sky child in a multitude of them.

If he was born a Royal-Sky, however, hiding him would be more difficult. Brenin had suggested if that were the case, she should consider going home. He'd brought that option up many times, not because he wanted to lose her, but because he desperately wanted her and their child to be safe. At the time, she'd refused to even consider going back to Vukel, but now, with the Tekhlan on their trail again and more Skies dying to keep them safe, she had to at least consider the possibility.

By any means necessary.

As if he'd heard his father's words, Arioan woke with a soft cry. Alatore hurried to his crib and lifted him into her arms. Crossing the room, she settled back into the rocking chair and settled Arioan at her breast. As she nursed Arioan, she became aware that the voices murmuring in the background had risen.

She'd used the excuse that Arioan needed a nap to escape the outer room and the discussions she knew would be taking place there. She'd hidden here in this small chamber and tried not to think about what they were deciding without her. The voices had grown too loud though and she could no longer ignore them.

"We cannot continue to protect her," Markyn said.

The five brothers were once more discussing what to do with her, where to go next.

Markyn had never been accepting of a Royal-Blue sister-in-law. He'd always felt she was not good enough, that she was too Royal, too different. He disliked her from the moment he met her. That dislike grew to hatred when four of his brothers were killed in their flight from Soryn, including Liden who had given up so much to accompany them on the journey from the palace to his home village of Soryn, where his life had ended.

When Brenin died to lead the Tekhlan away from her, Markyn began to actively speak out against her. He wanted his family safe. He wanted her gone.

"She must go," he said. "We cannot allow our entire family to be sacrificed for the sake of one child, especially for one of mixed blood."

"That child may one day rule this world. And his mixed blood may bring about true equality for our people." Torkyn was the most practical of her husband's family. He was rational and calm in the face of danger and was adamant that Arioan be protected for the good of all the races.

Alatore didn't care about politics. She wasn't interested in helping the Skies attain the throne anymore than she wanted to hold it herself. She wanted peace for the Blues and for the spinners, so many years in exile now. She wanted peace for her son. Her beautiful son.

Holding him in her arms, she contemplated the uncertainty of his future. Though Brenin had been pure Sky-Blue, her son's skin, hair and eyes were as royal as her own, a fact that might one day save his life. If she lied and claimed his father was a Royal, that his father was Vukel, who would dispute that? The proof was right there for anyone to see.

It filled Alatore with sadness to know that Brenin's gorgeous sky eyes had died with him, that his light blue hair and skin would not grace any of their children. Still, she could see something of Brenin in Arioan, something that transcended color. It was there in the tilt of his nose, in the texture of his hair, in the wide roundness of his eyes. She could see what many never would – her husband – in the face of their son, Arioan.

Filled with a kind of aching tenderness she'd never known she was capable of, Alatore gently kissed the riot of dark blue curls on top of Arioan's head. She would do anything, bargain with anyone, to protect her son.

"They say Volya has fallen," Markyn said. "An entire village sacrificed for what? To save a Royal-Blue heir and her son."

"That son is your nephew," Loren, another of the brothers, said.

A jumble of voices started talking, but Alatore could not tell who was speaking.

Volya has fallen.

What did that mean? Were the inhabitants of Volya dead?

She could not comprehend it.

Was this what had happened to Soryn? To Belia? To Kornal? To all the Sky villages she had visited this past year?

To all those wonderful, gentle, peace-loving Skies she had met along the way? Had all of them died for her and for Arioan?

Was this then their legacy? She and Arioan, spreading death and destruction everywhere they went?

It was too much.

It had always been too much. And it would never be enough.

She simply hadn't realized it yet. She'd been willing to watch the entire world burn for Arioan, but it wasn't enough to save him. All those losses would be in vain.

Vukel would never give up and the Skies would continue to pay the price for them to have just one more day, just one more hour.

"Oh, Arioan," she whispered, burying her face in his soft curls. "I'm so sorry, my sweet."

She stood and exited the back bedroom, Arioan snug in her arms.

No one noticed her arrival.

The men were seated around a large eating table and were fiercely debating where they should go next.

Should they head for Mozkola territory in the mountains of Lixor, attempting to cross its peaks toward spinner territory?

Should they seek the nesting grounds in Royal territory and beg the nargnets for protection?

The only thing they agreed on was they could not stay in Sky territory, but these other options involved huge risk as well. The Mozkola were dark beings of magick who guarded their territory fiercely and would destroy any caught trespassing upon their mountains. The nesting grounds were too deep into Royal territory to be anything but pure folly to head there. Besides, the Nargnet King was companion to the Royal King of Lutia, Alatore's brother. Could the nargnets even be trusted to help them?

"We cannot continue to protect her," Markyn said once more, bringing the argument full circle. "And why should we even try?"

"He's right." Alatore stepped further into the room. "It's time."

The brothers fell silent.

"Time for what?" Torkyn asked.

"For what must come next." Moving forward so that she stood at the end of the table and faced the five remaining brothers of Brenin, Alatore made eye contact with Markyn. "I cannot express how thankful I am, how thankful we are, for your help."

Markyn frowned and looked away.

"But Markyn is right. The time for flight has passed. There is only one way to end this. Only one way for me to save my son."

"No, Alatore!" Markyn leapt to his feet, shocking her with his protest. Of all the brothers, she had thought he was the one who would support this course of action. "Not after all of this! That bastard doesn't get to win you back, not after what he has done."

"I am so sorry, Markyn. You were right all along. You were right."

A door slammed open at the front of the building. "The Tekhlan are here!" A young Sky man barreled inside. "They are gathering everyone! They are here!"

Markyn leapt toward Alatore, grabbed her arm and dragged her toward the back of the building.

"Go, Markyn! Get them to safety!" Torkyn raced to the front.

"We will delay the Tekhlan!"

Markyn pulled Alatore out the back door. The nargnet, Klarina, stood waiting in her larger form, wings already launched, ready to take them away by flight.

"Markyn, no, please. Listen to me. None of this can end well."

"Be silent." He shoved her toward Klarina. "Give me the boy."

Alatore hesitated. She hated that she could not mount the nargnet with him in her arms.

"We must leave now, Alatore!"

Feeling as if her heart was being torn from her chest, she passed Arioan to Markyn, then turned and, reaching high, grabbed hold of Klarina's shaggy fur. She lifted a foot and set it against Klarina's side, lunging upward. Slinging one arm across Klarina's neck, she grasped handfuls of orange and yellow fur and pulled herself onto the nargnet's back.

Markyn held Arioan up to her and Alatore leaned down to take him.

Pffft!

An arrow slammed into Markyn's back, flinging him forward into Klarina's side. In one desperate lunge toward each other, Markyn and Alatore managed to make contact. She caught Arioan's body in her right arm and with her left, grasped hold of Markyn's hand.

"Markyn," she whispered, holding tight to his hand.

"Go!" He pulled his hand away and fell backward.

For a moment, Alatore was frozen. Somehow this death impacted her as much as Brenin's had. Brenin had loved her, had died for love of her, but Markyn – Markyn had hated her, had claimed she brought doom to all those around her and had wanted her gone. He'd been a well of bitterness against her and had made it plain he was not willing to sacrifice his brothers on her behalf, nor did he intend to die for her himself. Yet there he lay upon the ground, dead for her cause, and the grief was an endless tide rising to choke her.

Klarina rose to her feet and spread her wings.

A second arrow zipped through the air, tearing through Klarina's neck. Blood sprayed and Klarina collapsed.

"No!" Alatore cried out, barely managing to hold onto Arioan as the nargnet fell to her knees.

Klarina swayed there, blood pouring from her wound.

Alatore slid to the ground and Klarina toppled to the side in a thundering crash.

Cradling Arioan in one arm, Alatore sank to her knees beside Klarina and stroked a hand down her side. There was no movement. Death had taken another innocent, this time a nargnet who had been the kindest of companions.

Shaking, crying, Alatore looked up.

Vukel stood a few feet away, bow in hand, watching her grimly. He looked furious.

Oh, Vanadevi, help them. She had to make amends, somehow, for Arioan's sake.

"Vukel," she whispered.

"So. You are alive."

"Vukel, I—"

"Do you see what your running has done? Another man dead because of you. And worse, an innocent nargnet. Two who might have served in the war zone, fighting for the Blues, protecting our lands, instead lie dead on the ground. For what? So that you might defy your brother, so that you might defy me?"

Alatore shook her head. "I'm sorry, Vukel. I never meant for anyone to be hurt. I just wanted to be with—" She stopped at the look on his face.

"Yes. With your Sky lover. And how did that work out for you? The man is dead now, Alatore, killed because he dared touch you. And all those Sky men and women who have died protecting you, who might have served the throne, who might have protected our lands from the spinners, are lost to us forever. And do you hear that?" He cocked his head as if listening.

The sounds of battle carried to them from the front of the house.

"More innocents are dying for you. Is this what you wanted?" Spearing her with his gaze, he demanded, "Well? Is it?"

"No, Vukel. I am sorry. I just—"

Arioan opened his eyes and cried out in protest.

Alatore's arms tightened around him at the look on Vukel's face. *Oh, Vanadevi, please protect her son.*

Vukel strode toward her.

"Vukel, please, Vukel, wait! Listen!"

Vukel grabbed her arm and dragged her to her feet. When she stood before him, he snatched Arioan from her arms.

"Please, Vukel, no!"

Vukel turned and began to stride away.

"Vukel!" Alatore screamed, darting after him. "Please, wait! He's Royal, Vukel. He's Royal!"

Vukel stopped and turned to face Alatore.

Tears pouring down her face, Alatore skidded to a stop in front of Vukel.

"He's Royal, Vukel. Please, just let me—" With shaking hands, she reached out and carefully peeled the blanket away from Arioan's face, revealing his dark Royal skin.

Vukel drew in a deep breath. "Show me the rest," he demanded, handing the babe back to Alatore. With quick movements, Alatore stripped the swaddling cloth away from Arioan, revealing deeply Royal limbs, torso and body. Arioan cried out in protest as the cold air reached his skin.

"Shhh, Ari, it's okay, baby." Quickly wrapping the cloth around Arioan again, Alatore dared a quick look at Vukel.

"Give him to me."

Alatore hesitated, then slowly passed him back to Vukel. Vukel held the babe up in front of him and jostled him a bit.

Arioan whimpered and opened his royal eyes.

"Your genes bred true, then," Vukel said. "Your lover truly was inferior, for his blood has not tainted your son even a tiny bit."

Alatore swallowed the protest she wanted to make and instead answered quietly, "Yes, Vukel."

Vukel pulled the child to his chest and held him there with one arm, staring at Alatore silently, a cold and calculating look on his face. "If I accept this child, you will be mine. You will not fight. You will allow me to raise him as I see fit. You will marry me and you will proclaim to the world that this child is mine, that you were kidnapped by the Sky-Blues while pregnant with my child,

and that I saved you from them. You will never deny this truth.
You will never tell this child the truth of his origins. He will never
know of his Sky-Blue heritage. He will be Royal in every way
though he will never inherit the throne. And you, Alatore, you
will be mine. In every single way."

Trembling with fear, understanding that this moment would
determine the course of all their futures, that Arioan might yet
still die unless she was willing to make this deal, Alatore nodded
and whispered, "Yes, Vukel. Anything."

"Say it." His voice was cold and sharp as a blade.

"I will be yours." Alatore spoke woodenly. "Arioan will be
yours. I was kidnapped and you saved me. There is no other
truth."

"Good." Vukel handed Arioan back to Alatore, turned her so
that her back rested against his front, wrapped his arms around
her and the babe, and leaned down to settle his chin upon her
curls. Looking down at the babe in her arms, Vukel murmured
softly, "Now then, my dear. Introduce me to my son."

*

A short time later, Vukel led Alatore back into the safe house,
through the common rooms toward the front door. He carried
Arioan, though she had begged to keep him. Vukel stepped
outside onto the porch, and she followed. The safe house stood in
a long line of houses. Between that line and the houses across the
way lay a wide, dirt road. The Tekhlan lined both sides of the
road and on their knees between them, kneeling in the dust, were
the Skies of this village. Hundreds of men, women and children,
babes in their mothers' arms. They were staring at the ground in
hopelessness. Soft weeping met Alatore's ears. How many had
already died here? How many had the Tekhlan already killed?

Vanadevi, help them.

"My son!" Vukel raised Arioan high so that his blanket fell
away, revealing his darkly Royal skin.

Arioan cried out in protest.

"Vanadevi on high!"

Roars of triumph resounded as the Tekhlan warriors raised

their swords high and shouted back, "Vanadevi!"

Turning, Vukel placed Arioan in Alatore's arms.

Clutching her son close, trembling so hard she feared she might drop him, Alatore slowly looked up, her gaze caught by Torkyn's Sky-Blue one. Torkyn, the mirror image of Markyn, the brother whose body still lay behind the courthouse. She could barely face Torkyn after what had just happened, at the knowledge of what she had done. All those lives wasted. All those lives lost. For nothing.

She wanted to fall to her knees and beg his forgiveness. Explain that it was the only way she knew to save her son. Apologize for wasting so many lives. If only she had not run. If only she had stayed home. But then she would not have Arioan and she would never have known the joy of her husband's love.

Alatore's ears were ringing, her shame and misery almost drowning out what Vukel was saying. He was pacing between the rows of kneeling Skies, handing down the king's judgment.

"This entire village is in defiance of the throne. For holding the Royal heir and his mother hostage, this village and all its inhabitants are forfeit."

"What?" Alatore gasped. "Vukel, no. Mercy, please. Please, Vukel."

"Do you hear that? My beautiful betrothed pleads mercy on your behalf. And yet, I have none to give. You have offended the throne. You have acted against the Tekhlan, you have committed treasonous acts and you show no remorse." Vukel now stood at Torkyn's back.

"Oh, Vanadevi, no," Alatore whispered, staring into Torkyn's eyes. "I'm so sorry." Tears slid down her cheeks as Vukel gripped Torkyn's head and with one horrendous wrench, broke his neck. The sound echoed through the streets, again and again and again and again, until finally Alatore realized it wasn't an echo. It was simply happening over and over and over again, to many of the Skies who knelt there.

The remaining Skies lunged to their feet and rushed the Tekhlan, who pulled their korelian blades and struck them down.

Blood flowed.

Women screamed, men shouted, babes cried.

The world seemed full of madness, the wails of children overpowering even the sounds of death, then those too fell silent.

Alatore's knees buckled and she landed on the ground, Arioan still cradled in her arms. Burying her face in his softness, she tried not to hear the sounds of death and grief that permeated the air. "It's okay, baby. It's okay," she crooned softly as the world died around her.

When silence fell, Vukel's boots appeared before her. "Let's go, my dear." He reached down and gently helped her to her feet. Alatore kept her eyes on the ground as he turned her to march out of the village.

"Oh, no, Alatore, dear. You will look and you will see what your selfishness has wrought." Cupping her chin, he gently pulled her head up.

Alatore closed her eyes in reflex.

"Open your eyes, darling. You cannot learn this lesson if you refuse to see."

Alatore shook her head, trembling and incapable of speech.

"We will stand here all day then, surrounded by the dead, waiting for you to find your courage."

The silence around her had a weight and a presence. It thundered inside her like the heartbeat of death.

No one moved.

The Tekhlan, such killing machines, were still now. Waiting.

This was not her doing, not her fault. She had not done this. She had not.

Unable to stand the silence anymore, Alatore opened her eyes.

There were no words to describe what filled her vision. No words to describe the horror of her surroundings.

Rivers of blood in the streets. Bodies piled on top of each other. Eyes unseeing. Babies and children. Mothers and fathers. The elderly. The young. Innocence everywhere. And at the center of it all, Torkyn. His eyes open, unseeing, accusation in them. Accusation everywhere. In all the eyes sightlessly staring.

This was all her doing, all her fault. She had done this. She had.

As blackness swept Alatore's vision, she curled her body around her son, her last thought of him.

Arioan.

The son for whom she had killed thousands.

PRESENT DAY

JOURNEY'S END

TAKEEM'S EYES SNAPPED open. How long had they slept? Long enough for a Shrouded One to grow.

He leapt to his feet, dragging Samantha with him. "Samantha, come on. We've got to get out of here."

"What? Wait, again? We weren't resting that long, were we?"

"I don't know. Come on." He started pulling her toward the vines.

"Wait. Takeem." Samantha pulled her arm free.

"What is it?"

"Your mother, I mean—"

Takeem nodded. "I know. She wasn't a victim of the Skies after all. We should go now."

"Okay." Samantha caught his hand and they walked from beneath the Shrouded One to find the entire camp impatiently awaiting their arrival.

"I don't know how that happened," Marconen said as he mounted his krutesk, "and while it was amazing to watch a Shrouded One grow in less than an hour, we don't have the time to waste talking about it. Everyone mount up. We ride for the Shrine, no stops."

Takeem and Samantha climbed onto Hulak and within moments, they were on the move, racing toward the mountains in the distance.

Hulak pushed his way forward so they rode at Marconen's

side.

"The Shrouded Ones grow for Samantha," Takeem said. "The latest shared my mother's memories of the events at Lieria. They made me hate my father."

"You cannot possibly hate him more than I do," Marconen said.

Takeem nodded. "You probably think all those deaths were meaningless, but they were not. If Vukel had reached my mother before Arioan's birth, he would have either ensured the babe died in her womb, or executed them both. Either way, Arioan would not be alive today were it not for the Skies who sheltered my mother during those long months of her pregnancy."

"I do not resent her actions before Arioan's birth. We would all of us die to ensure his life. After he was born, though, she should have gone home and spared all those Sky lives immediately."

"Perhaps, but there was no guarantee Vukel would accept Arioan and that was a risk she would not take. It's so easy to look back and speak of what she should have done, but I cannot imagine the desperation she must have felt to protect Arioan from the Tekhlan. Regardless, my family owes you and all the Skies a debt we can never repay."

"Release the magicks, Takeem, and we will consider your debt paid in full." Marconen kicked his krutesk and rode away.

*

The sun was high in the sky when they reached the base of the mountain of Vanadevi. The Holy Shrine was at the very top of the mountain and the Trail of Truth began very close to its peak. Hulak could fly them to the base of the Trail of Truth, as he had done before, but they would have to walk the Trail to the Shrine, risking attack as they did so. To make matters worse, Hulak had flown them high enough to get a look and the Tekhlan were stationed along the Trail, all the way to the peak.

"We'll have to fight our way to the top," Takeem reported to the Skies when they landed, worry in his voice.

"That's not good," Marconen said. "You cannot keep purity in your heart while waging war. Your thoughts need to be focused when running the Trail, focused on your determination to return the magicks to the peoples of Lutia."

"I know."

"Is there a spot below the Trail where Hulak can carry us?" Revik asked. "Where we can gather?"

"There's a cliff not far below the Trail, beyond the bend. It should be out of sight. What are you thinking?"

"That it's time we Skies take a stand," Revik said. "If Hulak gets us to that cliff, we will clear a path for you to run the Trail of Truth."

Samantha worried her bottom lip with her teeth. "That sounds dangerous," she said.

Marconen smiled. "A little perhaps, but it will be our honor to serve the End Song and her king." His eyes met Takeem's.

Takeem hesitated then nodded.

"Takeem?" Samantha didn't like what was happening.

"Everything will be fine, Samantha. Do you want to stay here?"

"No! No, we go together, always."

"All right, then. How do you want to do this, Marconen?"

"Hulak can take, what, three at a time?"

"Yeah, I think so."

"Right, it should take about eight trips for him to get us all up there. I'll go up first, you come up on the fourth round."

"We'll see you up there." Takeem held out his arms in the classic warrior pose and Marconen did the same. The men clasped each other's arms in tribute and nodded their heads.

"Marconen!" A Sky-Blue rushed toward them. "The Tekhlan have been sighted. They're riding for us at tremendous speeds. They'll be here soon."

"Take four of the men. Hold them off as best you can."

The Sky rushed away.

Marconen ordered the other men into groups, readying them for the flight up the mountain.

Hulak had delivered Marconen and eight other men to the cliff above them when the Tekhlan arrived in a rush of movement and arrows. There was no sign of the five men who had been sent to hold them off.

"Go. Quickly." Revik pushed Samantha and Takeem toward Hulak before lunging for the Tekhlan, sword raised, a fierce look upon his face. He collided with one of the men in a resounding clang of steel.

"Samantha, come on." Takeem was already on Hulak's back, reaching toward her.

Samantha grabbed his arm and he swung her up behind him. "Come with us!" she cried out to Revik.

"Go!" he shouted, not even looking back.

Hulak launched them skyward.

The Skies and Tekhlan battled in fierce lunges below them, blood flying. The shouts of men and the sounds of battle faded as Hulak flew them higher.

A few moments later, Hulak landed. Samantha and Takeem scrambled off his back. Hulak immediately hurtled over the cliff, headed for the men they had left behind.

"The Tekhlan are below," Samantha told Marconen. "The Skies are battling them."

Marconen glanced down the mountain, a look of despair upon his face.

"We can go back, Marconen, help them, before we go forward," Takeem offered.

"No," Marconen said. "They are trained; they knew what they were getting into. Hulak will bring up as many survivors as he can and we will all engage the Tekhlan so that you can make our world right again." He glanced around at the eight other Skies who had made it up the mountain. "Are we ready, men?"

The Skies straightened their spines. "We are," they said.

"You two stay in our midst, at the center," Marconen told Takeem and Samantha. "We will run the Trail of Truth together, we will stand between you and the Tekhlan. You focus on reaching the peak, on making it inside the Shrine."

"We will," Samantha whispered.

At that moment, Hulak hurtled around the mountain and landed above them. Three men climbed from his back, Revik and two others. One of them was dripping blood from a wound on his arm.

"The others?" Marconen asked.

"They didn't make it," Revik said. "The Tekhlan are coming up the mountain on their krutesks, but it will take them days. We'll be long gone by then."

"Good." Marconen looked toward the injured man. "Are you going to be all right, Tomer?"

"I'll be fine. Just a scratch." Tomer gave a reckless smile.

"All right. All we have to deal with, then, are the Tekhlan above us. Shelter the End Song at all costs, Takeem as well."

"Wait," Takeem said. "The Mountain will test anyone on the Trail. I have no idea how the Tekhlan are even managing to guard it."

"Because they don't intend to enter the Shrine, Takeem," Marconen said. "As long as their intent is simply to stand and guard the Trail, the Mountain will not test them. It's a good point though." Turning to his men, he said, "Be careful in your thoughts. Keep them focused on protecting Samantha and Takeem. If the mountain chooses to judge us, we will not be able to defend the End Song."

"Samantha and I will be tested, though, perhaps Hulak as well," Takeem said, "which means at some point, we will probably be separated. We won't see you or the Tekhlan. We'll be blind in a fog as the Mountain judges our intentions."

Marconen nodded and assigned six men to Takeem and six to Samantha.

"What about Hulak?" Samantha asked.

"Hulak will be fine," Takeem said. "He can take care of himself."

"Are you sure?"

"I promise. He'll be fine."

Marconen made a sharp movement with his hands and the twelve men surrounded Takeem, Samantha and Hulak, who was now in his smaller form.

"Let's go." Marconen led the way.

And so it was for the second time in as many days, Samantha raced along a mountainous path. This time, though, the danger was worse than ever. When they reached the Trail of Truth, half the Skies raced forward ahead of them and half fell back to guard their rear. The sounds of battle rang through the air, steel crossing steel and men's shouts of pain and triumph.

The fog rolled in quicker this time and the sounds of battle faded. She no longer feared what was to come; her entire being had become committed to one question, one burning question that had to be answered.

Hwanon.

*

As they ran, Takeem tried to block out everything but the task they had set for themselves – release the ancestral magicks of Lutia.

The fog blanketed the world in seconds, the Skies and Tekhlan around him fading from sight. A Royal-Blue stepped onto the path. It was Zarkonen. Behind him stood a young, spinner boy.

"You are not allowed here, spinner," Zarkonen said.

Takeem raced by, refusing to engage.

The boy cried out and Takeem faltered. He whirled to see that Zarkonen had his hand wrapped around the boy's neck and was holding him high. "Would you have this child's death be in vain?"

Takeem took a step back down the path toward Zarkonen, but it was too late. The boy fell to his knees, blood pouring from a wound at his neck.

Zarkonen stepped over the child's body, a vial of blood in his hand. "This blood was spilt for a reason, young Takeem. You are not strong enough to undo the spell we have spun."

"Perhaps not," Takeem said, "but I'm strong enough to try." He turned and moved up the Trail once more.

He'd only taken a few steps when Kessink appeared, a young spinner girl, maybe 6 or 7 years old, at his side.

*

Jennifer appeared on the path directly in front of Samantha. "Aunt Jenny!"

"You left me, Samantha. Why?"

"I'm sorry, Jenny. Really, I am. Please understand. " Samantha pushed by Jennifer, only to have her appear again, directly ahead.

"Why did you leave?"

"I'm sorry. I have to do this." Samantha walked past.

"You left me all alone, with only my grief for company." Jennifer stood in the middle of the path once more.

Samantha stopped. "I'm sorry."

"You do not love me."

"I do, Jenny, I do. I just – I need to find Jonathan."

"Jonathan's dead, Samantha."

"No." Samantha pushed past. "He's here. I know it. I feel it. He's here."

"Samantha." Jennifer stood on the path, blocking it once more. "Come home with me, Samantha."

"I can't. Jenny, I can't. Jonathan's here. I have to find him."

"He's not here, Samantha. He's dead."

"You're the one who's not here." Samantha stormed past Jennifer. "I know you're not here."

"Samantha." Jennifer appeared in front of her. "Please, stop. Come home. Please."

"My home is with Jonathan." Samantha picked up her speed, almost running to escape the Jennifers that kept appearing over and over again.

"I thought your home was with me, Samantha."

Samantha skidded to a stop. It was. Of course, it was. She couldn't leave Jennifer behind. Could she? Samantha turned to face Jennifer, who had somehow gotten behind her. "You're right. Of course, my home's with you." The Jennifers were all around her now.

"Come with me, Samantha. Please."

Samantha held out her hand.

Jennifer stepped forward and her jeans and t-shirt morphed into the black tunic and pants of the Tekhlan, red sash around her waist.

Samantha jerked back.

A Sky-Blue appeared behind the Tekhlan, impaling him on his sword. The Tekhlan cried out and the coppery scent of blood tinged the air.

Samantha turned and ran. More Jennifers appeared on the path, but Samantha did not stop again. As she ran, she could not help but hear Jennifer's desperate pleas.

"Samantha, please. Take me with you."

"Jonathan isn't here. He's gone, but I'm not. I need you."

"Samantha, my home is on Earth. I can't stay here. Please."

Samantha stopped. She stood at the top of the Trail, the entrance to the Shrine directly ahead.

One final Jennifer stood in the way.

Samantha walked toward her. "I thought your home was with me, Jenny."

*

How many advisors had he passed? How many children's deaths had he seen? Was it five or only four?

Loxoryon and Ferilis stepped onto the path, two young boys at their sides, one maybe ten, the other so young, he seemed a toddler still. Not these two as well.

"You should not be here, spinner-born," Loxoryon said. "Leave this holy place before you defile it with your presence."

"Your time is past," Takeem said, pushing his way forward.

"Nothing you do here will change anything," Ferilis vowed. "These children will still be dead." The two boys fell to the ground, their blood staining the world red. "The magicks will still be gone. And you, boy, you will share their fate, another spinner sacrificed for the greater good."

Takeem shoved his way through the pink-tinged fog. The world was coated in the scent and taste of blood, metallic and raw. He stumbled forward and almost fell. He stood at the top of the Trail, facing the Shrine. Torel and a young nargnet, so young her legs wobbled and she had no wings, stood in the middle of the path, blocking the entrance to the Shrine.

*

Samantha stared into Jennifer's eyes. Was this really Jennifer or another Tekhlan? "Please, Jenny, come with me."

Jennifer took Samantha's hand in her own. "Where are we going?"

"To find Jonathan."

"Where is he?"

"Where he's always been. He's beneath the willow, Aunt Jenny." Pulling Jennifer behind her, Samantha crossed the threshold into the Shrine of Vanadevi.

The moment the cool air of the Shrine touched Samantha's hand, she lost contact with Jennifer. Samantha swung around, but Jennifer was gone.

*

Takeem approached Torel and the gnetti. He'd never seen a young nargnet before. They had all died before he was born. She was beautiful with fuzzy, pink fur and round, black eyes full of innocence.

"Nothing you do here will stop what has happened," Torel said.

"No one can change the past," Takeem agreed. "But maybe I can make the world a better place for the future."

"You sound like Malcor. Always wanting to make the world a better place. Unwilling to accept the world as it was. You will fail, young Takeem. The Tekhlan will see you dead if you continue on this path."

Takeem stared into Torel's eyes. "I will undo what you have spun, Torel. Your legacy dies today." He walked past them both, resisting the urge to touch the gnetti, to draw her near. She wasn't really there. Nothing he could do would save her now.

As he neared the entrance to the Shrine, he heard a soft sound, a whimper or a melody, but he did not turn around. He did not want to see the life bleed from an innocent gnetti's eyes.

A rush of movement warned him and he turned in time to see Marconen engage a Tekhlan whose sword had been aimed at his back. Takeem stumbled and then he was across the threshold, the cool embrace of the Shrine welcoming him home.

His heart clenched at the sight of Samantha, waiting for him there.

*

"Takeem!" Samantha launched herself at him.

Takeem wrapped an arm around her shoulders and pulled her toward the stairs. "Come, quickly. The Tekhlan are right outside the entrance."

"Wait! Where's Hulak?"

At that moment, as if her question had summoned him, Hulak barreled across the threshold and skidded to a stop at their side.

"Let's go," Takeem said. "We need to hurry. I don't know how long the Skies can keep the Tekhlan from attempting to enter the Shrine."

This time, as they raced down the stairs, they paid less attention to where they stepped, and instead, focused on moving as quickly as possible.

The light danced along the walls, lending them an eerie glow, almost as if the mountain itself welcomed their presence once more. Samantha's breath came shorter and shorter, not because she was running, but rather because she could feel the tension, the rising anticipation in the air around them.

Hulak flew beside them, gliding at their pace, in a great circle, around the interior of the mountain. He could have landed long ago, could have found shelter and safety beneath the Shrouded One. He would not leave them, however.

Then, finally, they were at the bottom. Takeem grabbed Samantha's hand and raced with her across the root-laden land. Their feet pounded the ground in the perfect spots, as if the roots themselves moved to allow their feet to land in safety. As they ran for the Shrouded One, a golden light burst from its center, beckoning them forward. They aimed for that light and upon stumbling beneath the branches of the Keeper, fell to the ground, gasping and clutching at each other for comfort and relief.

"Huk." Samantha's heart raced in worry, but then she saw Hulak stretched across the ground right below the glowing ember that shone from the heart of the trunk of the Shrouded One.

"He's here," Takeem murmured in her ear. "He's safe, and so are we." He pulled Samantha into his arms and kissed her. One hand clenched on her hip, the other sliding up her back to cradle her neck, his kiss burned Samantha's worries away.

*

Takeem kissed Samantha, pulled away, then kissed her again, unable to let her go. She was everything. *Everything.*

He was about to commit treason. They would be hunted. They would be declared enemies of the throne.

He buried his face into her neck, terrified at what he was about to do.

She clutched at his back, hugging him tight. Was she as scared as he was? He wanted to change his mind, but he couldn't.

This was the right thing to do.

He pressed a kiss into her neck and murmured, "Are you ready to ask our question of the Shrouded One?"

Samantha tilted her head to give him better access, but did not answer him. He pressed a second kiss into the hollow between her neck and collarbone, causing Samantha to shiver in reaction. He pulled away and stared into her eyes.

"Are you ready?" he asked again.

Samantha nodded, a dazed look in her eyes. "I am."

"Then let's ask the Book of Ages together."

Holding hands, they approached the trunk. Hulak stood and moved away. In his place, the pedestal with the Book of Ages appeared.

Takeem reached with their joined hands toward the Book of Ages, the question of how to restore the magicks burning bright in his mind as their hands fell upon the book. Once more the chamber was bathed in light and Takeem could see the future unfolding before him, revealing what he must do.

*

As their hands touched the book, Samantha's heart asked the question she had not intended to ask, the one question she had come here to know, but until now, could not bear to hear the answer. She asked, "Where is my brother? Where is Hwanon?"

A PLAGUE OF DARKNESS

JENNIFER WOKE WITH Samantha's voice ringing in her ear. "He's beneath the willow, Aunt Jenny." She had returned to her motel room, intending to shower and leave, but she'd ended up taking a nap filled with dreams of Samantha and Jonathan.

"He's beneath the willow, Aunt Jenny."

The only other weeping willows Jennifer knew about were at a local park. Feeling like she was grasping at straws, she headed for the park.

When she arrived, there were willow trees in every direction, but no Samantha. Heartbroken, Jennifer decided to sit beneath a willow one final time before heading home.

She chose the tree that most closely resembled the one they had all loved. It was an ancient tree whose roots were growing as much above the ground as below it. She entered beneath its branches and settled on the ground. She carried with her one of Samantha's stories and one of Jonathan's drawings.

His drawing was of the willow tree from their backyard. It was huge and wonderful and filled the page with the power of its presence, with the power of its ethereal beauty. The image was one she would hold with her always for it represented everything that was Jonathan, everything that was Samantha, everything that was this world, this Lutia, they had created together.

The story she carried, though the first one of Lutia, was actually the seventh version of it that Samantha's box had contained. Clearly it had been rewritten over and over again, through the years. The first version had been written in a child's hand, filled with a child's innocence and perception of life and death. The final version, however, the one she carried now, had to have been written in the aftermath of Jonathan's death. It was typewritten and held a deeply-rooted sadness and bittersweet longing that made her cry every time she read it.

Jennifer sat beneath the willow tree and contemplated the world that Jonathan and Samantha had created. How she wished she and Samantha could journey there now, together. It seemed such a magical world, even with its darkness. Both she and Samantha knew their own world had a plague of darkness itself. How desperately she needed a bit of magic now, a bit of magic to transport her to wherever Samantha stood right then. Turning her body slightly into the tree, she gently tapped her nails against its trunk, imagining as she did so that Samantha would feel her knocking, knocking to be let back into her life. Leaning her head against the tree's trunk, she imagined she could hear Samantha's voice whispering, "Hwanon."

EARNING THE THRONE

TAKEEM LET GO of the Book of Ages and leaving Samantha behind, walked toward the edge of the tree where he pulled off his tunic and grabbed a jeweled dagger from the bundle Hulak had dropped when he transformed. With the dagger in hand, he approached the tree. "With this blood, the blood of Zarkonen, we cast our fears into the light." Closing the palm of his right hand around the dagger's blade, he squeezed until the blood dripped, then slowly walked in a circle around the trunk of the Shrouded One.

Seven hundred and seventy-seven kilometers away from the palace, where the first gate of Lutia stood and not too far from where Takeem stood, a loud clanging sound was heard throughout the land as the gate finally unlatched and fell open. Springing from either side of the gate, in an ever-increasing circle, a ring of violet flowers sprang from the terrain into full bloom. Where the first wall of Lutia had once crossed through mountain ranges, rivers and forests, the flowers bloomed and thrived; even under water they flourished.

Having completed his first circle, Takeem began again. "With this blood, the blood of Kessink, we cast our hatred into the light." Closing the palm of his left hand around the blade of his dagger, he repeated his actions of before, dripping his blood around the trunk of the tree.

Seven hundred kilometers away from the palace, the second

gate of Lutia unlatched and a second ring of flowers bloomed.

"With this blood, the blood of Marel, we cast our fury into the light." Hand slick with blood, palm burning in pain, Takeem clutched the dagger handle tight and slashed across his right forearm, allowing the blood to drip as he walked.

Six hundred and twenty-three kilometers from the palace, the third gate opened and another ring of flowers sprang into being.

"With this blood, the blood of Nerys, we cast our vengeance into the light." Slashing across his left forearm, Takeem walked a new circuit around the Shrouded One.

Five hundred and forty-six kilometers from the palace, the fourth gate unlatched and another ring of flowers journeyed through the lands of Lutia.

Takeem removed his tunic, stumbling at the wave of pain and dizziness that followed. Continuing to walk around the Shrouded One, he set the tip of the knife at his right hip and drew in a deep breath. "With this blood, the blood of Petryus, we ask for forgiveness." He dragged the knife from his hip across his abdomen.

Four hundred and sixty-nine kilometers from the palace, the fifth gate opened and a new ring of flowers cut across the land.

"With this blood, the blood of Loxoryon, we offer reparation." Settling the blade against his left hip, Takeem dragged it across his abdomen and continued to walk his trail of repentance.

Three hundred and ninety-two kilometers from the palace, the sixth gate fell open and the sixth ring of flowers was born.

"With this blood, the blood of Ferilis, we renew the ties of blood and magick." Hand shaking, Takeem dragged the dagger downward from his right shoulder, blood dripping as he walked.

Three hundred and fifteen kilometers from the palace, the seventh gate unlatched and the final ring of flowers exploded from the ground.

Back at the beginning again, Takeem hesitated, a wave of dizziness making him sway in place. Redistributing his weight and planting his feet for balance, he slashed his dagger across his left shoulder and down his chest, so the blood pooled above his heart. "We make this blood offering to the light, this blood of my ancestor Torel, that it might bring light to the darkness, that it might tear down the cold metals of hatred my ancestors built, that warmth and light and hope shall live in their place, dominant throughout the ages."

Across the lands of Lutia, where the newly unlatched iron gates of hatred still stood, there came springing into full formation seven Shrouded Ones. Exploding from the ground beneath where the gates stood strong, the roots and trunks and branches of the great trees collided with the iron gates in a thunderous crash. The gates could not withstand the pure power of the Shrouded Ones and crumbled to dust. Those who were there to witness the births of the Shrouded Ones fell to their knees in reverence and wept in joy to see such glory thriving once more.

Back at the shrine, Takeem circled the tree one final time, blood dripping from his wounds as if in slow motion. "We offer our blood, that the magicks now sealed within the lands of Lutia might finally break free, that our brethren, of all colors and form and race and species, might live their lives as they were blessed to live them, unfettered by the chains of hatred."

*

Hulak would never forget what he witnessed that day. It was burned into his memory, into his very being. He witnessed the rebirth of an entire way of life. He witnessed a king become worthy of his throne.

HWANON'S GIFT

SAMANTHA PULLED HER hands from the Book of Ages, and sank to the ground beneath the willow tree. The book had promised her an answer, if she was ready to listen. She gently raked her nails across the bark of the Shrouded One, imagining as she did so that Hwanon would feel her knocking. Knocking to be allowed to know where he was, what he had become, how he had managed all of this. "Hwanon," she whispered, "speak to me. I'm ready."

And though she was no longer touching the Book of Ages, she read this world's beginnings the same way she once had written them.

*

This is the beginning, a voice whispered, *just the beginning, made for you.* And in that moment, she saw the building of their world from the simple molecules and particles and energy patterns that were the essence of her Hwanon, building and stretching and forming and *becoming.* All for her.

The essence of her Hwanon streamed forward away from that deadly crash, pulling with him the essence of both their parents. He held them tight as he hurtled toward their willow tree, pouring himself forward into its framework, then streaming outward again, a sleek arrow of light, the blue streak that was him, the swirls of purple and pink that represented their parents, the pure white that was the tree. He spun and went back, again and again, collecting the energy patterns of another willow tree, then of a deer felled by a hunter, then of all the life burning in a forest fire.

He spun the energy patterns of life, traveling amongst the stars, collecting the light from an exploding sun, the life force of a dying planet. The pure light that was Hwanon became so much more, whirling in place, then exploding into a million pinpoints of light.

She witnessed the formation of a world, a world that moved forward and backward from the same beginning point, a history unfolding in reverse, many potential futures spinning in place, awaiting the one event that would be the catalyst for all that was to come. Awaiting *her*.

Time that had doubled and tripled in place smoothed out and moved forward again, from the moment she arrived between the second and the third gates of Lutia. She stood in the middle of the deadened battlefield of Shorel and approached the dying forests of Bipin. She touched a leaf that fell behind her back and the world transformed. It breathed and lived again.

She saw that everyone's lives would eventually have spun in different directions, time would have eventually unfolded, and the futures would have written themselves, even without her arrival.

For Hwanon could not hold the fabric of his creation in stasis for all of eternity. It had grown beyond the realm and depths of either of their imaginations, but with the fortitude and will that made up the young man she once knew, he had held it just long enough for her to arrive at the middle point of their own story and begin to live it.

How was this possible? Oh, Hwanon, what have you done?

And the world answered in Jonathan's voice.

Love makes everything possible.

*

The truth was like an explosion, ripping apart her reality, then stitching it anew. She had finally found her Hwanon. Though he was forever changed, forever lost to her in one form, he had also become part of her everything in another. Digging her fingers deeply into the soil of the land that was him, she whispered his name and she wept.

*

"Sehmah," Jennifer imagined she could hear the sound of Samantha's sorrow, as she mourned all they had lost.

"Hwanon." Samantha's voice seemed so real, as if she were right there.

Jennifer opened her eyes and cried out.

Samantha knelt on the ground, not two feet from her, rocking and crying.

"Samantha!" Jennifer lunged forward.

"Aunt Jenny!"

The two came together in a storm of weeping.

"Aunt Jenny, I can't believe you found me."

"I'll always find you, baby, don't you know that?" Jennifer clung to her niece, rocking her gently and whispering words of comfort. "I'm so sorry I haven't been there for you, I'm sorry, I'm sorry, I should have talked to you more, oh, baby, I'm so sorry."

"I found him, Aunt Jenny, I found him, but how do you embrace an entire world?"

"What are you talking about, sweetheart?"

"Jonathan, I–" Samantha pulled away from Jennifer a little. "Did you–can't you feel him? Don't you feel–" She stopped, a look of confusion on her face. "Where are we, Aunt Jenny?"

"We're in Harrisonville, baby."

*

Harrisonville. Samantha looked around. She was still beneath a willow tree. Was it the same one that housed the Book of Ages? Or was it some other willow tree? And what of Takeem? If she had come home, who would help him? Who would help Hulak? Who would be the queen to stand at their sides? "Harrisonville?"

"Yes, darling, Harrisonville."

It was time. Regardless of where she stood, Lutia or

Harrisonville, or who was at her side, Takeem or her Aunt Jenny, Samantha knew it was time to stand tall and embrace the future. It was time to become the queen of her own fate, to become Sehmah in truth.

Movement caught her eye beyond her aunt's shoulder.

Takeem stood on the far side of the tree, arms wide, dagger in hand, blood dripping from his many wounds. His eyes were closed, head flung back toward the canopy of leaves above them.

Samantha pulled away from Jenny, eyes riveted to this bloodied Takeem.

The Shrouded One's leaves began to fall.

*

Jennifer turned her head to see what Samantha was looking at and gasped at the sight of a young man, wounded and half naked, dagger in hand. The leaves that swirled around him were neither falling to the earth nor moving with the wind, but rather were orbiting his form as if he were the center of their universe.

"Who on earth is that?"

Samantha grinned. "That, Aunt Jenny, is my Takeem."

*

At these words, Takeem's eyes sprang open. "Vanadevi, awaken." He slammed his hands together, trapping the dagger between the two before flinging it into the ground where it quivered, newly embedded within a root of the Shrouded One.

Staring at the dagger, it seemed to all three of them that the world wavered in silence, swaying upon the pinnacle of something great, waiting for the right moment.

Waiting.

*

Jennifer held her breath, uncertain what was happening, afraid to move. The hairs on the back of her neck stood up, and she clutched Samantha's hand in hers, staring at the dagger as it swayed, the jewels upon its hilt winking and beckoning. She waited, for something terrible or for something great. She waited for that moment, the one that would define her entire existence.

*

Takeem waited in silence. He waited for his birthright.

*

Samantha stared in fascination at the dagger that still quivered in the root of the world she and Jonathan had created together. Here was their beginning point, their end point, their middle point, here under this willow tree, here where it all began.

Waiting for Jonathan to show her the way.

Waiting for Hwanon to make a place for her in this world of change.

Waiting.

*

And then it happened.

The deafening roar of magicks poured across the land in a great wave of white exploding outward.

They were embraced

They were devoured

They were eclipsed

d e c o n s t r u c t e d

They were

reborn

ACKNOWLEDGEMENTS

I owe a huge debt of gratitude to a number of individuals who have contributed to the making of this novel.

For being one of the very first readers of this manuscript, in its earliest, roughest form, I must give my thanks to Dr. Greg Luthi. He provided endless feedback and encouragement as I participated in his creative writing workshops at Johnson County Community College in Overland Park, Kansas. Without his encouragement, I may never have finished even the first draft of this novel. Anne Kinskey and Linda Helmick served as my earliest critique partners at the college, becoming the very first fans of Samantha and Takeem.

This work eventually became my thesis project for the Writing Popular Fiction program at Seton Hill University in Greensburg, Pennsylvania. I owe a debt of thanks to the entire Seton Hill community for their encouragement and willingness to read endless drafts of this novel. In particular, I am indebted to my critique partner, Anna LaVoie, who accompanied me from the first draft to the very last draft of this manuscript, and my fellow Secret-Keepers, for making the writer's journey one of companionship and fellowship and general awesomeness.

At Seton Hill, I was blessed to have an incredible mentor, Heidi Ruby Miller. Words simply cannot express how much she contributed to the making of this novel and how eternally grateful I will always be for her belief in me and for her endless words of wisdom around character development, story, writing and the art of living as a writer. Her keen editor's eye and attention to detail improved this novel in countless ways. Through her eyes, I came to know my characters and to understand their journeys in deeper ways than I ever would have believed possible. Her contributions are literally immeasurable.

Finally, as always, my family lies at the heart of my writing. Without the encouragement of my parents and my G.T.E. to pursue my dreams, I might never have started this novel, let alone finished it. I am also grateful to my niece, Tobi, for her enthusiasm and excitement about this novel and her willingness to read several versions of it. To Tobi, Ariana, Josie and Calvin, I am deeply indebted. Without their presence in my life, Jennifer's character would not have been so rich and without their many requests over the years for "just one more story," I may never have indulged the fire in me that burns to write.

OTHER BOOKS BY A.J. CULEY

can be found at www.ajculey.com

AVAILABLE NOW FOR EARLY READERS:

A Fairy's Job

Salsa Visits the Zoo

Taco Runs Away

Tyrabbisaurus Rex

COMING SOON FOR EARLY READERS:

If My Cat Could Fly (May 2016)

COMING SOON FOR YOUNG ADULT READERS:

Jennara in Flux (Summer 2016)

The Trouble with Antlers (Summer 2016)

ABOUT THE AUTHOR

A.J. Culey is a teacher, world traveler and writer. She lives with a number of very bossy cats and can be found at her website www.ajculey.com. She can also be followed on Facebook at www.facebook.com/ajculey.author and on Twitter @ajculey.

T-Rab from *Tyrabbisaurus Rex* is also on Twitter @Tyrabbisaurus and can be found there when he manages to coax the laptop away from A.J.

Made in the USA
Lexington, KY
11 April 2016